SMART MOVE

WORK FOR IT
BOOK SEVEN

AMANDA PENNINGTON

WWW.SMARTYPANTSROMANCE.COM

COPYRIGHT

For my Rupp and Pennington parents, who show me what it means to be caregivers.

CHAPTER 1

IVY

Mel: Good luck with registration opening today, Ivy!
Ivy: Thanks! Keeping my fingers crossed that our portal doesn't crash like last year.
Cameron: I can guarantee that if you promise to let only the best students sign up for my classes.
Ivy: You know I'm an equal opportunist.

Gray upon gray upon gray. The inside of my head was charcoal, dusky heather, and soot. The monotonous sounds of the registrar's office, with shuffling papers, clicking mouses, and hushed voices, all amounted to a single, unfulfilling collage of gray.

I faced the printer, discreetly texting my best friends and coworkers, Cameron and Mel, while I waited on copies for the student who'd just registered for classes. If I tilted my head just so, the intricate designs of my silver earrings would chime, and if I listened just so, some of the gray would fade into lilac, and I could clear the monotony out of my head and breathe a little easier.

Ah, the joys of living with synesthesia, where every sound in my ears painted colors in my mind. Some days I handled it better than others. Today was not one of those days. Now that I thought about it, I hadn't had one of those better days in a long time.

Before I could enjoy the lilac for long, the printer jammed.

Cursing under my breath, I opened various compartments. Three flimsy plastic doors later, I gripped the twisted page by its edges and managed to coat my fingers in ink.

The door to the registrar's office opened and closed.

A man spoke. "What a great day to register for classes, right?"

The student, who waited for me at the counter, answered, "Especially since I got the last seat in Dr. Whitacre's class. You?"

The man spoke again. "I'm here for continuing education credits. But I know Dr. Whitacre, and you're lucky you got in."

The student replied, but I didn't care to listen to her.

That voice. That sound.

The gray in my head was completely, instantly wiped out with bold shades of paprika, scarlet, cobalt, and emerald. The colors shifted in endless change and movement.

No single sound ever created more than one color for me before. And for the colors to change like this? Impossible.

I needed to hear more, needed this voice, needed to know who this was.

No, I didn't *need*. I didn't do desperation. Just because a stranger's voice had washed away the gray didn't mean anything. I, Ivy Lunden, was a strong, independent woman with artistic dreams. My mom, a single mother, had taught me to squash spiders by myself and change engine oil without help. She'd raised me on sheer willpower, hard work, and devotion. Mom wasn't quite the same lately, given she was in her early seventies now and had never taken care of herself. Still, the principles she taught me remained the same. I was capable. Hardy. Tough.

But I was also curious.

Carefully, I glanced under the arm that gripped the mangled paper. It wasn't my most flattering position, and it put the man upside down in my line of sight. But at least I caught a glimpse. And was it ever worth it. Even upside down, he was tall, handsome, big-shouldered, and giving a friendly smile. His words didn't register in my mind. Just shades and hues—

No wonder his voice puts colors in my head.

Even strong, independent women could appreciate a gorgeous man.

I straightened, wrenched the paper free, and restarted the print job, still listening. With the new copy in hand, I turned to the waiting student. "Here's your registration paperwork. Your book list and classroom assignments are on the second page."

As the student thanked me and moved away, I gave the man with the voice my best customer service smile. "May I help you?"

If his voice hadn't already made me notice he was different, his smile would have. It stretched in brilliant white across his dark brown face.

He stepped closer to the counter, resting his forearms on the edge. "I should ask if *I* can help *you*." He nodded toward my hands. "Looks like you had a fight with an octopus."

I snatched a tissue from my desk and blotted at my ink-spotted hands. *Real smooth, Ivy.* "Octopus, evil overlord printer, same thing."

He laughed, and the colorful image in my mind brightened. "Should I even ask how your day is going?"

I forced a breath into my chest. "It's going fine." *Get yourself together.* I tossed the ink-covered tissue into the trash can beside me. "Anyway. May I help you?"

"You're not going to ask how my day is going"—he glanced at the lanyard around my neck—"Ivy?"

If he didn't have a magical voice, if there had been students waiting in line behind him, if I hadn't been bored senseless moments ago, I never would've played along. But I did. I leaned my own forearms on my side of the countertop. "How's your day going?"

Narrowing his eyes, he considered. "It's about an eight."

"A what?"

"An eight."

Huh. He may have had a gorgeous face and a fascinating voice, but he was…strange.

"On a scale of one to ten, one to one hundred…?"

He grinned. "One to ten."

Nodding, I cleared my throat, ready to pass him the student catalog and chalk this up to a bizarre conversation with a good-looking man.

"Don't you want to know why my day is an eight?"

There were better things I could be doing instead of playing games with an adult man. But then I remembered all the gray inside my head before he walked through the registrar doors, and I looked at his brilliant smile, and…well.

"Why an eight?"

"I'm so glad you asked." He gave me a teasing grin. "My day started off much lower than an eight; it was more like a four, because I knew registering for CEs meant filling out paperwork. I already fill out paperwork all day at work.

But then I ran into some students in the parking lot"—he jutted a thumb over his shoulder—"and they let me try out their hoverboard. I'd never tried a hoverboard before." His dynamism took on a boyish eagerness for a moment.

"That bumped up your day to an eight?"

"No, that bumped my day to a six." He paused, clearly waiting for me to ask where his other two points came from.

Lucky for him, I felt intrigued enough to play along. "So the other two points came from where, exactly?"

"Meeting you, Ivy."

From anyone else, the line would've felt rehearsed, forced, fake. But somehow, between his enthusiasm over trying a hoverboard and his teasing me into a more-than-generic conversation, he came across as sincere. His unwavering eye contact certainly helped his cause. He studied me like he thought I was more than just university staff at a dead-end job at the registrar's office. Like he saw details others missed, like I was interesting, like I was worth noticing.

"How would you rate your day, Ivy?"

He was a relentless optimist; that was obvious. He saw students with a hoverboard and, one way or another, tried the hoverboard. I saw students with a hoverboard and took the long way around them to avoid their noisy laughter filling my head with chartreuse. He met someone new and lured her into a conversation that felt like a game. I met someone new and suspected him of being strange.

We couldn't be more different, and it wasn't like I'd ever see him again. Might as well be honest from the start.

"My day is a three."

"A three?" He leaned a little closer. "Tell me more."

I leaned a little closer too. "It's a secret."

"I can keep a secret."

"It's very important."

"I won't say a word."

Something in me longed to tell him the whole truth: *You see, it's this job that leaves me feeling empty, discarded, and vaguely depressed at the end of the day. It's my failed art career that—get this, I* chose *to fail for reasons I don't want to go into right now. It's my love life that I've given up on. And it's my mom, the only family I have, who is now a seventy-three-year-old woman so feeble I barely recognize her. That's why my day feels like a three. Actually, can I make that a negative three?*

But I couldn't say all that to a stranger.

Instead, I whispered, curving my hand around one side of my mouth like we were kids swapping rumors on the playground. I didn't miss the way his eyes glanced at my lips. "I hate my job."

He tilted his head, frowning a little. "Why?"

I'd expected him to laugh, offer some generic sympathy, or shrug with a good-natured "Don't we all?" That was the typical response people gave when someone complained about work. Face it, work sucks some days even for people who like their jobs. Most reasonably adjusted adults are used to this by a certain age. But genuine interest, free of judgment? I hadn't expected that.

I shrugged, playing off my surprise at his response. "The drudgery. It's paperwork and processes and politics, and it drains the color from my life."

He nodded. "What would it take to get your day to a ten?"

I place my chin on my hand, tapping my lower lip, pleased to see his eyes flicker there again. "I'm not sure. Maybe a spontaneous half-day? Like take my lunch break and don't come back for 'personal' reasons?"

"Then do it."

"Just…take a half-day?" My tone was skeptical, but now that I said it aloud for myself, the idea carried weight, significance, maybe even possibility.

He shrugged. "Why not? Do you have vacation time for it?"

"Well, yeah, but—" *But I need to save it to go with my mom to her doctor appointments, because I'm all she has, and she's all I have, and it's complicated.*

"Take a day off. Go home. Go on a spontaneous hour-long road trip. Do something fun." His gaze wandered over my face, studying me with a look of… affection? "What's stopping you?"

I allowed a coy smile to curve my lips. "The day is still young, isn't it?"

This time, his eyes didn't dip toward my mouth. They stayed fixed on mine, a smile teasing his face. "Yes, it is."

"Tell me," I whispered, "what it would take to get your day to a ten?"

"I'm doing it right now."

I rolled my eyes. "I'm serious."

"So am I."

We locked eyes. Was all that warmth in his face for me? Did a little flirting really mean that much to him? Considering my own improved mood since we met, I was hardly one to judge.

Flirting was fun. I did it all the time. It helped me get along with almost anyone, helped me skip a few places in line at catered meals, and helped turn my day around, like it was doing now. I'd honed my flirting skills for years. If flirting had a pro league, I'd be the team captain.

"I'm flattered," I teased, "but surely there's something else."

This time the coy smile was his, and he lifted a brow suggestively. "Like you said, the day is still young."

I laughed. It was my real laugh: big, unfeminine, with a faint snort—in that moment, I didn't have the wherewithal to taper it into something more attractive like I normally did—and his face lit up.

We registered him for CEs next semester. I noted his name, Tobias "Toby" Azumah, and saw his address wasn't far from here. Maybe he would become a regular at the registrar's in future semesters. I printed his class schedule and receipt. He accepted both from me, his fingertips lingering at the top of the page, where a line identified me as the registrar staff who had helped him.

When other students began entering the glass double doors behind him, he smiled reluctantly, backing away from my counter with a grin. "My day is a ten because of you, Ivy Lunden."

I didn't take that half-day, but later that night, after I called Mom to check in with her, I stood in front of my easel, nestled in the spare bedroom I'd converted into a soundproof studio, and painted something worthwhile for the first time in years. I dared to dream of a future where I had my own art career. I painted the saturated colors his voice had splashed in my mind, adding all the brightness of his last words: *My day is a ten because of you, Ivy Lunden.*

CHAPTER 2

TOBY

Several Months Later

Cameron: Continuing education registration opens today.
Toby: Thanks! I'll let you know when my class is, and I can stop by your closet-office for a visit.
Cameron: My door is always open for my favorite physical therapist.

I make my living reading the human body.

That sounded better in my head. I could already hear my best friend, Cameron, poking fun at me for sounding so laughable.

Let me explain that a bit more—I read the human body for a living because, when a patient walks through the doors of Better Movement, I not only go through their paperwork to plan our sessions, but I also watch how they move, whether they hold eye contact, if they smile or frown, how their posture compensates for the hip surgery they're recovering from. But it's not just their bones, joints, and movements that dictate how they're feeling. I write fake "prescriptions" for them to spend more time with loved ones or watch a new comedy show to get their spirits up. Physical therapy is more than weights and bands and pain. It's emotional therapy too.

Sometimes reading bodies extended outside of work. Like, for example, the pretty blue-eyed blond at the registrar's office, who moved like each motion was part of a dance. *My day is a ten because of you, Ivy Lunden.*

Movement caught my periphery. It was my new supervisor, Deke, lecturing an intern. What doesn't help patients get better? Managerial lectures from Deke. I kept my head down as I focused on cleaning the therapy bench, willing him to stay on the other side of the room and leave me in peace.

I glanced at my Garmin watch, noting the time. How many more hours until I could take my lunch break and see Ivy? Today was different from the other few times I'd seen her when I signed up for my continuing ed credits at the nearby university. Today I would ask her to dinner.

I didn't have much of a plan, but I didn't mind. I would drive to the university to fill out registrar paperwork, and I would flirt with her, like I had for the last few semesters. Then I would oh-so-innocently ask her if she'd been to that new sushi restaurant. I could hardly wait.

As soon as I finished cleaning my station, I turned toward the break room and my work locker. Last night I'd stayed up late reviewing my plans for my first three patients of the day, the low hum of my TV providing the perfect white noise. Technically, paperwork isn't supposed to leave the premises of Better Movement. But I couldn't let down my patients, and if that meant their files happened to be in my work bag when I left at 5:30, so be it. A few wrinkled pages was a small price to pay for a tailored physical therapy program. I'd crinkled a few corners when I fell asleep sprawled next to my coffee table, pen still in hand, dreaming of Ivy's blue eyes, blond hair, and red lipstick—

Focus, Tobias Azumah.

Moving casually through the main therapy area, I smiled at a fellow therapist counting reps with a patient, joked with an intern about wearing the wrong scrubs to work, and tried to look as inconspicuous as possible as I strolled to my locker. I checked to my left. I checked to my right. The staff room was clear. Opening my locker and reaching into my bag, I withdrew my file folder to—

"Toby."

The booming voice of Hudson, owner of Better Movement and literal giant of a man at six foot six inches tall, didn't scare me at all. Doesn't everyone enjoy interrupting their morning with an adrenaline rush and girlish squeal? Just me?

Having turned midair when I jumped several inches into space, I pressed the folder between my back and my locker. "Morning, Boss!"

He grinned, making his eyes disappear into his cheeks. "I can always count on you to be chipper in the mornings, Toby."

It was the adrenaline flooding my system, but he didn't need to know my secrets to a "chipper" morning. "You know me, always ready to change the world."

"Even if it means taking home patients' files, right?" His smile shifted from jovial boss to amiable mentor.

Reaching behind me, I retrieved the folder. "I know, I know, but I needed to focus, and you know how it is at work, when there are patients to talk to, and then coworkers to talk to, and then…well, people to talk to."

He nodded. "Extroverts like us find it harder to focus on monotonous tasks when water cooler chat is so much more fun. That same friendliness is what makes us great with our patients."

I relaxed. This was precisely why Deke would never understand the relationships I had with my patients, because he was too busy clutching his clipboard like a lifeline. This was also precisely why I sometimes found Deke's patients looking longingly at other therapists, like we were sundaes with all the toppings and Deke was boiled Brussels sprouts. A little friendliness and a little compassion went a long way when people felt pain and frustration.

Hudson stuffed his large hands into his scrubs pants. "That same friendliness is why I wanted to chat with you today. It's about Deke."

Please, anyone but him.

"I'm concerned about him fitting in with our culture here," Hudson said.

No kidding. The rest of us got along and loved our work for the work itself. Deke, with his clipboard and frown, was everything I *didn't* want to be as a physical therapist.

"He's more reserved than you and me," Hudson said, "so he has a little trouble making friends. What would you say to making a bit more of an effort to include him in talk around the office?"

Deke was already plenty involved in talk around the office. Nobody could find anything else worth gossiping about lately.

"Or, if nothing else, set a good example of respecting him as a supervisor, even if you disagree with his methods. You're a favorite with all of our patients and your peers. Your vote of confidence means a tremendous amount to your coworkers. To me."

To me. How could I say no to that? As much as Deke was everything I didn't want to be, Hudson was my hero.

"I'll do my part." The words were out before I could stop them.

Hudson smiled, his eyes disappearing into his cheeks again, and he clapped a giant but gentle hand on my shoulder. "I knew I could count on you." He turned back to his office.

I stood in front of my locker, baffled by my own words. What exactly was "my part," and how would I do it? When would I ever learn to think before I spoke?

Maybe I could take the easy way out, just this once. When Deke handed out his laminated checklist for the staff kitchen, I would smile and not ask overly innocent questions about how the foil-wrapped lunch had gotten in the microwave in the first place, because we all knew it was Deke who'd caught the staff microwave on fire. When he clutched his clipboard in his white knuckles, I would nod and do what he said. When my coworkers gathered around the water cooler and complained about his newly revised employee handbook, I would stay silent. That would follow the letter of what Hudson asked me to do.

There. Problem solved. We would all win. Hudson would see less dislike of Deke in the workplace. Deke would feel more respected. And I could do the job I loved.

I loved my work. Honest. It was just, right now, the thought of another late night of paperwork at my coffee table didn't sound all that great. Going home to a too-quiet apartment wasn't appealing. I pictured my beige carpet, beige walls, beige kitchen cabinets—what was with apartment complexes and the color beige? I might've been a stereotypical bachelor with junk mail piling up on my counter and clothes flung everywhere but the hamper, but I aspired to something more. I *wanted* something more. I felt ready to get back out there, and my first step was to ask Ivy on a date.

My last girlfriend was Yvonne, a brunette who worked as a CPA in the industrial complex across town. After a year of dating, I'd been ready to dive headlong into the next step. I'd been ready before then, but I didn't want to rush her. I knew I tended to leap forward when others were still ten steps behind me.

When I'd handed Yvonne a key to my apartment, her body stiffened with discomfort. She wouldn't hold eye contact. Her smile was delayed a moment too long as she explained it wasn't me, it was her. She wanted to take things slow. She wanted to keep other avenues open a little longer, just until she was sure about us.

Her tense posture told me more than her words. We'd been together for a year. If Yvonne loved me enough to live with me, she would've known by then.

If she were ever going to love me at all, she would've loved me by then. But she didn't. She saw me as just one "avenue" while she waited for someone better.

I hadn't dated anyone since Yvonne. I'd been a little crushed, honestly. But now…

A memory surfaced from my dream last night: shiny blond hair, red lipstick, and a dancer's grace. Ivy.

Today was the day.

CHAPTER 3

IVY

Mel: I saw continuing education registration is open today, Ivy. Sending you good vibes that the portal doesn't crash today.
Cameron: I could crash the portal on purpose if you really wanted…
Ivy: I don't know if that thrills me or terrifies me.
Mel: You have a heart of gold, but you're also a rebel. You know it's a thrill.
Ivy: How much do you charge, Cam?

The voice came from behind me, diagonally from my desk. I didn't need to turn around to know who it was. Only one person's voice did this to me, painting a mental image in rapid, broad strokes and brilliant colors. This painting happened the first time I heard his voice, and it happened now, two semesters later.

I continued my mindless, fog-gray work: stapling, stamping, noting, filing. I ignored text notifications from Cameron and Mel in favor of collecting my composure. These moments mattered because, as I straightened my paperwork, I straightened my face into a neutral customer service expression, and, more importantly, I straightened my mind. Reveling in the colors was only a distraction from the centerpiece: flirting with Toby.

Pulling back my shoulders, I turned to the student standing at my desk. "You're all set for this semester. Here's your schedule. This column shows your classrooms, and this one shows your professors' names. If you have any questions, give us a call."

The freshman student nodded and shuffled away to wrap her head around her second semester of college.

I glanced over to make sure Clarice, my lazy coworker who was never happier than when she was pointing out others' mistakes, was on the other side of the room, sitting at her desk and staring at her phone. Then I let myself look at him.

As usual, he stepped close and leaned his elbows on the counter. His forearms edged the boundary of professionalism, the sleeves of his coat landing a few inches short of the middle of the counter. He always gave me just enough space to let me know that I was still the one in control of our flirtationship.

That's right. I, Ivy Lunden, have a flirtationship with Toby Azumah, the man whose voice draws more colorful images in my head than any other sound ever has.

For the last few semesters, he leaned across the registrar counter, and he flirted with me, and I flirted back, and then we parted ways until the next time the university opened registration for physical therapy CEs.

Toby always came just after noon on opening day. Always.

Not that I kept track. And not that I wore my best red lipstick and sexy heels for the occasion.

This, whatever it was, was all just a game. My favorite kind of game.

"Hey."

More bright splashes. More beautiful colors.

I smiled. "Hey."

"How are you?"

From anyone else, this was a pat question expecting a pat answer. But not from Toby. This was all part of our routine, and it never bored me.

I pursed my lips and pretended to think, not missing when his eyes flicked to my mouth for a moment. *Yep. Still got it.* "I'm feeling about a seven right now." I definitely felt worse than a seven, but our flirtationship was my escape, and I wanted to pretend for a few precious moments.

He nodded like this was the most interesting statement he'd heard all day—and his interest didn't feel artificial. In a world of fake dating profiles and pretended sincerity, I reveled in his focused attention.

"What'll it take to get to ten?" A grin teased the right corner of his lips.

My answer was instant. "A box of wine that lasts until I clock out at five."

He laughed. "A whole box? Your day must be much worse than a seven."

That kind of openness wasn't part of my game, so I shrugged. "What can I say? I'm a simple woman."

"I doubt it," he whispered, and the sound put a delightful haze in my head.

"What about you?" Now I leaned across the counter, our forearms mere inches apart. "How's your day?"

He pretended to think about it before saying, "Nine."

Of course. He never rated his day any lower than an eight.

"Don't you ever have a bad day?" I picked up the catalog from my desk, turning to the CE page.

"Never when you're around."

My eyes widened.

He winced. "That was pretty awful."

"Maybe your bad day is showing after all." Smiling, I handed him the catalog.

"I don't believe in bad days."

Lucky. Bad days were all I knew anymore, between this job that filled my head with gray and my mother who became more and more frail each time I saw her—and more and more needy. A few months ago, I'd made the mistake of mentioning my plans to go on a date, and she'd shown up at the restaurant. The guy had been just as slimy as all the others, so it wasn't a real loss; it was just the principle of going on dates *without* my mother.

I studied Toby as he glanced through the CE catalog. What did it feel like to have only good days? Was his life filled with unicorns and puppies? He probably had flirtationships with women all over the city. Not that it mattered. It definitely didn't matter.

Then again, this was Toby, the man who was determinedly optimistic and extroverted. He actually *liked* people. Why else did he register for classes in person instead of online like every other student under the age of sixty? I wasn't vain enough to think he registered in person because of me. He just wanted to talk to someone. Anyone. *Extroverts*, right?

His bright smile stretched in clean, symmetrical lines. "Aren't you going to ask me?" he asked without looking up from the catalog.

I ran my fingertip along the side of the catalog he held. The corner of the paper edged into my finger, grounding me in reality when all I wanted was to float into a fantasy where I flirted with Toby, didn't work at this depressing job, and…

I pushed the corner deeper into my fingertip. I glanced at him through my eyelashes.

He stared back at me.

"If your day is a nine, what'll it take to get you to a ten?"

He paused, studying my face so closely that I couldn't doubt his intentions. Instead of turning the next page of the catalog, his hand brushed against the same edge of paper I toyed with, his finger breaths away from touching mine.

"I'm doing it right now," he said.

I smiled.

"Even better."

I blinked. "What?"

"I made you smile." He looked smug. "Now my day is a twelve."

I rolled my eyes. "Since when can a day be better than a ten?"

"Since now." He tapped a finger on the catalog and slid his credit card across the counter. "This one. 'Functional Geriatrics and Fall Prevention Strategies.'"

I turned toward my computer and began entering the information. "Are most of your patients geriatrics?"

My fingers faltered on the keyboard. Where had that come from? This was a superficial flirtationship. It'd lasted a ridiculously long time with zero progress, but that was the fun of it. No strings, no pressure. Asking questions about his work would signal that I welcomed questions about my own work, and then I'd face the dilemma of whether to tell him about my failed art career, and all the associated disappointment and guilt, and—

He didn't seem to find my unscripted question strange. "No, I have patients from all over. Adolescent athletes, middle-aged surgery recoveries, geriatrics, everything in between. Sometimes we have pediatrics. A few weeks ago my coworker had a kid with gait dysfunction."

"Is the kid better now?"

He shrugged. "It'll take some time. But I think he'll be fine in a couple months. The dysfunction isn't too major."

I felt him watching me. Like every encounter I'd had with Toby, he brought a physical force with him, that megawatt smile impossible to resist.

I handed him a freshly printed schedule for his class and a receipt for the course. "Here you are. Your classroom is in the basement of Goldner Arena, which you're familiar with."

"Don't you need to confirm my information? Are you sure you spelled my last name correctly? 'Azumah' isn't your average 'Smith,' you know."

"Of course I spelled it correctly." I slid the catalog from his hands. "I remember my favorite students."

His face lit up.

Now there was that irresistible, megawatt smile.

If only these entertaining moments with him could stretch a little longer than a few minutes every few months. They were the highlights in my world of working at the registrar's office and visiting Mom to make sure she was okay.

But even if Toby and I had more time together, this flirtationship couldn't grow into anything else. I'd seen how Mom struggled, both emotionally and financially, to raise me on her own, since my dad was never a part of our lives. I'd seen how her only boyfriend broke her heart when I was in high school, making her more codependent than ever. Mom gave two men her all, and look what happened. I couldn't open myself up to the possibility, the vulnerability, of following in her footsteps. I'd never met a man who was worth the risk.

So it was a good thing I didn't anticipate these few minutes with Toby like they fueled me until his next visit. Good thing I didn't look forward to Toby so much that I wore heels to stand a little more eye level with him. I had no problem keeping a thick barrier wrapped around my heart to guard against the feelings our flirtationship stirred up—and this was *definitely* just a flirtationship.

CHAPTER 4

TOBY

Deke: Let me know when you're back from lunch and registration. I developed a new spreadsheet to track continuing education credits.

Good thing I had an excuse to look away from her as I slid my credit card into my pocket. I willed myself to stay calm and put together. Ivy looked prettier than ever, her black outfit a stark contrast to her blond hair, her lips a precise red bow.

Nobody had ever looked so good in fluorescent lighting and office greige. But ogling like a creep wouldn't help my cause.

I would ask her out, and we would go on a date, and we would have a great time, and I would kiss her red lips goodnight, and after a few more dates, we would fall in love, and—

I took a deep breath. No sense getting ahead of myself. Again. The worst that could happen would be a flat-out rejection. Just because she flirted with me a few times a year didn't mean she wanted a relationship. Maybe she already had a boyfriend, and I was her secret dalliance. If what we had could even qualify as a secret dalliance. But if I *was* a secret dalliance, maybe I could become her *only* dalliance.

Tobias Azumah. Cool your engines. You haven't even asked her yet.

"Actually, I lied a little. My day is a zero." The words blurted from my mouth without any conscious thought from myself.

Maybe my engines aren't meant to be cooled.

Her brows drew together. "Are you okay? You never rate your days lower than an eight. What's wrong?"

Her coworker, Clarice, remained at her desk on the other side of the room, but I still leaned closer to Ivy across the counter and lowered my voice. "What's wrong is"—*be cool*—"I don't have your number."

Ivy's frown cleared by degrees, her pretty lips gradually lifting at one corner. "We rate our days from one to ten, and not having my number puts you at a zero?"

She sounded skeptical, amused. Not a hopeful start to this conversation.

"Are you challenging my daily rating?" I teased.

"I'm saying I doubt you literally fell off the end of our rating scale over this. If your grasp on numbers is so tenuous, I don't think I should trust you with mine."

Clarice stirred in her desk chair. We glanced at her. She never looked up from her phone, idly fiddling with a paperclip.

"I'm giving you a compliment," I whispered to Ivy, drawing her attention back to me. "Your phone number is worth ten whole points."

The lift at the corner of her mouth turned into a teasing smile. "Well, when you put it like that..."

I set my phone on the counter and slid it toward her, never breaking eye contact. When she didn't move, I raised an eyebrow at her. "Are you saying you don't care whether I have a zero day? Heartless."

"I'm not heartless; I just don't understand what kind of man plays this game just to get my number."

"A man who knows what he wants." I turned my Casanova voice to something more serious. "A man who plays the long game."

Just like that, her face changed. Her coy smile flattened. Her baby blues dimmed. Her body changed, too, becoming rigid beneath her black top. Her throat moved in a swallow.

What had I said wrong?

I leaned a little closer across the counter. "Come on. What's the best that could happen?"

"I think the phrase is, 'What's the *worst* that could happen?'"

"I only believe in the best."

She rolled her eyes, an exasperated smile on her lips. But it was a smile, and her expression had softened, so I'd take it.

"Okay, let's think through the pros and cons. What's the *worst* that could happen?" I lifted one hand, palm facing up. "You give me your number because you can't resist me. I text you a few times, you warm up to the idea, we go to dinner, you're miserable, and we part ways. We only see each other for CE registrations, so if it doesn't work out, you'd only be seeing me a few times a year. That's not so bad."

"What kinds of texts do you send?"

I frowned, thinking back to my last few texts to Cameron and wondering how this was relevant. "Uh, GIFs of cute cats landing on their feet against impossible odds?"

She narrowed her eyes. "You promise never to send me nude selfies?"

My head jerked back. "What? No!"

"Because I'm sick of getting unsolicited nude selfies."

What kinds of people did she give her number to?

I placed a hand over my heart. "I promise I'll never send you nude selfies. Unless you ask for one, of course."

Ivy smiled a little then, her gaze darting toward my chest. My own teasing smile faltered.

Focus, Tobias.

"Stop undressing me with your eyes, vixen," I whispered, winking at her and lifting my other hand, palm facing up. "What's the *best* that could happen? You give me your number, we have a great time and enjoy getting to know one another better."

Her skeptical tone was back. "Just getting to know one another? No strings attached?"

I thought of Yvonne explaining that it wasn't me, it was her, and who needed apartment keys to limit what we had?

No. Ivy was the opposite of Yvonne. Yvonne was a tailored pantsuit with a tightly knotted bun; Ivy was all-black clothes with funky earrings and bold lipstick. I studied Ivy a little closer, taking in the remaining rigidity in her posture, the subtle way her lower lip shifted as she nibbled at it inside her closed mouth.

What I saw standing in front of me wasn't a woman who was noncommittal because she was waiting for someone better than me to come along. I saw a woman who was scared to try in the first place.

I lifted my hands in surrender. "If no strings attached is what you want, that's what we'll do. But I have to warn you, dating me is like opening a can of Pringles. You can't have just one."

Still she hesitated. Still I waited.

Unable to resist any longer, I leaned against the counter again. "Look. I know we've only spoken twice over two semesters, but I think we have some real potential, and I think it'd be a shame not to give it a shot. What do you say?"

I watched her. She watched me. She probably didn't know her internal debate played clearly across her pretty face. Normally she hid her thoughts and feelings better than this, using our flirting game as a barrier between us, but I'd surprised her and slipped past her defenses. I watched the uncertainty in her eyes and basked in this moment; if a coy Ivy was beautiful, then an unguarded Ivy was breathtaking.

She shrugged one shoulder. "I always have fun talking to you, so why not?"

"That's not exactly a resounding yes, but I'll take it."

I smiled and tapped at my phone screen until it unlocked. Our fingers touched, and I hoped she didn't notice my hand flattening against the countertop, seeking balance.

After entering her number, she slid my phone back to me, the screen still lit up, and her last name spelled out as No Nudes.

I laughed, tapping out a quick text to her so she'd have my number too.

A phone behind the desk vibrated. Ivy ignored it.

The glass door opened behind me, and I glanced back at the student who walked in, her fingers tangling in her black braid and an enormous backpack slung over her shoulders.

Turning back to Ivy, I tsked and angled my head toward her phone. "Ivy, is this the kind of effort you're going to give our one shot?"

She rolled her eyes and picked up her phone, unlocking the screen and passing it to me without reading my text. "You can have the honors of entering your name, since you don't trust me to spell 'Azumah' correctly."

Moving quickly, I added myself as a contact and then backed toward the exit, navigating around the waiting student. "I'll be in touch, Ivy Lunden."

As the door closed behind me, I heard her laugh. She must've read my text, complete with a GIF of a nude cartoon character.

Success.

CHAPTER 5

IVY

*Seven missed calls from Mom. Dial * to listen to voicemails.*

Maybe I speak for overworked women everywhere, maybe it's just me, but nothing feels better than knowing I can go home and be alone. All day in an office with fluorescent light bulbs buzzing, students complaining, bosses demanding—*people*, right? Going home to peace and quiet at the end of the day was my reward for smiling through it all.

Tonight was no exception. Just imagining walking through my door melted away some of the tension in my shoulders. Van Gogh would be waiting for me, as always, sitting erect and watchful. I would tell him about my day—yes, I'm *that* kind of cat lady—as I put away my purse and keys, pulled on my leggings, and heated up dinner. We would sprawl on my couch and watch some TV before I went upstairs to my studio.

Home couldn't get more perfect than that.

Actually, one thing could make it more perfect: not having to go to work at all the next day. I dreamed for a moment, picturing a world where I painted and worked with art galleries and never had to step into the registrar's fluorescent lighting again. I wouldn't go back to my earlier art career that I hated, that was based on uninspiring commissions. This art career would be new. Different. Exactly what I wanted. I would finally channel the colors in my head into a solid, creative path.

The colors were such a natural part of me that it took years before I realized not everyone saw the world like I did. We'd been learning phonics in school, and each time the teacher asked us to match a vowel sound to its corresponding letter, I said the wrong answer.

"*Ay?*" Ms. Harlow over-enunciated.

"Pink," I'd said, immediately wishing I hadn't said it so loudly. No child wants to be different in front of her friends.

"*Ee?*" Ms. Harlow had asked.

This time I kept my voice quieter, hoping to blend with my classmates. "Green?"

The boy sitting directly in front of me turned to stare at me with wide eyes.

I'd whispered from then on, which worked until I had to take the test.

Mom had frowned at the letter grade scrawled at the top of my paper. "What happened?"

But how could a child explain that she saw colors when she heard sounds? How could a little girl understand that the way she looked at the world was different? I'd assumed everyone was just like me.

I was so drained from today and wrapped up in my art career dream that I almost drove past my exit ramp. Fortunately my cue, a giant billboard, was impossible to miss. It was the largest one on the highway. The logo of the community center downtown overlaid an image with poor enough quality that it had probably been taken with a phone. I could picture it now, unwilling volunteers gathering on a weekend to wrap their arms around one another in a stereotypical stock image pose. In Times New Roman font as large as a car, the billboard screamed *We Are Better Together!*

Better Together? More like extrovert propaganda.

I turned onto my street.

My house was a simple, two-story brick home, and it was filled with everything that brought me peace: calming white walls, warm lighting, art supplies, and a box of wine. My home was quiet; it was zen; it was exactly what I wanted.

But maybe I wanted Toby too.

Lately, when my mind had an empty space, it filled with Toby.

I felt equally panicked and flattered at how he had weaseled his way into my day. He'd texted me regularly since we exchanged numbers. He kept the conversation light and vague, sharing a corny joke from one of his patients, telling me how he was waiting for the first snowfall of the season so he could build a snowman draped over the hood of his best friend's car like it was a hit-and-run scene. (Did he plan to do this to Cameron's car? I knew he was close to Cameron, but neither Toby nor Cameron knew I was a link connecting the two of them. It wouldn't hurt if Cameron knew, but I also liked keeping this flirtation-ship away from his and Mel's prying eyes.)

The next thing I knew, Toby and I were exchanging dozens of texts, and then he was asking me to dinner with an oh-so-casual *Have you been to that new sushi place downtown? I've heard the lighting is dim enough that you can undress me with your eyes without embarrassing me so much this time.*

That was when I caught myself smiling at my phone. The conversation was fun. *He* was fun. Most surprising of all, *I* was having *fun*. Texting a man. A man who, for the record, hadn't sent a single nude selfie.

I'd heard of the new sushi place downtown, with its fabric menu and relaxing water displays and low lighting. It sounded romantic. But I liked keeping my first dates brief, with set cutoff times and clear exits for a quick escape in case the guy was a creep. For me, first dates were casual, not romantic.

Besides, I'd noticed a rewards card on his keychain, the well-worn plastic a silent witness to how much he loved gourmet grilled cheese sandwiches from Take It Cheesy.

I didn't need to unlock my phone to remember what I'd replied. *I'll meet you at Take It Cheesy for lunch at noon on Friday. Maybe I like embarrassing you in broad daylight.*

I also didn't need to unlock my phone to remember how he'd saved his name in it: *Toby - 10/10 Smile.*

I jolted when my phone vibrated with a call. Not just any call. The sixteenth call I'd had from that same number today.

I imagined hurling my phone out the window. I imagined the sharp cracking sound it would make hitting the pavement, the satisfaction I would feel. I imagined the hassle and expense of buying a new phone.

Shame on you. Remember, you're all she has, and she's all you have.

I answered on the fourth ring. "Hi, Mom."

"Oh, good, you're home. I worried you'd died in a ditch somewhere."

The tart yellow of her voice choked my breath. I swallowed. "Just turned onto my street. Made it home safe and sound, like always."

"Not like always. You know anything can happen in today's world. I like to know you're okay."

So what had the other fifteen calls been about? Her car remote stopped work-ing; an unfamiliar truck had circled her cul-de-sac; her showerhead dripped slightly more frequently today than it had yesterday… Just imagine if she learned how to text.

She could never learn how to text.

I stopped in front of my garage door, watching it slowly open. "No need to worry."

Mom began explaining the way the elastic in her pants seemed a little looser today. Maybe she'd worn these pants earlier this week, so they were already "lived-in," but also maybe her latest diet was working wonders already. She'd have to wait a few more days to be certain.

All I wanted was some quiet time to myself, but I loved my mom, and I did my best to patiently listen. Though Mom never discussed details, I was the product of a brief but intense relationship she'd had in her forties, so the two of us were the only family we had. I couldn't let the meaningfulness of that dim because of how poorly we got along.

Movement from my neighbor's house caught my periphery, but I stared straight ahead.

Avoid eye contact. Avoid eye contact. Avoid…

Now my neighbor progressed from waving on her front stoop to shuffling across her yard toward me.

I willed the garage door to open faster.

Hurry hurry hurry…

Phyllis knocked on my car window, the rap of her knuckles startling me from my telepathy. I smiled, waved, and gestured to my phone. She smiled, waved, and gestured for me to roll down my window.

I sighed. Yes, I spent my weeknights pretending to be a hermit. But, no, I wouldn't be mean-spirited.

Phyllis knocked again.

"What's that noise?" Mom asked.

"My neighbor. Just a sec."

Phyllis started talking before my window rolled down even halfway. "Who are you talking to?"

"My mom."

"What does your neighbor want?" Mom said in my other ear.

"I don't know," I said to Mom.

"Is your mom doing well?" Phyllis asked. "I'm so sorry I've never gotten to meet her."

"Yes, she's great."

"Your neighbor is great?" Mom said. "Wonderful. I can't wait to meet her."

I thought of Mom and Phyllis meeting. I thought of my life being under not just two individual magnifying glasses, but one giant stereo microscope wielded by two well-meaning but extremely bored women. I didn't need them exchanging numbers and comparing notes.

Mom and Phyllis could never *ever* meet.

"I noticed you changed your drapes," Phyllis said.

"I'll have to come over," Mom said.

"Yes, this weekend," I said to Phyllis.

"Perfect," Mom said. "I'll be there Saturday afternoon."

What. A. Mess. I hadn't muted my phone because the last time I did, Mom almost called the police because she assumed I was dead. Again. We only lived across town from one another, but she worried over me worse than a mother hen.

"No, not that, just a second, Mom." I covered my phone's speakers with one hand and smiled at my neighbor.

Phyllis made a show of studying my house, eyeing the suspected new drapes. "Are they room darkening? They don't look like they're room darkening."

"They're blackout curtains." Because it was my guest-room-turned-art studio, and I didn't need my neighbors—aka Phyllis—wondering why that room stayed lit up late into the night.

"I remember that room when Janet lived there. She had it painted the prettiest blue."

I also remembered Janet's blue. It was turquoise, bright enough to singe my retinas, and it was the first room I'd repainted. But Phyllis didn't need to know what I thought of the previous owner's paint choices. Janet had been Phyllis's friend, and Janet's family had put her house on the market so they could afford to move her into a nursing home. As much as I sympathized with the sadness of Phyllis losing her friend, I didn't sympathize enough to invite her inside my home. She would not find a speck of turquoise paint on my walls.

The hazards of moving into a neighborhood of almost entirely elderly people. The hazards of having Phyllis as my neighbor.

I smiled and gestured toward my garage again. "I should head inside. Van is probably clawing at the door since he heard my garage open."

"Oh, of course, don't let me hold you up!" She took half a step away, smiling and waving, her gaze tracking over the items in my open garage.

I tamped down my annoyance as I pulled forward. My garage was filled with shovels and rakes and weed whackers. Phyllis could gawk all she wanted, and I could have the quiet evening I wanted.

I pushed the garage door button and watched it slowly descend, still sitting in my car, using my rearview mirror to watch Phyllis continue her inspection.

I uncovered my phone. "Okay, Mom, I'm back."

She was still talking. She hadn't noticed I was gone.

"—chicken salad sandwiches and—"

"What?" I said. "When?"

"Saturday afternoon," she said. "Haven't you been listening?"

"No, my neighbor—"

"Your neighbor can come over Saturday afternoon, and I can't?"

I gripped my steering wheel tighter, feeling like the stereo microscope loomed overhead. "No, nobody is coming over Saturday afternoon."

"Then what's happening this weekend?"

So, so many reasons for Mom and Phyllis to stay strangers.

Taking my purse and keys, I made my way toward my door. "It was last weekend. My neighbor asked about my drapes, and I said I'd changed them this weekend."

Mom huffed. "I wish you'd said *last* weekend and not *this* weekend. It would've saved this whole 'who's on first' situation. What did you do with your drapes?"

"Just found a sale on blackout curtains. No big deal."

Van greeted me at the door, weaving between my legs and telling me how much he missed me. Just kidding. He didn't miss me; he wanted dinner.

"I'd love to see them," Mom cooed. "Good drapes change the entire feeling of a room."

"They're really not a big deal. Just some simple drapes is all."

"And I just have some simple interest in my daughter's life is all," she said, ever the expert at turning my tone back on me.

Other than a potential run-in with Phyllis, I didn't mind if Mom came over. We lived across town from one another, but the short drive didn't bother me. What I minded was the memory of the last time Mom had tried climbing the stairs to the second floor. She'd looked frail and trembling and withered. I'd walked directly behind her, hands outstretched in case the worst should happen. I'd never been so grateful for her single-story home before; now I did my best to plan all our visits at her house, not mine.

"I'll bring pictures when I stop by tomorrow night, okay?" I said.

"I'd still like to come over Saturday afternoon," she insisted.

"Let's talk about it tomorrow night."

"We can finalize our plans tomorrow night then. How was your day?"

Not at all what I'd said, but this was how Mom worked, pushing and pushing at even the hint of a boundary between us. Moments like these made it harder to remember that Mom was aging quickly, and we were the only family we had, and we wouldn't have one another forever. And these moments were growing increasingly frequent.

"Same old, same old, just buried the latest dead body in the quad." After picking up Van, I made my way to the kitchen, turning on table lamps and adjusting the thermostat as I went.

She ignored my outrageous comment. "Speaking of old, I ran into your old gym teacher at the grocery store the other day, and I must say, all that exercising she used to do didn't make her age any better than I'm aging. Not that I'm judging, but her face is as spotted as an overripe banana."

I kept my voice light. "It's probably from all the sun when she was exercising outside."

"Her cousin—you remember her cousin?—has a friend whose brother-in-law is opening a new art gallery downtown."

I tried to follow the story. "So…my gym teacher's friend's cousin's brother-in-law?"

"No, her cousin's friend's brother-in-law, and the new gallery is accepting artwork in a couple months."

I knew what she was hinting at, but I played dumb. When in doubt, always play dumb. Petty people will feel good thinking they know more than you, and helpful people will tend to over-explain so you'll know even more at the end than you did at the beginning. Or maybe it'll just buy you more time so you can brace yourself for what's coming next. Playing dumb is a win-win. In this case, a win-win-win.

"Spring is a good time to open a gallery," I said. "More people out and about."

"So I told her you were an artist—"

I buried my face in Van's fur, losing myself in the thrum of his purring.

"—just like you'd always dreamed of being, and you'd love to submit something."

"No, I wouldn't," I mumbled into my cat's side.

"What was that?"

I lifted my face from Van. "No, I wouldn't like to submit anything."

"Why not? I know commissioned pieces ended up not being your favorite, but you could sell original pieces too."

Not being my favorite? I'd worked myself into a state of creative burnout and depression, which I was still recovering from years later. Sure, I'd paid off my college debt in record time, and I'd started to make a name for myself. But commissioned art, as much as there was nothing wrong with it, was just that. I wanted more.

"I don't have anything original worth selling." I thought of the half-finished pieces in my upstairs studio. Another reason to take pictures of my drapes and keep Mom on the first floor.

"Surely you have something," she insisted. "Your house is like an art gallery itself."

"Nothing is ready, okay? I'm working on stuff, but it's nothing good yet."

She sighed, long and loud and directly into her phone's receiver. "I was just trying to help."

"I know, and I appreciate it." I dished some leftovers onto a plate and added thirty seconds to the microwave. "Look, I'll stop by tomorrow night. I need to go feed Van and salt my sidewalk before tonight's snowfall. I'll see you tomorrow, okay?"

"I'll make a tuna casserole for dinner tomorrow night."

I grinned, grateful to be back in our conversational routine. Mom always offered to make tuna casserole, which she knew I hated, and then she acted pleasantly surprised when I insisted on bringing dinner instead. "No, it's okay, I'll pick something up on my way."

"Are you sure?" she dithered.

"Yes, I'm sure."

"I hate to be a bother."

"You're not a bother."

"I guess I wouldn't mind some eggplant parmigiana from Sal's…"

I smiled at her feigned truce. "Yes, I can do that. Bye, Mom."

"See you tomorrow! I love you!"

"I love you too."

Minutes later, enveloped in silence, my home was the cozy haven I loved, with me eating leftovers at the coffee table and Van chowing down at his cat dish.

Satisfaction ebbed through my body, my limbs growing heavy. Van soon joined me on the couch. He curled into the curve between my shoulder and neck, purring while I searched Netflix.

"What are you in the mood for tonight?" I asked him. "Romance? Action? Horror? I picked last night, so it's only fair I give you a chance."

Starting up an episode of a show I was partially through, I texted Cameron and Mel. My best friends would sympathize with my neighborly woes.

Ivy: Phyllis noticed my new curtains.

Mel: That gives me the heebie-jeebies. Does she have X-ray vision? Super strong binoculars?

Cameron: Definitely X-ray vision.

Ivy: This calls for drastic measures.

Mel: Moving across town? No, wait, move in with me!

Ivy: No. Taking down all my curtains, turning on all my lights, and walking around naked. Maybe that eyeful would finally be enough for her.

Cameron: You might end up trading in Phyllis for your own stalker.

Mel: That's Cam's way of telling you you're hot stuff, and creepy men might see your streaking.

Cameron: Isn't that what I said?

I smiled. The one Cameron needed to call "hot stuff" was Mel. I'd spent the last five years watching the two of them covertly stare at one another, and they still showed no signs of confessing their feelings.

A new text notification lit my screen.

Toby - 10/10 Smile: It's Wednesday.

Ivy: Your point?

Toby - 10/10 Smile: Then it's Thursday, then it's Friday.

I knew what he was getting at, but razzing Toby was half the fun.

Ivy: You need new underwear.

Toby - 10/10 Smile: Why are you always trying to get me naked?

Ivy: I'm talking about the underwear labeled with the days of the week. Brilliant scientists designed them so regular people like you and me don't have to keep track in our heads anymore.

Toby - 10/10 Smile: Yuk it up, smartypants. The joke will be on you when I wear my favorite Friday undies on our date. How do you think I became an expert on the days of the week in the first place?

I snorted a half-laugh, and Van blinked at the sound. Despite Toby's joking, despite our flirtationship being a game, I knew the truth: Toby was anything but playful about our date. He was counting down like a little boy at summer camp.

It was adorable. It was genuine and kind of weird in its sincerity. In a world of superficial dating, Toby's all-or-nothing enthusiasm felt...well, I felt butterflies at the moment, but I wasn't about to admit that to him.

Ivy: Ah, the lunch date. This Friday, you say? I have a scheduling conflict. I forgot I'm busy for the next three to nine Fridays.

Toby - 10/10 Smile: Hilarious.

Ivy: It's called playing coy.

Toby - 10/10 Smile: Is that what the kids are calling it these days?

Did he see my flirting for the illusion I wanted him to see or for the truth I wanted to hide? The way his eyes fixed on me at the registrar's office, the way he watched my every gesture like he cataloged my movements—under his attention, I felt like the only woman in the room. Under his attention, I felt visible. It was unnerving.

Ivy: Goodnight. See you not today, not Thursday, but Friday.

Toby - 10/10 Smile: Goodnight, Ivy. Sweet dreams.

CHAPTER 6

IVY

Zero missed calls from Mom.

Even though it was only temporary relief, I sat in my car for a few extra moments and just breathed. With the ignition off, the cold made short work of invading my car. But the brisk air gave me something to focus on other than the next hour of my Thursday night that I would spend with Mom.

I wouldn't think about how I felt trapped by her need for me. Don't think about how I feared the worst when I saw the ways she wasn't the vibrant woman who'd raised me. Don't think about the times I'd canceled plans with Cameron and Mel because Mom needed me at the last minute.

I'd think of it as a game. A sort of Russian roulette. Only, you know, a non-lethal Russian roulette.

I climbed out of my car, focusing on the winter air prickling my skin. My shoes made a tapping sound as I walked the sidewalk up to Mom's small, vinyl-sided house. I opened her door with the key she'd given me several years ago.

The usual musty smell assaulted my nose. I ignored it, toeing off my boots and resting them next to the door.

Turning, my eyes surveyed the living room. Picture frames and knickknacks filled the shelves. Artwork hung in perfect groupings. Each throw pillow was in place. A single porcelain teacup rested on its matching saucer on the coffee table. Her favorite recliner, where she always sat, stood empty.

To an outsider, my perfectionist mom's home proved she was a woman in her seventies who was self-sufficient enough to live on her own.

But I'd spent the last few years noticing the changes. They were subtle at first, and they stretched over a long period of time. A single dirty fork in the sink. Two days' worth of newspapers on her front stoop, soggy with weather. A couple of weeds popping through the sidewalk.

To an outsider, this was normal living. To me, the soft sheen of dust that covered each picture frame showed Mom was feeling each one of her seventy-some years.

She'd never admit it.

But why these changes? Was it difficult for Mom to get around? Did she need new glasses and couldn't see the dust flecking her shelves and the food sticking to her plates? My worst fear: was she developing dementia and forgetting about things like dishes?

This was part of my game, trying to figure out why the most perfectionistic person I'd ever known was now letting dust and dishes build up in her otherwise flawless existence. Asking her directly was no use. How did you convince someone as independent as Mom to admit she needed help—and that there wasn't anything wrong with that?

"Work went a little late today," I said to the empty living room. "Mom?"

Setting the takeout containers of eggplant parmigiana on the kitchen table, I glanced around the empty room. Where was she? Chest tightening, I hurried down the hall. The half-bath beneath the stairs was empty. The guest bedroom, now converted into a knitting room, was empty. Her bedroom was the same. Only one room left—her master bathroom.

Even with my rising panic, the last thing I expected to see that Thursday night was my mom, curled into a ball on the floor of the bathroom, her face pale and wet with tears. Her steadily shrinking frame looked even smaller when she was half naked and collapsed on the floor.

My knees cracked when I hit the linoleum. "Mom? Mom!" I searched for pulse points in her neck and wrists. Was that the flutter of her heartbeat? Or was it my own trembling fingers?

I fumbled for my phone in my pocket, but my hands didn't seem to work.

A half-functioning part of my brain noted I'd left the door open, and snow would be swirling inside, and Mom would sit up at any moment and tell me, "I raised you better than that, silly girl," and I would close the door and go count the dirty dishes in the sink and then heat up dinner for her.

That same part of my brain started lecturing me in a voice that sounded like hers. *If I'd been a better daughter, I wouldn't have rolled my eyes when she called me sixteen times yesterday. I would've checked on her earlier instead of staying late at work. If... I...*

She was my only family. She was all I had. I couldn't lose her.

I blinked, and then I was on the phone with an emergency dispatcher. How had I gotten my phone out of my pocket? How had I managed to call 9-1-1?

"Where is your emergency?"

The voice was detached, cold, professional. It filled my head with glacier blue. It was a beacon in my drowning mind.

I must've answered with Mom's address, because the voice asked a different question. "What is your emergency?"

"My mom. She's on the floor. I don't know what happened. I came to check on her like I do most nights, and she's pale, and—"

"Is the scene safe? Do you see any broken glass, blood—"

"No, nothing like that."

"Does she appear to be injured in any way?"

My eyes began at the top of her head, darting around what I could see of her body. "No, I don't see any blood or anything."

"Thank you, ma'am. I already have someone heading your way. They'll take a good look at her and see how they can—ma'am, please take a deep breath."

A deep breath? I didn't need to take a deep breath. But I needed these wheezing sounds to stop, because they were lighting up the inside of my head in a putrid color that slashed and cut and—

"Ma'am, please breathe for a minute. Follow me. Inhale. Exhale. Inhale. Exhale."

I *knew* how to breathe; I didn't need her telling me to breathe. I needed her to tell me—

"—Inhale. Exhale—"

Okay, fine, I'd breathe like she said just to get her to stop chanting like a yoga instructor. A yoga instructor was not what I needed right now. I needed—

I breathed, the wheezing slowed, and I realized it'd been me making those putrid slashes in my mind.

"Ma'am, I'm going to stay on the line with you until the team arrives. Just keep breathing. Inhale. Exhale..."

CHAPTER 7

TOBY

Toby: It's Friday, Ivy Lunden. See you soon.

Of course my last patient of the morning ran late on Friday, making me late to meet Ivy at Take It Cheesy. I rushed through the entrance, the bell above the door chiming after me. I noticed a Thor look-alike with his arm around his pretty girl-friend, a few college-age students slouching over dirty plates and textbooks, but no Ivy. I glanced at my Garmin. I was only a few minutes late. Surely she didn't leave because of just a few minutes.

I claimed a quiet corner table, nodding to the cashier as I walked past the counter. Take It Cheesy had the best gourmet grilled cheeses, and if you entered a sandwich idea in the box by the register, they put it in the running to become the special of the month. My sandwich idea became a regular menu item—raisin cinnamon swirl bread with sharp cheddar cheese, the perfect mix of sweet and salty. Making it onto their menu might be the crowning achievement of my life, now that I thought about it.

After hanging my jacket on the back of my chair, I settled in. *Ivy should be along any minute.*

I spun my phone in a circle on the table, tempted to go back through our texts. You couldn't blame me for at least trying for the sushi restaurant. I wasn't embarrassed to admit I'm a romantic, and it would've been a perfect first step in what I hoped would be a great relationship with Ivy.

She'd killed off the sushi idea in no time. She'd opted for a *lunch date*. The flirty line about embarrassing me in broad daylight didn't fool me. Lunch dates were for people who didn't want to go on the date in the first place.

Ivy was skittish. She was keeping her guard up. She might say she was giving us a chance, but I knew the truth. Holding me at arm's length was her first line of defense.

We'd see how long that lasted. We would be great together. I could see it now: date nights at Take It Cheesy *and* the sushi place, cooking at her house on the weekends, maybe going to Trivia Tuesdays with Cameron.

Cool it, Tobias Azumah.

Back to my point: I liked a challenge. I wouldn't give up until I'd charmed her to the best of my abilities.

I checked the time on my Garmin. I checked the time on my phone. I compared my Garmin and phone to the sandwich-shaped clock hanging behind the cashier. All the clocks seemed to be working correctly.

Any minute now, Ivy would walk through that door in a swirl of snowflakes. Maybe she'd wear that knit hat and scarf I'd noticed on her desk last week. Maybe she'd wear that red lipstick—no, that seemed like a dinner date move, and since she'd relegated me to a *lunch date*, that was unlikely.

Any minute now.

How soon was too soon to text and ask if she was still coming? We'd agreed to meet at ten past noon. I'd gotten here at fifteen past. Now it was almost 12:30. Any sign of impatience would probably scare her off. But lunch dates were designed to be fast, and now we had so little time left together.

I tapped out a text.

Toby: Feel free to send me your order, and I can have it ready for you when you get here.

I waited.

And waited.

Maybe it was for the best that she'd wanted to meet here. The sushi restaurant had servers who would've given me knowing looks about the empty chair across from me. The dim lighting would've hidden Ivy undressing me with her eyes, sure, but it also would've screamed that it was a place for dates. At a grilled cheese diner in broad daylight, it was more believable that a friend might bail at the last minute. That was more palatable than the truth: the stunning blond I'd been obsessing over had ditched me.

She said she'd give us a shot. Well, her exact words were "Why not?" I'd had to talk her into it. But still, there had to be a good reason she wasn't here. I only knew Ivy through a few conversations and some vague social media stalking—hey, we've all done it—but this didn't feel like her. She might be noncommittal, but she wasn't forgetful or mean.

Lunch breaks don't last forever. At 12:50, after a few more casual texts to let Ivy know I was waiting for her, I had no choice but to order a sandwich and scarf it down on my drive back to work. Maybe the grease would numb the sting of rejection.

I should ask Cameron. He worked in the computer science department, which was…well, okay, nowhere near the registrar's office. It was close to the tutoring center, which he regularly mentioned because the woman of his dreams worked at the tutoring center, and he delighted in every excuse to stop by her desk and see her. Still, maybe Cameron knew if Ivy was okay.

Since I couldn't stop by his office and still get back to work on time, I called him.

He answered at the first ring. "I'm not complaining, but it's very weird for you to call me in the middle of the workday."

"Do you have a minute to talk?"

I heard some papers rustling, and then silence. I pictured him straightening his glasses and settling back in his chair to focus on our conversation. "What's going on?"

"A girl just stood me up."

"Is this the lunch date girl?"

"Yeah. She didn't show up. No text, no call, nothing."

But she wasn't just the woman who'd stood me up. She was Ivy, who seamlessly engaged with each student at the registrar. Who made time to talk to me about her day.

Did a person like that leave a man at Take It Cheesy for nothing? My gut instinct told me something was wrong.

But I wasn't just thinking of Ivy. I was thinking of myself. Because Ivy was *also* the woman who'd stood me up. Who was so jaded she hesitated to give out her number for fear of unwanted nude selfies. Who flirted with me but didn't want any strings attached. Wouldn't a woman that cynical use any excuse to avoid a date? My ego, petty as it was, urged me to charge into the registrar's office and demand answers. Let her know she was better than this.

"Sorry, Toby. That hurts." Cameron paused. "This would've been your first date since Yvonne, right?"

I stopped at a red light, frowning as I remembered one fight in particular with Yvonne. She didn't want to rearrange the furniture in her living room. I thought it would be a nice change, really open up the room, give her more time sitting in the sunshine, which would help her vitamin D levels—everyone knew vitamin D was healthy. I started moving the couch with her still sitting on it, laughing because it was funny. Instead, she'd jumped up and hissed at me, "Don't you know when to stop?"

No, actually, I didn't know when to stop.

I sighed. "Yeah, it would've been the first date. Riddle me this, how do people know whether they need to show determination and keep going, or give up and walk away? Do I try to reach this girl or call it quits?"

Every day I taught my patients to fight against the temptation to give up. How hypocritical would it be to do exactly what I tell them not to do? But if Ivy didn't want to see me...

"I don't have a good answer for that one," he said, his tone kind. "You know I've been hung up on the same person for years. Clearly I don't know when to walk away either."

Good point. Did I want to wait around for a woman as long as Cameron had? Hard pass. I should have felt grateful that disappointments *early* in a relationship were better than knives through the heart *later* in a relationship—or years spent with unrequited feelings.

"I guess it's best to know now," I said. "I have better things to do than try to see the woman who stood me up on a lunch date. Right?"

"Right," Cameron said.

Still, I couldn't help thinking about it, and when I thought about something, I talked about it. "You know, I met her when I was signing up for CEs."

What I was really doing: digging for information and excuses. *Hey, Cameron, have any of your coworkers had last-minute emergencies that would've prevented them from taking a lunch break? A coworker from the regis-trar's office, perhaps?*

Seriously, what was my plan here? Make sure she was healthy and whole? Vent to him about the ache in my diaphragm that hadn't let up since she left me stranded, and how could she do such a heartless thing?

"You were going on a date with a student?" he asked. "I wouldn't have guessed you would go for someone younger."

"She's not a student; she's staff." I pulled into my parking spot at Better Movement.

"Really? Maybe I know her. I can tell her she missed out by standing you up, put in a good word for you. If you're still interested."

Before I could answer him, I felt it, the spine-crawling awareness of managerial eyes on me. I looked up. Deke stood in the waiting room, his eyes moving from the parking lot to the clock above the receptionist's desk. Hudson wanted me to be nice to this guy, who was more robot than human? *This* guy?

My annoyance fizzled into chagrin when I glanced at the time on my Garmin. Deke was right. I was a few minutes late—but only a few.

I unbuckled my seat belt. "I'm sure she'd appreciate you hassling her at her workplace about the date she ditched. Anyway, I just got back to work. See you at basketball?"

"Of course."

I hung up, knowing that even if Cameron did know her, even if he could help me understand her better, I'd love answers directly from Ivy. I settled on texting her again after work today.

Don't you know when to stop?

No. I still didn't.

CHAPTER 8

IVY

Mel: We missed you at the staff meeting today, Ivy!
Cameron: If you played hooky to do something fun and didn't invite us, please know we're deeply offended.

Withdrawal is my knee-jerk reaction to stress. After a lifetime of only me and Mom, the two of us prefer to do it on our own, whether it's cooking or shopping or waiting in the ER, where I happened to be reliving the last several hours while I watched Mom sleep.

The ambulance ride was an experience I'll be happy never to repeat again, with Mom pale and silent, and the two paramedics talking between themselves. I held her cold hand in mine the whole time, wishing she would sit up and ask me why I wasn't wearing a coat on a freezing night like this. I would explain I'd forgotten it in my haste to climb into the ambulance with her, and please don't worry, I would go back to get it now that she was awake and well.

Mom was groggy but conscious by the time we reached the big ER downtown. She blinked in confusion at the fluorescent lights and doctors. Numb, I filled out her paperwork and answered questions for her the best I could.

That's where her passivity ended. When the nurse left us behind a cloth partition in the large ER room, Mom insisted she didn't need to be there. She wanted to go home. She had a little sprain, nothing more; the swelling in her ankle just meant she needed that bag of frozen peas waiting for her at home, and she laughed and said we could cook the frozen peas with dinner.

Then she tried to climb out of the hospital bed on her own. I caught her when she fell. I felt her trembling, her limbs weak.

Now Mom's quiet snores painted soft, buttery yellow in my mind. I watched her, wondering over our reversed roles. How many times had I woken up to find her watching me sleep? When I was little, I'd bolt upright and ask if it was time to play; when I was older, I pretended to still be asleep, embarrassed and annoyed to see her so needy. Now the child watched over the mother.

I should spend less time feeling annoyed with her millions of questions and more time trying to understand her. I would ask her what she'd dreamed about doing when she was my age. I would tell her about my art, how I was afraid to show my new canvases to anyone, to take that chance after I'd already failed once, because my day job was depressing, but at least it was low risk.

The next time she wanted to come over on a Saturday afternoon to make the precarious climb up to my second floor, I would welcome her with open arms. Who knew how many Saturday afternoons we had left together?

I couldn't dwell on that though. Not right now.

Mom woke up, blinking at her surroundings. "Since when is a sprain worthy of a hospital stay?"

When they took her for X-rays, I left the partitioned area to sit in the larger waiting room down the hall. Thankfully there were a few windows to see the outdoors, which were washed in early afternoon light. An entire night and most of a day had passed because a serious car accident pushed Mom's emergency to the bottom of the ER's priorities. Time moved on while we waited.

Maybe taking care of Mom in the evenings wasn't such a good plan. I couldn't continue juggling this schedule, frantically keeping multiple glass orbs in the air, hoping I didn't drop something breakable, like Mom's heart. If I'd been there when she fell, she wouldn't need X-rays right now—but I couldn't quit my job to stay with her nonstop. I also couldn't afford a nursing home or a visiting nurse.

Stressing like this wasn't helping Mom; it was only muddying my thoughts. I tried to focus on the colors in my mind, wishing for a pleasant sound, like Cameron and Mel's laughter.

Cameron and Mel.

Resisting the instinct to handle this on my own, I unlocked my phone to text Cameron and Mel. Instead I found a voicemail from Phyllis about Van being on her roof. In typical cat fashion, he refused to climb down. As much as I loved Van, I wasn't leaving Mom's side.

I texted my two best friends, forcing the words through my numbness. Each thumb press against my phone screen felt exhausting.

Ivy: My mom fell. We're at the ER. I'm freaking out and need someone to check on Van because my neighbor called to say he's stuck on her roof. Help?

Their replies were instant.

Cameron: I'll rescue Van and set out fresh cat food and water for him. I'll meet you at the hospital after. Anything I can bring you from home?

Tears dripped onto my phone. It took a moment to realize they were mine. As much as I made fun of the lovable goofball, Cameron was good people.

Mel: Be there in a few minutes.

Only then, when I was relieved enough to take a couple deep breaths, did I notice the texts from Toby. Only then did I realize it was Friday, early afternoon, and I'd missed our lunch date. His messages were spread out over the last few hours, proving he'd given me plenty of time to reply, but I hadn't been answering my phone.

Toby - 10/10 Smile: Feel free to send me your order, and I can have it ready for you when you get here.

Toby - 10/10 Smile: I know you like playing coy, but this takes it to a whole new level. I'm impressed!

Toby - 10/10 Smile: So do you have any other openings coming up in the next three to nine Fridays?

Toby - 10/10 Smile: All joking aside, are you okay?

I'd completely forgotten. My emotions were crowded with worry and fatigue and daughterly remorse, so why not add another layer of guilt to the mix?

I should text Toby. I'd been ditched; I'd been ghosted; I knew how that knife could twist in your feelings. I didn't want to hurt him. But I also didn't have it in me to text him anything deeper than the most superficial reply. It took concentrated effort to simply sit here and wait for my friends. My very essence felt watered down and faded out; I couldn't give any more, even just for a simple text.

I managed to type out a quick *Something came up.*

Closing my eyes and letting the ER fade away, I imagined how our date would've gone. He would have arrived at Take It Cheesy before me because he was the type to always show up early. Our table would have been one of the booths in the back, where it was quiet enough for real conversations. He would have teased. I would have evaded and flirted, denying exactly how much I enjoyed every minute with him.

He would have gradually peeled back my layers. He would have seen more than I meant for him to see. And in the end, I would have given in to another date, and then another, and maybe that third date ended with a kiss. A long, deep kiss? A quick peck? Maybe more than a kiss—

A hand rubbed my back, just as soothing as Mel's teal voice. "I brought snacks."

I blinked out of my daydream and smiled. "Sugary ones?"

"Of course. I'm many things, but I'm not a monster." She paused the back rub, which I immediately missed, and withdrew a chocolate-covered pastry from a Bluesy Bean bag, which I immediately drooled over.

"I can't remember when I last ate," I said, already chewing a mouthful of delightful sweetness.

Mel held up two carryout cups. "I brought coffee and tea. I didn't know if you'd be exhausted enough to want caffeine or stressed enough to want some chamomile."

In a few moments, I would need to walk back through those doors to see Mom after her X-rays... "Caffeine, please and thank you."

I found myself rambling about Mom and private X-ray rooms, how much morphine they'd given her, and I needed a break, so here I sat. The ramble culminated in an apology. "I'm sorry for ruining your day if you had plans for the weekend. I was worried about Van with how cold it is, and then Mom, and then I couldn't think of anyone else, and I'm sorry—"

Mel's hand returned to my back. "It's okay. I'm here because I love you. You can always call me for anything."

This was what love looked like: dropping everything to show up at the ER for your distraught friend on a Friday afternoon, bringing her coffee and tea and pastries. No questions asked. No judgments passed. Just pure love. I needed her, and she showed up.

With a friend like this, I could confess my fears that extended beyond the ER's walls.

"I noticed she was getting older," I whispered. "I just...I didn't realize how much older, you know?" My throat tightened around my next words. "But if I put her in a nursing home, she'll hate me. I'll feel guilty, and I just—"

Cameron, bearing his own delivery from Bluesy Bean, interrupted me with a grand entrance of sliding doors and swirling snowflakes. Perfect timing, because

I was about to become outright emotional. Ivy Lunden didn't get outright emotional.

But then he made my raw emotions worse.

Cameron set the Bluesy Bean packages on an end table and crouched in front of me, his gaze concerned. "What do you need? Is there anything I can do?"

Gratitude swelled in my chest until it stuck in my throat and pricked tears in my eyes. I would *not* cry… "Just having you both here is more than enough. Thank you."

A nurse slouched into the room, her voice beige and exhausted. "Ivy Lunden."

Cursing under my breath, I rushed away from Cameron and Mel. If I could be in the room before Mom got there, then she'd never need to worry about why I'd left for a few minutes.

But Mom was already in the room. She sat upright on the bed, hands folded in front of her, her knuckles white from clasping together so tightly. A few stray hairs puffed out of place, but otherwise, she looked good.

"Where were you?" she asked.

"I just needed to walk around for a minute."

The doctor strode into the room, turning through papers on his clipboard. Mom sat straighter. The doctor explained that Mom had a broken ankle, something called a Pott's fracture, and he would refer her to a surgeon. After her surgery, she would need physical therapy. Did either of us have any questions, he seemed to wonder aloud to himself more than to us, while his eyes darted toward the gap in the partition at the sound of another ambulance arriving.

My phone vibrated. *Toby - 10/10 Smile* spelled out on my screen, but I looked away. I couldn't think about Toby right now. I would fix my mistake of missing our date later. I needed to focus on Mom right now. She needed me to face this with her.

I looked at Mom. She looked at me. I took one of her white-knuckled hands in mine, feeling her papery skin beneath my palm.

Together. We'd figure it out together.

CHAPTER 9

TOBY

Deke: I'm following up about the spreadsheet I made to track continuing education credits. Please let me know as soon as you're available to review the new process.

Crossing my arms over my chest, I leaned against the staff lockers and watched Deke and Hudson walk through the therapy room. Deke moved unnaturally, his robotic movements stiff and impersonal, his posture uncomfortably straight; Hudson gestured around the room and smiled at everyone who glanced his way. How could such opposites manage to work well together? How could I manage to do the same with Deke?

Still puzzled, I reached into my locker for the patient files I'd taken home yesterday for another late night of work in front of the TV. Beneath the patient files sat my phone.

I paused, my hand hovering. Hudson had a strict policy against phones in the therapy room—a policy I fully agreed with because our patients deserved all of our attention. So as much as it pained me, I hadn't been able to check my phone to see whether Ivy had replied about our lunch date.

But thanks to a rare last-minute cancellation, I wasn't in the therapy room now. I unlocked my screen.

Ivy: Something came up.

Three words. They could mean anything. Was it something simple, like work was too busy so she couldn't get away? Or was it something complicated, like she'd had second thoughts?

Details, woman, I needed details.

I tapped out a text.

Toby: Can I help?

No. Too pushy. I deleted and tried again.

Toby: What happened?

Vague indifference sounded even worse.

I settled on sending *Are you okay?* and instantly wished I hadn't.

Long moments passed as I debated. My thumb hovered over the call icon. A multitude of emotions could hide in a text. But emotions couldn't hide in a person's voice unless they were really, really good. As much as Ivy might play coy, I doubted she could act well enough to throw me off.

I walked through the break room, stepped out the back door and stood under the eaves to avoid the steadily falling snowflakes.

It rang four times before she answered. "Hello?"

One word was all I needed to gauge the exhaustion and stress in her voice. But she also sounded…wary? Was she worried I was calling because I was mad at her?

Not wanting to scare her off, I kept my voice soft. "Hey."

"Hi," she repeated, a sure sign I was right about that exhaustion I'd heard.

I frowned. "Are you okay?"

"I'm fine," she said, although she sounded anything but. "Sorry about our lunch date."

Just lay it on me. I thought before I spoke for once. She'd grudgingly agreed to one date with me. Asking too much too soon wouldn't help my cause.

I cleared my throat. "That's okay. Want to tell me what happened?"

She hesitated, then sighed. "My mom fell. She broke her ankle. We've been at the ER since late last night, and she just went to sleep a bit ago."

The ache in my diaphragm eased with relief. I'd been wrapped up in our failed lunch date, in how I felt about getting stood up, in my own insecurities, and now I knew the reason wasn't Ivy second-guessing herself or me. She'd missed our date for a real emergency. We still had our one shot.

Wait a second. While I'd been sitting at Take It Cheesy, Ivy had been sitting at the ER. How could I be relieved for myself in light of this?

Shame on you, Tobias Azumah.

I refocused. "Is your mom okay?"

"I guess so," Ivy said around a shuffling noise in the background. "We're still at the ER. I guess the fact that there are more urgent patients than us is a good sign, right?"

I glanced at my Garmin watch, making some quick calculations about the hours she'd spent at the ER. "Sorry you've been there for so long." My inner healthcare worker started kicking in. "Did your mom say how she fell?"

"She said she got dizzy. Maybe it was low blood sugar or blood pressure. One of the nurses said it's not unusual for someone in their seventies."

I frowned. Falls were common for the elderly, but had the doctor mentioned that one fall usually meant there were more to come? I wasn't about to bring it up now. Ivy already sounded exhausted and worried. I wouldn't add to her fears. The doctor had more firsthand knowledge than I did anyway, so I shouldn't get involved.

I settled for repeating, "Are you okay?"

"I'm fine."

But I could hear the truth behind her voice. She was far from fine.

I imagined her scenario playing out in my own life, if my mom had fallen and broken her ankle. My family was large and close-knit, so the ER would've been flooded with my dad, me, my two brothers, and their families. We were big. We were loud. The nurses would've kicked us out in a matter of minutes.

"Do you have anyone else there with you? Any other family?" I asked.

"It's just me and my mom, but my closest friends are here"—her voice softened—"and they're like family to me."

I mentally erased the picture I'd drawn of my boisterous relatives descending on the unsuspecting ER. Ivy's family life was nothing like mine. I imagined her sitting next to her mom's bed, just the two of them. Alone.

"Is there anything I can do? I get off work in a few hours."

"No, thanks."

"I can bring you dinner."

"Please don't worry yourself. We'll be heading home soon, I hope."

I heard the stubbornness in her voice loud and clear, but that was something Ivy Lunden hadn't learned about me yet: I could match her stubbornness with more to spare.

"What about ice cream? Is that your comfort food? Or are you more a bottle-of-wine kind of woman? Because I can definitely sneak whatever you want in a paper bag."

Her laugh was humorless. "More like a box of wine."

I grinned. "I knew we had a connection. But, really, is there anything you need?"

"I promise I'm okay." She paused at a muffled voice in the background. "Mom is awake—can you hold on a second?"

I listened to the hushed sounds of Ivy offering to find another pillow for her mom, asking if she needed some water from the drinking fountain. I smiled despite the circumstances. Hidden behind Ivy's coy texts and bold lipstick was a daughter who loved her family in the hardest moments. This new dimension of her sent warmth curling through my chest.

"Sorry about that," Ivy said, her voice clear again. "I need to go."

"Please keep me updated about your mom and how you're doing."

"I will. Talk to you later."

Despite my concern for her, despite how much I hated the idea of Ivy and her mom sitting alone and overwhelmed in the ER, my brain focused on her last word. *Later*. She took it for granted there would be a next time.

I smiled up at the falling snow.

CHAPTER 10

IVY

Mel: We shoveled your sidewalk so it'll be ready for you and your mom. I'll stop by tomorrow with a frozen meal.
Cameron: Phyllis says she might hire us to shovel her sidewalk too. We found our calling.
Ivy: You two are the best. Thank you!

Rushing between home, work, the hospital, and Mom's house, I felt perpetually behind. I would forget my purse at work and have to drive back, or I would doubt whether I locked my front door and ended up calling Phyllis to ask her to check for me.

Around noon I'd left work so I could pick up Mom from the hospital. Clarice had stared at me as I walked out the door, clearly unhappy about covering for me while I was out.

Guilty, worried thoughts filled my head. I wasn't there enough for Mom. I wasn't able to focus at work. I hadn't painted anything since she fell, my current work in progress collecting dust, and the longer I ran on too little sleep and too little creativity, the more my head packed itself with dizzying colors. I couldn't manage all the loose ends in my life, and the ones I did happen to manage, I didn't manage well.

Now Mom and I drove in silence, the sound of the pavement passing below us the only gray background noise to our trip home.

Twenty-four-hour care, the surgeon had said, because it was essential that Mom not overdo it as she healed. Later, the round-faced nurse practitioner mentioned that I should start thinking about long-term care solutions, not just during surgery recovery, because the elderly shouldn't live alone, particularly when falls were a risk.

Surely the doctor and nurse didn't mean *literal* twenty-four-hour care. I could accept that Mom needed me for more than just a couple hours each night, but twenty-four hours? How was I supposed to work? Maybe it was medical humor, and I'd missed the punchline.

The added stress of insurance hadn't helped; trapdoors and hidden spikes seemed to be lurking in each form I filled out. Thankfully the surgeon was willing to work with us so Mom could stay home and not pay for an expensive stay at a rehab facility. So now we just had the perfectly affordable hospital bills, surgeon bills, ER bills, and normal physical therapy bills.

Yes, that was sarcasm.

Not for the first time, I wished our family was bigger than just the two of us. Maybe if I had a father around, he could have eased Mom's constant worries about me, soothed her with the reassurance that he loved her. Maybe siblings could have taken turns caring for her in the evenings or during the workdays. Maybe Toby could help take turns instead—

Useless, wishful thinking. I mentally shook my sleep-deprived brain into some state of wakefulness and reminded myself that Mom was aging. She needed me now more than ever. I couldn't let her down.

But when I spoke, my voice sounded rusty with exhaustion. "You need more care than just me checking on you in the evenings."

"I know." Her voice was much too chipper for my already-frazzled patience.

She'd refused the wheelchair in the doctor's office, preferring to fumble with the crutches. Her stubborn independence would've been endearing if it wasn't so terrifying to watch her wobble like a baby colt learning to walk. Each step with those trembling crutches was another step she could fall again. The nurse urged Mom to try the walker instead, but Mom said the crutches would make it easier to climb stairs.

What stairs? Her house didn't have stairs.

But my house did.

Why did I have a feeling she was three moves ahead of me, broken bones and all?

I frowned at the crutches propped in the back seat, as if it was their fault. "You can't think that's a good idea, being alone after a major surgery like this."

"Of course it's not." She turned to blink at me with wide, innocent eyes.

Right.

We couldn't afford hiring out twenty-four-hour care, a rehab facility, or a visiting nurse, and my nightly visits wouldn't be enough. The only other option was a plan she'd already set in motion when she forfeited the walker for the crutches.

I breathed deep, telling myself the walls closing around me shouldn't be my only concern. This was hard for Mom, too, because it was a rude awakening for both of us that she wouldn't always be here. What did it matter that my studio was collecting dust when my mother's life as she knew it was over?

I cleared my throat. "Then you can move in with me for a little while—"

She beamed. "What a lovely idea!"

CHAPTER 11

IVY

Mel: I restocked my Moscow mule ingredients for tonight.
Ivy: I know you said not to bring anything, but I had a craving and ordered us
some chow mein.
Mel: Perfect!

Some of my favorite memories happened in Mel's apartment. It was the setting of our inaugural Monday night gatherings, which was really just an excuse Cameron made up to spend more time with Mel, but it ended in so much bonding and hilarity that we decided to make it a weekly event. From that first night, to countless others since then, where we vented and laughed and cried and vegged, the highlight of my time at the university was Cameron and Mel on Monday nights.

Mel's apartment was the picture of coziness, and—the best part—it was quiet. I could focus. I could breathe easily. I could simply be a friend without multitasking through the jumble of colors inside my head. After several long days adjusting to my new caretaker role, Mel's apartment was heaven.

Tonight was also a perfect time to push Toby out of my mind, and my feelings, for a little while. When Mom was still in the ER, he'd called, softening the harsh edges of that day by asking if there was anything he could do. Since then, his texts had quickly become the best parts of my day.

Tonight was actually a Wednesday, not a Monday, and it was a little bit more special because it was just me and Mel. She'd called for an emergency girls' night to "destress" me. Cameron had plans to play basketball with some friends —Toby, maybe?—doing whatever it was men did together. I wouldn't bother giving them a second thought.

Mel, on the other hand, spent quite a bit of time thinking about them.

"What do you think Cam is doing?" She set my Moscow mule on the coffee table, making the flame of her vanilla candle flicker.

I sipped my drink, savoring the ginger and lime flavors. "Picking up a girl at a bar."

Mel's head swiveled toward me, eyes wide. "You think so?"

"Of course not," I scoffed. "He's too lovesick over you to do that."

Mel set yet another vanilla candle—how many did she have?—on an end table and lit it. "That's not true."

"If you're so worried about him, text him. See what he's up to."

One of my favorite parts of our friendship: nudging Cameron and Mel together. They'd thank me someday.

My phone vibrated on her coffee table, gently rattling the plate of cookies.

Mel glanced toward it. "You're getting a lot of texts tonight. Is it your mom?"

Picking up my phone, I read the notification for a text from *Toby - 10/10 Smile* and locked the screen again. "No, I'll keep an eye on my phone, but she should be okay."

This weekend I would move more of Mom's belongings to my place so she wouldn't need to live out of an overnight bag anymore. So long, peaceful home. Hello, chaos.

Mel set another newly lit candle on a windowsill. "So if it's not your mom, and it's not Cam, is it a new guy? You know I love your dating horror stories."

I enjoyed scandalizing Cameron and Mel just as much as they enjoyed the drama of my love life. But for now, my dating apps and the men I'd been messaging could wait. Mom came first. In the meantime, I texted Toby. He was a significant upgrade.

"I've sworn off the apps," I said. "There's nobody good left. Other than Cam, and he's reserved for you."

Other than Cam…and Toby. Dark eyes, big shoulders and hands, and a smile that was contagious. He'd had every excuse to hold a grudge over our date. But he didn't. His forgiveness had washed me in relief. That mattered more than I was willing to admit.

Mel shook her head. "Cam isn't reserved for me, but he's definitely not your type. We'll find you someone amazing. Someone who's fun to be with. He'll be dashing too."

I choked around a sip of Moscow mule. "Dashing? Please. I'm not one of your Jane Austen heroines."

"Every woman is a Jane Austen heroine."

I laughed. "The ideal man is the fictional kind invented by a woman."

"Now you sound like a meme."

"No meme," I said, "just real-life experience in the barracuda-infested waters called the dating pool."

Her lip pouted in sympathy. "A couple of bad dates shouldn't ruin your opinion of love forever."

"A couple?" My laugh sounded harsh. "Have you forgotten about the one who demanded a striptease after one date? Or the guy who ditched me in the middle of dinner because his ex called him? Or the three men who ghosted me after they got bored with sex?"

She lifted a finger. "Don't forget the random nudes."

"Yes," I said, lifting my glass in a mock salute. "Thank you for agreeing with me."

"You've had a few bad runs, but I think you should keep trying. Everyone wants to be loved, despite bad dates. Even you."

"I know what those men wanted from me. Distraction. Sex. An ego boost. Whatever. Once they got it, they left. You're the romantic, not me. I prefer to think of myself as Georgia O'Keeffe." I twirled my hand in a dramatic flair.

Mel squinted, sorting through our years of conversations. "She was an… artist. Painter, right?"

I nodded. "She had a sweeping romance with Alfred Stieglitz, a photographer. They wrote more than five thousand letters to each other, and some of those letters were forty pages long. Sometimes they wrote two or three times a day."

She oohed. "You're right, that is romantic."

"All we get now are texts and memes and GIFs. I want a man to be so enamored with me that he writes me a forty-page letter. Is that too much to ask?"

Mel smiled around her copper mug. "We may need to adjust our expectations. And, in case you didn't notice, you just referenced a real-life man, not a fictional one, that you see as a romance model. You're still hopeful; you're just hiding it."

I considered telling her Cameron would happily write her a forty-page letter, three times a day. But I'd already nudged her enough tonight. Besides, as much as I relished dramatizing the men I'd dated, I was at fault too. I certainly wasn't planning to write forty-page letters to anyone. Or even show up to a lunch date.

"I did have a date the other week." I wrapped my fingers around my cold copper mug. "I accidentally stood him up because Mom was in the ER, and I completely forgot to text him."

Mel made a sympathetic humming noise. "You couldn't help the timing of that."

If Cameron were here, I'd cling to my tough persona and crack a joke. With Mel, my toughness dwindled to regular hurts and disappointments, both in others and in myself.

I shrugged. "I should still take responsibility for sometimes being thoughtless about dating."

"What was his reaction?"

Technically, there wasn't anything to stop me from mentioning Toby. It would be natural to say, *You know how Cameron talks about his friend Toby? He was my date, and he was so understanding and nice. But I don't want to bring him up by name and potentially complicate the wonderful friendship I have with you and Cameron if Toby ends up being yet another dud.*

I drained the last of my Moscow mule. "I sent him a vague text that something came up. He called me, asked if I was okay. When I explained, he was…kind."

"That sounds promising."

"It's certainly not a forty-page letter." But being on the receiving end of his kindness had felt good. Too good.

"Like I said, adjust your expectations. Do you think you'll try to see him again?"

If he had anything to say about it, definitely.

I shrugged. "Maybe."

Mel stood, recognizing I'd closed the door on the dating topic for tonight. "Refill?"

As soon as she disappeared into her kitchen, I reached for my phone.

Toby - 10/10 Smile: Playing basketball with some friends. You like sports?

Ivy: I'd rather die in the zombie apocalypse than run a single step.

Toby - 10/10 Smile: Really? Not a single step?

Ivy: Well, I would make it look good. I'd sacrifice myself for my friends to give them more time to escape. Gotta go out with a bang.

Toby - 10/10 Smile: I wouldn't give you the chance. I'd fight the zombies off.
Ivy: Have you ever heard of a hero complex? You might have it.
Toby - 10/10 Smile: Sounds serious. Maybe I should look it up on WebMD.

"What are you grinning at?"

I nearly dropped my phone in the fresh drink Mel set in front of me. "Just thinking how grateful I am that my mom doesn't know how to text."

Like the best friend she is, Mel cringed with appropriate dramatics. "Can you imagine?"

I slid my phone under my leg so I wouldn't be tempted to check notifications. "Remember years ago, when I tried to teach Mom to email? Sometimes she still sends me those 'forward to a friend or you'll die at midnight' threads."

Mel frowned. "I haven't thought of those in years. They're still going around?"

I raised a brow and whispered, "I bet you she's the one who starts them."

Mel laughed, and I laughed too, even though I felt another pang of guilt. Yes, Mom made me want to hug her and throttle her at the same time. But she was at her most vulnerable right now. And here I was, poking fun at her behind her back. She would be crushed if she heard me.

"How are you handling all the caretaking?" Mel asked. "It's a lot of responsibility."

I nodded. "It is."

When I didn't elaborate, she prodded me with her foot. "So how are you feeling?"

Leaning my head against the back of the couch, I slumped lower in my seat. "You know I suck at talking about my feelings."

"That's why you practice with me. So when you do meet Alfred Stigly—"

"Stieglitz."

"—you'll be able to tell him in fluent English exactly how much you love and adore him."

I made a gagging sound. "Excuse me while I puke."

She laughed. "Come on. Stop playing tough. It's just us. How are you feeling about caretaking?"

I sighed and ran a finger around the rim of my copper mug. Would it be too obvious of a deflection to ask for another refill?

"It's hard," I said. "She's always been exhausting, and now it's much worse. I'd thought I was drained running between work and my house and her house. Now she's living with me. I have to plan every detail to make sure her food and meds and drinks and crutches are within reach at all times. You know I'm not a planner."

Mel nodded sympathetically.

"So this is really pushing my mental, emotional, and physical limits. I'm exhausted all the time. If I could give this zero stars, I would. Do not recommend."

Our conversation paused. I stared at a vanilla candle, watching the flame move. It was oddly hypnotizing. Maybe this was all part of Mel's scheme to play therapist. It was nice, to be honest.

"So that's what you're *doing*," Mel said. "How are you *feeling*?"

Never mind. This wasn't nice. "You're annoying."

"And you love me for it."

"I do."

I stared into my Moscow mule, watching the bubbles from the ginger beer drift toward the surface, popping with teeny bursts of silver sound. I thought of walking into Mom's home, of dawning horror and guilt and fear when I found her collapsed on the floor, so pale, so cold. She'd been like that for hours.

I cleared my throat. "I'm feeling tired. I'm feeling worried that she'll fall again someday, and it won't be just a broken ankle."

"Is that likely to happen?"

I shrugged. "Anything could happen."

Mel hugged a throw pillow to her chest. "But if it's unlikely, statistically speaking, then maybe it's one less thing to worry about." She hesitated before speaking again. "Sorry, I should be listening and not trying to fix this for you. I just hate seeing you stress so much."

I shrugged. "I don't mind your fixing. You know I'd rather talk about solutions than feelings. Especially since Mom needs twenty-four-hour care. I brought her overnight bag to my house, but she needs more of her things from home, so I make an extra stop at her place every day to pick up what she needs. It's not a big deal, but on top of everything else…I feel too thinly stretched. The best solution is to have her move in with me on a bigger scale."

"You can't be serious."

Mel was appropriately horrified. Of course she understood how much my space and independence meant to me. Of course she knew how much I craved alone time at the end of my long, gray workdays at the registrar's office. She understood my art and synesthesia better than most did, and she understood as a fellow introvert. The silent haven of my house was about to be invaded by a chatterbox.

I continued watching my Moscow mule bubble. "The other solutions are more expensive than I can afford."

"But she'll be so…in your space. And for a long time."

Or for as long as Mom had left. The thought made my heart ache.

"It'll be really difficult," I admitted, "but I'll make the best of it. Having Mom barrel over the few boundaries I've managed to establish will be rough. She's already shown up on a date. Who knows, she might show up at the registrar's office next. But there isn't a better solution. At least I won't be running myself ragged anymore."

Mel slowly nodded, processing the news with me. "Okay. How can I help?"

My fingers paused their tapping on my mug's rim. "With what?"

She blinked at me like it was obvious. "With your mom. Cam and I have been helping with Van as much as possible, and dropping off meals and such, but there has to be more we can do."

"There isn't anything else."

"Are you sure?"

I didn't pause to think. "I'm sure."

Mel didn't let it go. "When are you planning to move her in on a 'bigger scale'?"

I tapped on my phone, happy for an excuse to check for another text from *Toby - 10/10 Smile*, and then I was peeved with myself for putting so much stock in silly messages from a silly man.

I opened my calendar and weather apps. "Probably this weekend. There's no snow or ice on the forecast."

"Good. Cam and I will be there."

My head shot up. Too late, I saw what I'd walked into. "What?"

"A moving party. I can bring boxes from work—you wouldn't believe how many boxes of paper we go through—so that'll help with packing. Cam can help with the heavy stuff. He has more muscles than you'd think."

My knee-jerk reaction kicked in, this deeply rooted need to do everything on my own. "You don't have to do that."

"We don't have to, but we want to."

Accepting Cameron and Mel's help would mean being a nuisance to them. They'd already pressured me into accepting frozen meals and other help. Now they wanted to spend their weekend moving boxes? They couldn't do that.

"You haven't even asked Cam yet," I countered.

She picked up her phone, tapping rapidly. "You know he'll say yes."

Before I could protest, my phone vibrated with a text.

Mel: Any plans this weekend, Cam? We're having a moving party for Ivy's mom.

"You're fast," I mumbled.

The thought of moving everything on my own had weighed on me. Packing boxes, making trips, and loading and unloading cars, draining what little stamina I had left. As much as I bristled at taking up my friends' time and energy with my issues, my slight tension headache was already easing with relief.

My phone vibrated.

Cameron: I'm in. Thanks for the chance to show off my biceps, Ivy. You're the best.

I smiled. Not at his lame joke, though. I smiled because I couldn't ask for better best friends.

So of course I needed to tease Mel. "Let's circle back to those muscles you mentioned earlier. How do you know what's happening under Cam's clothes?"

CHAPTER 12

TOBY

Ivy: I'd still rather take my chances with the zombies than with exercising.
Toby: What's so bad about it?
Ivy: What's NOT bad about it?
Toby: Exercising is good for you.
Ivy: That's what they said about leeches a few years ago. Hard pass.

I couldn't ask for a better night spent with my best friend and my brothers. Sweat stung my eyes, my legs and arms ached, and my chest rose and fell with deep recovery breaths. Our sneakers squeaked on the basketball court as we exchanged hand-claps and "good game" congratulations with the other team.

"You all played great," I said to my teammates.

My oldest brother, Silas, shot me a look. "We lost."

Cameron, more appreciative of my optimism, nodded. "Thanks, Toby. Your assists were perfectly timed."

I grinned. "Thanks."

"You two are ridiculous," Silas muttered.

Amos, my middle brother, spoke as he tapped out a text. "Don't be a sore loser, Silas."

"I'm not a sore loser. The only reason you're happy to lose that game is so you can go home to your woman sooner."

Amos shrugged, not bothering to deny the truth.

I couldn't resist teasing Silas, the perpetual grump of our friend group. "You're just jealous because Estelle is mad at you."

Cameron shifted his stance to face Silas more directly. "What happened?"

My oldest brother sighed. "I taught the kids how to layback climb the doorframes in the house."

Cameron frowned. "And that rock climbing term means…?"

Silas demonstrated with his hands. "They curl their fingertips around the ledge of the trim on the doorframe, then brace their feet inside the doorframe, and they use that tension to climb their way up."

Laughing, Cameron removed his glasses to wipe the sweat from his face. "Climbing every surface in your childhood home is a rite of passage, but you tell Estelle that's what I said, and I'll deny it. I'm staying out of this one."

Silas grumbled, shoving his belongings back into his duffel bag. "I need to teach them young. I'm raising the next generation of world-class climbers."

Finding my phone in my duffel bag, I unlocked the screen, worry about Ivy at the front of my mind. Caretaking is one of the hardest jobs there is, in my opinion. She didn't have any other family to share all that responsibility. I'd offered to help, but of course she'd turned me down. I got it. She barely knew me. If only we could've gone on our date before her mom fell. If she knew me better, maybe she would accept my offers.

I couldn't say that to her, though. Building a relationship with Ivy felt weirdly similar to building rapport with a cat. If I came on too strong, she shied away. If I held out my hand and waited for her to come to me, I might manage to get a little closer. Might. There was no guarantee.

I didn't mind. I enjoyed the challenge of earning my place in her life. She was worth the extra effort.

Still, I couldn't leave her hanging without any backup. So if my support was limited to texting lame jokes in hopes she would smile, that was what I would do.

Toby: Just finished the game.

Ivy: Did you win?

Toby: Do you doubt us?

Ivy: Since you didn't immediately answer with gloating, yes, I doubt you won.

Toby: Fine. We lost. But we don't have enough players for an official game, so we just play pickup. It's hard to mesh as a team if you're always rotating through random people.

Ivy: Excuses.

Toby: Careful you don't hurt my feelings. I might not carry you through the zombie apocalypse if you're too mean to me.

While I was still looking down at my phone, Cameron's sneaker-clad foot came into my line of sight. I locked my screen.

He slung his bag over his shoulder. "What are you smiling about?"

Silas shrugged on his coat. "He's been grinning like that since he came out of the womb."

Amos cringed. "Please don't talk about Mama's womb."

Silas launched into full-on ribbing. Amos tuned him out, his eyes getting that hazy look he had when he was too busy running numbers through his genius brain to bother with regular conversations.

Cameron pulled on his coat, too, and dug for his car keys. He hadn't stopped watching me.

I indicated my phone. "It's the girl from my lunch date."

Cameron's brows rose. "Did she explain what happened?"

Ivy's family emergency wasn't my news to tell. Normally I told Cameron everything. I told my brothers everything. Actually, I told everyone everything— I was an open book. If Ivy was a cat, I was a carefree golden retriever. But I wanted to play it close this time, since it was what she would probably want.

"She said it was a family emergency."

He nodded. "So when is the make-up date?"

"We haven't gotten that far yet."

Silas interrupted to announce that Estelle had called a truce for the sake of basketball night, so we could crash at their house for dinner.

My phone vibrated again.

Ivy: I'm not mean. I'm snarky.

Toby: And the difference is…?

Ivy: The difference is you feel charmed and not offended.

Toby: Maybe my feelings are deeply hurt. Maybe you need to meet me for post-game drinks tonight to help me feel better.

Ivy: Can't. Gotta head home to be with Mom.

Right. Caretakers didn't get breaks. Hopefully she had someone she could count on for relief—

Wait. If she wasn't home with her mom right now, then where was she? She couldn't be on a date with someone else. Then again, what if she was? I didn't have any claim on her. I just had a lot of hopes, and my hopes weren't any reason to expect her to see us as an exclusive relationship when we had yet to go on our first date.

I caught the train of my thoughts and reeled them back. I'd just been worried about her stress levels, and now I was worried about her going out. *That* was irrational. She needed a break. This was good.

Toby: Glad you could get away for a little bit.

Ivy: Me too. Driving now.

Toby: Be safe. Talk later.

I looked up to see my friend and brothers staring at me.

Silas folded his arms across his chest in his favorite big-brother pose. "Care to join the team, Toby?"

Cameron grinned. "You can text your woman over pizza just as well as you can text standing by the bleachers. I'm hungry."

Amos paused, his fingers still on the zipper of his coat. "Woman?"

"Please tell me she's nothing like Yvonne," Silas said.

"Alexandra was worse," Cameron said helpfully.

They turned toward the exit, discussing my love life like I wasn't standing right there. That's family and friends for you.

I looked back to our seats, reached for my duffel bag, and realized I'd been too distracted with texting to pack up my gear. Snatching up my belongings, I jogged a few steps to catch up with my teammates.

"Have I told you guys we played really well tonight?" I joked.

Cameron smiled. Amos laughed, his head still bowed over his phone. Silas wrapped his arm around my neck in a fake chokehold.

Pretending to fight off Silas, I patted my pocket to be sure my phone was there. I'd revisit that date with Ivy later.

CHAPTER 13

IVY

Cameron: How much coffee do we need for this venture?
Mel: I vote two to-go cups for each of us.
Ivy: Such restraint, Mel. I vote all the coffee.
Cameron: Coffee IV, coming right up.

When Cameron and Mel showed up at my front door at 8:00 a.m. on a weekend, their arms filled with coffees and pastries, I could've wept, both with relief and embarrassment. Today I needed them more than ever, and today they would see me at my absolute worst.

They greeted Mom, who reminded them to wrap their scarves tight or they'd get pneumonia.

Cameron and Mel chattered as we drove. I let the sound of my friends' voices loop curls of aquamarine (Cameron) and teal (Mel) into my thoughts.

Mom had given me a long list earlier. It took up an entire notebook page, front and back, and included clothes, shoes, jewelry, makeup, and the books on her nightstand. The rest of her house would remain unpacked, ready for her to move back home after she fully recovered. The doctor and nurse practitioner might call it irrational, but I held out hope that Mom could regain her independence.

Until then, how could I help her be happy at my house? As much as I didn't look forward to more of her nosiness in my life, I wanted to make the best of it.

At her house, she had an entire room dedicated to knitting—something she'd tried to teach me years ago—so I'd added yarn and needles to her list. What about bringing her favorite mug, or some of her framed photos?

As I added a few notes to Mom's list, I eavesdropped on Cameron and Mel.

"Did you see Dr. Freisen's bowtie yesterday?" Cameron asked.

Mel made a face. "The bowtie with embroidered images of tiny bowties? He has some new ones in his rotation, and I have to say, I'm not a fan."

Cameron laughed. "Come on. It's a good thing he's switching up his routine a bit."

"Dr. Freisen doesn't do change; you know that."

What needed change was Cameron and Mel's friendship. Mel might not see Cameron's longing looks in her direction, but I did. I knew my tropes. They were the dictionary definition of friends-to-lovers.

What trope fit me and Toby? Opposites attract? Flirts-to-lovers? I remembered how his voice first transformed my thoughts from charcoal to layers of cerulean, emerald, and scarlet. If I were honest with myself, we were love at first sound.

What a terrifying thought. Complicated emotions and the idea of opening up, only to be hurt, like my mother, were the last things I needed in my life right now. I should be focused on Mom, not tropes and Toby.

Cameron parked in the narrow driveway. The three of us stared at the house for a moment. Just like they volunteered to help me move Mom's things without me asking them, Cameron and Mel instinctively gave me a moment to brace myself for the next few hours.

Somehow the vinyl-sided home looked deflated, like it knew Mom, the person who saw this perfect little house as one of her biggest accomplishments, wasn't filling the structure with her pride anymore. But she would be back soon. Hopefully.

Cameron broke the silence. "The neighborhood is really nice."

Mel nodded. "I wonder what houses go for in an area like this."

He nudged her with his elbow. "Now isn't the best time to play House Hunters."

"Sorry." She glanced at me in the rearview mirror.

Blinking, I tried to see my mom's house and neighborhood through Cameron and Mel's eyes. Unlike other areas in the city, Mom's neighborhood had improved over time. The street was still lined with trees and sidewalks, and several houses had literal white picket fences.

I reached for the door. "Let's do this."

The three of us packed as much as we could fit into Cameron's car. Mel and I packed the last of Mom's novels from her nightstand before we found Cameron in the kitchen, sorting through the refrigerator.

I rested my elbow on the fridge door and squinted at him. "Moving a few boxes of my mom's shoes triggered your teenage-boy metabolism?"

He grinned. "I'm always up for snacks, so that's not a bad idea, but I was seeing if any of her food would expire and stink up the house while she's gone."

I nodded. "Good thinking. Thanks. I should empty the trash cans too."

I turned to see Mel glancing away from Cameron's backside as he bent inside the fridge. These two.

I found a few dirty dishes, toast crusts, and a moldy mug of coffee on a side table in the living room. In the bedroom, a cluster of water glasses crowded Mom's nightstand and dresser. I remembered how she always got up around 2:00 a.m. for a drink of water. Had she been feeling so poorly that she now kept a collection of water glasses in her bedroom to save herself the trip?

When I entered the kitchen, Cameron and Mel were leaning toward the window above the sink. "What's so fascinating?"

"We can't just leave these here." Mel pointed to a small potted plant. "But I remember your mom acting like I'd murdered a puppy the last time I touched one."

"I'll make sure she knows you voted to leave them behind to die. It'll earn me some brownie points." Cameron picked up the smallest plant. "Ivy, your mom is mostly sweet, but I always feel like she's watching for me to make a mistake. I wouldn't have guessed she was a plant lady."

"It's shocking when someone doesn't fall for your puns, huh?" I teased.

He smirked and shrugged, nonchalant and confident. "It just means I haven't figured her out yet."

I nodded toward the plants. "Well, here's your first clue to figuring her out: she only likes African violets. Let's bring them with us. Maybe they'll help her feel a little more settled."

When we arrived back at my house, the lights in my art studio were on, and the drapes were wide open. Surely Mom hadn't climbed the stairs alone, with crutches and a broken ankle? Since my house was small and didn't have bedrooms downstairs, every night I escorted Mom up the steps, ready to catch her if she slipped or fell. Now I panicked, racing into the house and up the stairs, only to falter at the threshold of my studio.

Mom sat on my artist stool, her crutches helping her balance on the narrow seat. I breathed a little easier when I saw her in one piece—but only a little. She knew how I worried about her. How could she be so reckless?

Phyllis stood near the window, grasping a corner of my drapes between two fingers. Behind her large glasses, her eyes gawked around the room. "I had no idea you were an artist, Ivy."

Mom smiled over her shoulder at me. "She's the most talented artist of her age."

Flatter all you want, Mom. It didn't cancel out the fact that she'd needlessly put herself at risk.

"She can paint and sculpt anything she sets her mind to," Mom was saying to Phyllis, "but she stopped because commissions weren't fulfilling for her creatively. Creatives need—"

"Please explain to me how you two got up here." My voice sounded steady for how many emotions clogged my throat—worry, relief, anger, to name a few.

Cameron and Mel's footsteps creaked on the hallway floorboards behind me. They whispered and then fell silent, probably when they saw Mom, broken ankle and crutches and all, on the second floor of my home. Justifications ran through my mind in a bulleted list: my house was small, so there wasn't any space for a bed downstairs; I wasn't strong enough to move a bed and mattress down a floor anyway; and Mom insisted she could manage the steps twice a day without a problem. I was doing the best I could.

I glanced at my friends. They weren't looking into the room with judgment; they were looking with concern. They were here to support, not condemn. What a relief that I didn't need to justify my every decision to them.

"Phyllis stopped by to borrow a few eggs," Mom said. "We got to chatting, and it was cold outside, so I invited her in."

Right.

"And you thought eggs would be in my upstairs guest bedroom?"

"Well, no, but Phyllis mentioned your new drapes, and I remembered I hadn't seen them for myself yet. Remember that Saturday afternoon we were planning to spend together? So, we thought, why not explore on our own? What, do you have secrets up here you don't want us to see?" She smiled like it was a joke.

I looked at Phyllis then, the knobby joints on her thin arms and legs, which looked hardly strong enough to hold her up, let alone catch my mother if she fell down a flight of stairs. Could she sense the lightning bolting from my eyes?

Phyllis couldn't, but Mom could.

"We made it in one piece," Mom chided me. She peered into the hallway. "Though I would appreciate Cam's help on the way back down."

The four of us went downstairs, with Cameron carefully guiding Mom, and Mom enjoying the extra attention. Once Mom and Phyllis were settled in the living room, the eggs completely forgotten by Phyllis, Cameron and Mel unpacked some of Mom's things in her bedroom upstairs. I placed the African violets where Mom would see them every day, on the windowsill next to her recliner.

"They look especially beautiful in your house," Mom said, "almost like they're at home here."

I wasn't falling for that bait after the adventure she'd just had.

Once I locked my studio door—it would stay locked from now on, preserving what little privacy I had left, because *boundaries*, thanks very much —I found my friends upstairs. Cameron was hanging up clothes in Mom's closet, and Mel was lining up shoes along the floor.

"Did she like the plants?" Cameron asked.

"She did. I'm glad you two suggested it." I thumped Mom's books onto the nightstand. "Thanks for helping her down the stairs. I can't believe she did that."

Mel's arms wrapped around me from behind. "I know none of this is what you planned to be doing with your life right now, but you're handling everything like a champ."

I was turning to hug her back when Cameron's much larger arms also wrapped around me from behind, sandwiching Mel between the two of us. Mel might not have known what he was up to, but I did.

Mel made spitting sounds. "Sorry, Ivy, I didn't mean to eat your hair."

"Way to ruin a good hug." Cameron squeezed one last time before letting go. "Have you found a rehab facility yet, Ivy?"

"The doctor gave us a few recommendations. I'll make an appointment tomorrow."

"Try Better Movement." He tapped on his phone screen. "I just sent you the link to their website. They're great."

"That's where you went after your stroke, right?"

"Right. You've heard me talk about Toby before. Make sure to ask for him. I know I'm a little biased, but he's the best."

I felt my phone vibrate in my pocket. Did I want Toby and Mom to meet? Exactly how nosy would Cameron and Mel be if they knew about the connection between me and Toby? Would it change our flirtationship, or whatever it was, if Toby found out I knew his best friend?

"Call them first thing tomorrow morning," Cameron continued. "Explain about your mom. I'm sure they can fit you in on short notice."

I nodded. "Thanks."

"We're here for you, whatever you need," Mel said.

Cameron and Mel's footsteps thumped down the stairs, and soon their voices drifted up from the living room, asking Mom where she wanted her favorite pictures set up once we came back with our second load.

If anyone could help Mom, it would be Toby. Cameron always talked about him like he was magical, and it probably had taken a fair bit of magic when Cameron needed physical therapy. But Mom would require a lot of patience and attention. She didn't follow exercise programs; she did what she wanted, when she wanted.

So why, at 11:00 at night, when I should've been helping Cameron and Mel carry boxes, was I staring at Better Movement's online scheduling system on my phone to see if I could book an appointment?

CHAPTER 14

TOBY

Toby: How is your mom? Is there anything I can help with?
Ivy: There might be something you can do.
Toby: Name it.

Ivy. How did she manage to look so good, standing at the counter in the Better Movement waiting room, signing paperwork? She wore all black, and her blond hair twisted away from her face in a messy bun. So pretty.

The picture wasn't so pretty to her left, where Deke stood, turning pages over the top of a form. He glanced at her between page turns.

I'd just emerged from the therapy room having cleaned the equipment from my last session, and I was supposed to start my lunch break, but no lunch could distract me from her. I strode toward the waiting room.

"Ivy."

She instantly turned toward my voice. Her lips curved into a smile when she saw me—not the flirty smile she usually gave me but a genuine, happy smile. I liked this look on her even more.

"Hey," she said. "I wasn't sure you'd be here today."

"I'm here every day. How are you?" My eyes scanned her body, purely for the sake of physical therapy reasons, but maybe also to appreciate how her black jeans hugged her lean legs.

"I'm good."

Tell me more, rate your day, let's catch up over lunch, I wanted to say, but Deke stood close by, and she looked away and gestured behind herself.

"I'm here with my mom, Irena."

Ivy's mom wore an old-fashioned cardigan and leaned on aluminum crutches, but she had Ivy's blue eyes and wary look and held her daughter's arm in a death grip.

I stuck out my hand. "Pleased to meet you, Irena."

"Mom fell," Ivy explained, "which you already know."

I took in her mom's stance. Tremors shook the hand that gripped her crutches. Her spine was straight, but her shoulders dipped forward. Standing seemed to take significant effort.

I looked back to Ivy, noting the dark circles beneath her eyes. Her body had always been long, smooth lines, but now it looked hollowed out, too thin. Any lingering disappointment I felt over our date the last few weeks took a back seat. Concern was driving now.

Ivy was having a hard time, given how she looked, and she'd only sent me goofy little texts. I could've been there for her. Why hadn't she told me?

Ivy's mom held a limp, trembling hand in my direction. "And you are…?"

"Toby Azumah. I'm your physical therapist."

Deke cleared his throat.

"If that's okay with my supervisor, of course," I amended.

Deke tilted his head to the side in a clear "come this way" gesture. I followed him a few steps' distance from Ivy and her mom.

He tapped on his clipboard. "Your schedule is already full, Azumah."

I shrugged. "That's what lunch breaks are for."

"That's what HR policies are for. You're required to take a lunch break."

"I won't say anything if you won't say anything."

He straightened to his full height. "This isn't a playground, Azumah. We have policies for a reason. Our patients deserve the best, and they don't get the best if we're not at our best."

"I agree. Because I have a personal connection with the Lundens, I think I can best serve them, with or without a lunch break." I flashed my most charming smile. "I'm sure I can work something out with one of the other therapists. The interns are always looking for extra sessions, right?"

He frowned.

Didn't he know this was what friends did for one another at work? They covered. They swapped. They cheered each other on and cut each other slack.

Hadn't he noticed I'd been including him around Better Movement, just like Hudson had asked? Okay, maybe I only passively included him, but still, give me some credit.

"Fine. I need to walk the interns around in a few minutes anyway. I'll tell Lucy she won't be working with the Lundens since she's behind on paperwork." He was already turning away.

"Thanks, Deke. I really appreciate it."

Moments later, the three of us stood in the therapy room, me skimming through the paperwork for Ivy's mom, Ivy's mom sitting on the therapy bench and casting nervous glances at her daughter, and Ivy standing next to her. I watched Ivy in my periphery. She stood still, her posture straight, but the fingers of her right hand tapped rhythms against her thigh.

I set aside the file folder and rubbed my hands together. "Let's get started. We'll begin with some exercises to help me see where we're at now, and then we can make a plan for where to go from here. Sound good?"

If I flexed a little more than usual during the exercises, so be it. Ivy was watching, after all.

I noticed Deke and his entourage of interns making their rounds through the therapy room, but they didn't register in my mind. I was a little distracted. For every movement I went through and suggestion I made with her mom, I gauged Ivy's reaction. Did she look pleased? Worried? Impressed? I hoped for impressed.

Admittedly, it was difficult to focus with Ivy on my mind. She didn't move from her post, silently watching. Her fingers hadn't stopped tapping that rhythm.

I nearly tripped over Deke when he materialized next to me. "Hi, Deke."

"Here is one of our newest patients," he monotoned to the interns. "Irena Lunden, age seventy-three. She fell and broke her ankle a short while ago, had surgery to repair the break, and now she's with us. Keep several things in mind with female geriatrics. First, osteoporosis. It's particularly common among women due to hormonal changes and the lifetime their bodies have spent pulling nutrients from their bones to allow for menstruation."

He stood a little straighter, his tone high-handed. "This likely won't be her first broken bone as she grows older. Remember this when you're assigning therapy to do at home, because she will need to be especially careful.

"Second, remember her lifestyle. If she's in a state where depression could be an issue—widowed, living alone, etc.—her health will decline much more rapidly than her coupled or cohabitating peers."

As a physical therapist, everything he said was correct. As a human being, I wished his voice was a few tones better than robotic. The interns stood behind him, expressions serious as they took notes. They followed Deke's lead, studying Irena like an animal at a zoo.

Should I stop him? What would I say? "You're right, but be nice about it"? That wouldn't help our faux coworker relationship I was trying to build. I'd been doing so well, asking his advice about a patient even though I already knew the answer, including him in lunch break conversations, which he ignored in favor of paperwork. Just last week, Deke started to show his humanity when his upper lip twitched into the start of a smile. Or maybe it had been a grimace. Still, for the first time since I'd met him, he'd had some kind of facial expression, so I counted that twitch as a win.

The other physical therapists were watching too, and so were the interns. If I questioned his authority now, in front of people he considered beneath him, it would go directly against what Hudson asked me to do. Deke would feel under-mined, and rightly so. Leadership supported leadership. Wasn't that why Hudson asked me to help Deke in the first place, to respect his new role as an example to our colleagues?

Then again, watching the way Irena's gaze shifted from Deke to the floor, her posture stooping…this felt wrong. Ivy stood behind her, mouth slightly open, staring at my supervisor in open horror.

Deke had just objectified her mom into a number. Into statistics and diag-noses. And he'd done it in the coldest way possible.

But what could I do? My options were to go against Hudson and jeopardize the progress I'd made with Deke, or to wait out Deke's monotone lecture and move on with our session.

Deke and his posse disappeared as quickly as they'd arrived, shuffling away to the soundtrack of pages turning on his clipboard.

I released the breath I'd been holding. What a relief that was over.

CHAPTER 15

IVY

Mel: Just left some Thai takeout in your fridge, Ivy.
*Cameron: Just shoveled your sidewalk, Ivy. And I scratched Van's belly, so I'm
the chief friend today.*
Mel: What he means to say is, let us know if there's anything else.

This was over.

I refused to do nothing as Toby let Deke belittle Mom into an even worse
state. She was a human being, with hopes and hurts and everything in between.
She was a force of nature—a stubborn force, yes, but that same stubbornness
was how she'd managed to accomplish everything she'd done, how she'd raised
me alone, with nothing to rely on but her own determination. She deserved better
than Deke treating her like nothing more than a textbook case. Remind me again
how much we were paying for the privilege to be treated like this?

Fury hummed in my veins. Fear joined in as Deke's words echoed in my
head—*This likely won't be her last broken bone.* Would I have to repeatedly live
through finding Mom unconscious, her half-naked body curled up on the floor?

I picked up Mom's crutches from the bench and thrust them into her hands.
"We're leaving."

"Thank goodness," she sighed. "Phyllis and I are planning to watch a new
show today—"

"You're leaving?" Toby towered over us. "But—"

I whirled on him. "Don't 'but' me. You just stood there while that weasel of a man trivialized my mother. He belittled her. He took away her hope."

Maybe it was my hope more than hers, but that wasn't the point.

My fingers curled into fists. "He made her less than human. He made her a nobody. And you did *nothing*."

"Is there a problem?" Deke had turned around to stare at us.

Oh, *oops*, was my voice loud enough he'd heard me? *So* sorry.

"No," Toby hurried to say. "Everything is fine—"

"Yes, actually, I have a problem," I said. "You owe my mom an apology."

Deke blinked. "Excuse me?"

"What you said about my mom. You need to apologize."

He fiddled with the papers in his hands. "Everything I said has been proven by extensive research—"

"I'm sure it has been. But you were rude."

He frowned. "I don't understand."

"I'm sure you don't. It's this little thing called compassion. I've heard it's great for patients. You know, patients? The people you're here to help?"

"I didn't realize I came across so poorly." Deke's frown pulled his brows even lower. "I was teaching the interns, so I was focused on the facts."

How typical of management—no apologies, only excuses.

I turned to Mom, tucking my arm under her elbow. "Let's go."

Toby's footsteps followed close behind me. "I understand you're upset, but it's not that simple—"

"Of course it is. There's the right way to treat people, and there's the wrong way. You're supposed to look out for your patients, remember?" I glared over my shoulder at him.

Before he could answer, I guided Mom toward the exit, ignoring the chipper receptionist who asked us about rescheduling.

Toby's tree trunk of an arm swept open the door ahead of us. "Please listen for a second. Deke is my boss, and I can't just say whatever I want to him. His voice is the final say unless the owner is around."

What a lie. I'd heard the story from Cameron. Years ago, after his stroke, Cameron came to Better Movement so he could relearn how to walk, and Toby had stood up for him, even when Toby's boss encouraged him to choose more lucrative, more promising patients. Toby had stuck with Cameron anyway. He'd changed my friend's life. But he didn't know I knew that.

And you don't know whether Deke was his boss back then.

It doesn't matter who his boss was. Gumption is gumption.

But maybe he stood up to his boss after the fact. This time his hands were tied, professionally speaking.

Hush, logic. I'm too angry to listen to you right now.

I ignored Toby and navigated Mom toward my car. At least there weren't any ice patches or slush to evade on the sidewalk. That was one thing Better Movement had going for it—a squeaky clean parking lot. I imagined writing a scathing Yelp review about Better Movement's unsatisfactory management, spineless employees, and, oh, pristine pavement to avoid slip and fall lawsuits after their patients leave their miserable physical therapy sessions.

Once Mom could lean against the support of my car, I dug in my purse for my keys. Mom's rapid breaths puffed clouds of steam in front of her face.

Toby stood next to me, shifting his weight from foot to foot. He had to be freezing in his khakis and short-sleeved polo with its Better Movement logo stamped across his right pec. But he stayed.

"Look, I can help." His gaze darted between Mom and me. "I can work with you three times a week, for as long as it takes. Whatever it takes."

"We don't need your help."

He focused more fully on Mom. "If we don't stick with a physical therapy program, you'll never fully heal. Your mobility will never go back to normal. You'll completely lose your independence over time. With my help, you can regain what you've lost and also grow stronger than you were before, helping prevent future falls."

She lifted an eyebrow at him. "According to your friend, my bones are already dust anyway."

Mom's sass is a delight when it's directed at someone other than me.

"He's not my fr—" Toby scrubbed a hand over his face. "Deke is a textbook genius. He's not so genius about, well, relating to people. But you're not working with him; you're working with me. I'm not like Deke. Please come back inside."

"We're not going back inside." I finally located my keys, tangled in the lanyard of my university ID. The car door clicked as it unlocked.

"Okay, fine, I'll come to your house."

Mom's eyebrows skyrocketed. If she were wearing pearls, she would have clutched them at the scandalous idea of a man inviting himself into her single daughter's home. "Excuse me?"

"I'll do at-home sessions. I'll bring all the equipment, and I'll help you with your physical therapy at home, three times a week. Please don't let Deke's text-book scenarios become your normal. You can do anything."

Mom scoffed. "Can I turn dust back into bones?"

The sound he made was a half-groan, half-laugh. "You can have good quality of life. You can improve your balance and—"

"You didn't care enough to stand up for her. We need someone to invest." My voice sounded flat. "You're not that person. Clearly we chose the wrong place."

After opening the car door, I helped Mom lower into the passenger seat. I tucked her crutches into the back. With a little work, we turned her so she faced forward, her legs tucked in with plenty of space for comfort.

His voice came from behind me. "You picked up her legs wrong."

The nerve of this man.

"I'm doing just fine, thank you." I closed the car door with more force than necessary.

"You need to lift by her calf and her thigh. And you need to use your legs, not your back, or you'll hurt yourself."

"Like I said, we're doing fine."

I moved to walk around the car, but he stepped in front of me. We stood inches apart. Our breaths clouded together in front of us, and I noticed the skin on his neck was raised in goose bumps from the cold. His dark eyes stared into mine. I moved to the right, but he followed, blocking my way.

"Let me help you. Let me help your mom. This is what I do." His voice was filled with certainty, the confidence of a man who knew who he was and what he was good at. "I really want to help."

I tilted my head further back to hold direct eye contact so he could see I wasn't wavering in the least. "No."

He frowned, but I didn't give him a chance to reply. I stepped around him. I was too angry to have the presence of mind to watch out for slick spots like I'd done for Mom, so when my foot slid out from under me, my arms pinwheeled wildly. Of course there'd been one teeny-tiny patch of ice, and of course I'd found it. The horizon of business buildings spun around me until I face-planted into Toby.

He steadied me, held me upright. Because what else would someone as good as Toby do after I'd ripped his head off?

Despite the cold, despite the fact he wore only a flimsy polo t-shirt for his work uniform, his skin was a furnace. I felt the heat instantly. It was one of the greatest injustices in life that men hogged all the genes for body heat, and women froze until they got menopausal hot flashes.

"Are you okay?"

Azure and jade dyed my thoughts. How dare his voice draw beautiful colors in my head right now.

"I'm fine." My words sounded breathless, even to me.

My lack of oxygen had nothing to do with his arms, one wrapped around my upper back and one wrapped around my lower. It wasn't like we stared into one another's eyes, or I watched his throat work in a heavy swallow, or his gaze dipped to my lips.

He let go the instant I resisted his hold. I saw myself clearly in that moment, like I was an outside observer: a grown woman desperate to protect herself from too many feelings, scrambling away from a kind man who only wanted to help her.

How humiliating. But it would be even more humiliating to apologize, so I kept moving.

"I don't want your help," I said—to remind myself as much as him.

I climbed into my car and started the ignition. I left the parking lot with only one glance in the rearview mirror. Toby stood in front of the curb. I couldn't make out his face, but his stance was strong and sure.

I straightened my own shoulders in response. Toby could take his good intentions to someone who ignored the fact he didn't walk the talk. That someone wouldn't be me.

"Well"—Mom patted at the front of her coat—"at least we'll be home in time for me to watch *Swamp People* with Phyllis."

Mom chatted the entire drive home, talking about how the *Better Together* community center billboard needed to be straightened, but of course they would never hire someone who could do the job well, like her friend's son's nephew, who could tell at a glance whether a roofline was slanted by the slightest degree.

Once we were home, I helped her out of the car, making a point to myself to do the exact opposite of what Toby had said. I lifted her legs how I wanted, using only my back, and if I felt any twinges, he would never know because I would never tell him because I wasn't talking to him anymore. *Take that.*

Childish? Yes. Satisfying? Very much yes.

Phyllis must've been watching my house, because she slipped in after us before the door could close completely. She chatted with Mom, and even though I didn't like their cumulative nosiness into my life, I was grateful Phyllis could carry the conversation. I desperately needed some space right now.

Once Mom was comfortable in her favorite recliner Cameron had set up a few days ago, and once she and Phyllis turned the TV to full volume to watch the latest episode of *Swamp People*, I went to my bedroom for a moment to breathe and escape the algae-green background noise.

My disappointment in Toby pricked sharply under my ribs. How dare he act like he cared about his patients and then let Deke treat them so poorly? It echoed the way every man I'd dated said I mattered, only to prove through their actions that I didn't.

I'd thought Toby was different. Before now, we'd only interacted at the registrar's office, and exchanged one call and several texts. But he'd been genuine. He'd been kind. When he asked me to rate my day, he thoughtfully listened to my answers. He'd been everything my exes weren't.

It was my own fault for expecting him to be different. He was just like the others. I didn't need more shallow relationships in my life. I'd had my fill.

I felt my phone vibrate in my pocket. It was probably Toby. Again. He didn't know how to handle rejection, did he?

Maybe it was a good thing we hadn't gone on that date. If I'd let him deeper into my life, and then later on, he turned out to be like the other men I'd dated, the disappointment would have escalated to full-blown hurt. I let it play out in my mind. The dates. The kisses. The sex. The heartbreak when he inevitably got what he wanted and left.

I let my disappointment harden until it restricted my breath. Good. I would direct my anger at Toby. All the unspent emotions I'd felt with Mom—the anxiety, the petty frustrations, the fear about losing her someday—could now be reshaped into anger toward Toby, and it felt so, so good.

We would be just fine without him. I didn't want to put Mom at another physical therapist's mercy. Surely it wouldn't be that hard to recreate my own physical therapy session with Mom. I'd watched Toby carefully during our appointment, and maybe with a little help from Google, I could tackle it on my own. Ivy Lunden, moonlighting as a physical therapist.

Taking painter's tape from my studio, I went downstairs and marked lines along the kitchen floor. I cleared the countertops in case Mom needed support to keep her steady. I wished we'd completed the full appointment with Toby so I had a bit more to go on, but wishing wouldn't get the job done, and Google could fill in the gaps well enough.

I was in my studio looking for another roll of painter's tape when Phyllis called for me from the bottom of the stairs.

"Ivy! Someone's at the door!" Her voice trembled, either with fear over a knock after dark or with excitement from getting a firsthand scoop on whatever was about to happen. Most likely the latter.

Mom's voice, definitely panicked, joined in. "Ivy?!"

"Coming!"

Phyllis peered around the edges of my living room curtains to see who stood on the doorstep. "He's very large," she whispered, like she hadn't just been screaming for me to come downstairs.

Mom craned her neck from her recliner, eyeing the glass transom at the top of the door like it would defy physics and show her the man who stood a full foot below the transom's view. "What does he look like?"

Phyllis squinted. "Just…big. And dark. But it's dark outside, so I can't see. Ivy, why haven't you fixed your porch light yet?"

"Your porch light is out?" Mom's eyes widened comically. "That's not safe. Anyone could—"

"I'm sure it's nothing." I strode to the door.

"But we don't know who it is!" Mom cried. "Quick, Phyllis, find a weapon."

Hand on the doorknob, I looked back at them.

"Got it!" Phyllis lifted her weapon of choice above her shoulder.

I gave her a skeptical look. "That's what you're going with?"

"I'm ready!" she cried.

My concern wasn't the crutch-turned-weapon, it was the way her arms shook when she held it overhead.

Toby would know the physical therapy she needed to strengthen—

Stop it. You're mad at Toby, remember? Because he turned out to be just like all the others.

I rolled my eyes at Mom and Phyllis, scowled at my thoughts of Toby, and opened the front door.

CHAPTER 16

TOBY

Toby: Need to cancel tonight. Something came up.
Cameron: We can postpone for next week. You okay?
Toby: Next week it is! I'm good, just a work thing.

The door was yanked open so hard that I feared for its hinges. Taking a startled step back, I looked up to see Ivy glowering at me.

"You." Her voice was a growl.

Now was the time for my plan. My plan to…um…

I'd justified my motives to myself so many times throughout the day, I hadn't considered this exact moment.

My line of thinking was this: Ivy needed help, her mom needed physical therapy, and I needed to restore my professional reputation. My professional reputation, that was it. My showing up on her doorstep wasn't an overstep. It was purely a professional service.

My plan had sounded much better in my head, before I had Ivy glaring blue lasers at me.

Truthfully, I'd agonized over this since Ivy left Better Movement in a flurry of anger. She hadn't answered my texts or calls, and, as usual, I didn't know when to stop. I couldn't stand by when I knew she needed me, whether she would admit it or not. I'd argued with myself when I looked into her mom's file and mapped out her address. I'd debated over the pros and cons of waiting another day versus stopping by her house as soon as I could.

My only misstep, from my perspective, was my spontaneous purchase at a grocery store, where I'd bought a bouquet of mixed flowers. I didn't know what her favorite kind was, so why not buy a variety and hope one of them was right? The decision hadn't felt like a misstep at the time; now, looking into her flushed face, regret gripped my throat. I should've stuck with the "professional service" excuse.

I'd pictured this going so differently. In my imagination, she opened the door with a surprised and wary smile, and she maybe wore those ridiculously tiny pajama shorts some women liked, and I gave the apology I'd been rehearsing all day, and she welcomed me inside. We had an evening that started off a little awkward but quickly grew comfortable; she accepted my proposal for at-home physical therapy; and then, fast-forwarding a few weeks, we were making out like teenagers.

Pathetic. What a relief she couldn't read my mind.

Ivy didn't speak, just crossed her arms over her chest and stared at me. And, no, for the record, she was not wearing ridiculously tiny pajama shorts.

"I'm sorry." I didn't wait for a response. "You're right. I should've defended your mom to my boss. I should've reminded him that patients are people. I didn't do that, and there's no excuse. If I say I love my patients, I should be there for them. I'm sorry for my actions—or lack of actions—and I'm sorry my boss is a robot, and I'm sorry for hurting you and your mom."

She continued staring, but her head tilted ever so slightly, which I took as a sign to keep talking.

"I'm here to make it up to you. I'll grovel if you want."

The winter air bit at my neck beneath my coat, but I refused to show any weakness. Now was not the time to complain about the weather. Now was the time to convince her I was the only one who could do at-home physical therapy.

"What makes you think I need you?" Her voice was colder than the New England winter.

This moment required tact. I couldn't leap forward like I normally did, or I would scare her beyond ever letting me close to her again.

"You might not need me," I said, "but your mom needs physical therapy. I'm offering you at-home sessions. Free of charge, because I'll log my hours pro bono to impress my boss. I can be here any time that's convenient for you."

Her posture lost some of its stiffness.

"Please, let me make it up to—"

"No strings attached?"

I frowned, not having predicted the conversation would take this turn. "No strings attached to what?"

"Your offer for free at-home sessions. Nothing is free."

I shook my head. "Ivy, I'm just trying to do the right thing. I promise I'm not trying to screw you over."

How many people had hurt her that she was so suspicious of everyone? How many of those hurts had she never let go, holding them close and watching them grow? Equally important, how long would she keep me standing in the cold, holding this bouquet like a fool? Not much embarrassed me, but I was still tempted to crawl back to my car.

I studied her, watching for any signs of softening. Her expression was less angry, but it definitely wasn't flooded with forgiveness and goodwill. Except for a single crease between her brows, her face was blank. Her arms still crossed over her chest, but that could've been because of the cold, not me.

"How did you know where I live?"

"Your mom's patient file. When you didn't answer your phone—"

"You're letting all the cold air in," a voice from behind her complained.

For the first time, I noticed the watchful set of eyes on us. She was probably in her seventies, wearing fluffy pink socks and sparkly purple glasses, and she wielded a crutch overhead with great effort. Her stance was throwing her off-balance.

I smiled at her in greeting. "If you spread your feet a little farther apart, it will give you more power when you swing that crutch at my head. Like this." I demonstrated with my feet.

The woman hesitated a moment before mimicking me.

"And bend your knees a little bit for some momentum. Perfect." I smiled at her. "I'm Toby, by the way."

"I'm Phyllis. I live next door."

"Toby from physical therapy?" another voice called from the living room. "Let him in, Ivy; I'm freezing."

Ivy rolled her eyes. "Come on in. Don't get too comfortable."

I expected her to turn and walk away without another word, but she opened the door wider. Look at that positively friendly gesture.

I stepped inside and thrust the bouquet at her. "I wasn't sure what you'd like."

She blinked at my offering before taking the flowers from me. "Thanks."

I shoved back the urge to fist-pump and reminded myself I had a long way to go before she considered letting me into her life again, or going on a date with me, or moving in together—

Cool it.

I could cool it. I could be the coolest cool kid on the block.

I nodded at Irena as I followed Ivy past the living room, where her mom and Phyllis watched me with wide eyes, to the kitchen. All of her walls were painted white, but the artwork was so bright and full of life, I would never consider her home boring. Each canvas was covered with thick, bright paint in a swirl of colors and range of styles. I knew next to nothing about art, but even I could tell the artist was talented. Everywhere I turned, I saw a new one.

"These are beautiful," I told her.

"Thank you."

I peered closer at a picture in a thin black frame. In the lower right-hand corner, whirling letters spelled out *I. Lunden.*

"Did you make all of these?" I didn't try to keep the wonder from my tone. She deserved to know she was amazing.

Ivy cleared her throat. "Yes, I did."

"I had no idea."

She stood at the counter, fussing with the bouquet. She methodically cut each stem to a specific length before dipping it into a vase. Each movement was slow and intentional, almost meditative. A cat perched on the top of her refrigerator, its unblinking eyes fixed on her flower-arranging progress.

When she noticed me watching, she stiffened and set aside her scissors. "Free, or pro bono, at-home physical therapy. Starting when?"

"Whenever you want."

"Tomorrow night."

I nodded.

"Should it be three days a week? Four?"

Every single day. Purely for professional reasons, of course.

I cleared my throat. "Let's start with three and see how that goes. We can increase or decrease from there."

The tape on the floor caught my attention. "Redecorating?"

She crossed her arms over her chest again. "Something like that."

Excuse me for not realizing the neon tape on the floor was a touchy subject. I jumped back to physical therapy. "What time do you want me here tomorrow?"

"By the time I get home from work, and depending on traffic, it's around six. Let's plan on that."

"I'll be here. I can bring dinner if it helps—"

"I can handle dinner."

I restrained a smile. Tiptoeing around Ivy would be my new challenge. I looked forward to tapping on her walls until I found a way through.

"Let him bring dinner," Phyllis called from the living room. "We're almost out of canned soup."

"You don't even live here," Ivy muttered in Phyllis's direction.

"We don't like him, remember?" her mom stage-whispered, unaware we could hear them from the other room.

"We don't need to like him for him to bring us dinner," Phyllis whispered back.

"I do love Sal's eggplant parmigiana," Irena murmured. "But with the penne noodle, not the spaghetti noodle."

Their conversation dissolved into debating the merits of traditional spaghetti or penne, and which type of noodle held more sauce. I smiled when Ivy made eye contact with me, and even though she didn't smile back, her gaze warmed enough that I knew she was laughing at the overly serious noodle argument in the other room.

I also knew I'd found my way in: food.

CHAPTER 17

IVY

Mel: First, you're right, Cam loves me, we're together now, and we're going to live happily ever after. Second, how's your mom?
Ivy: Excuse me?! You just dropped that and think I'm not going to comment?!

My life felt like a minefield. Then again, so did my emotions.

The good news: Cameron and Mel were finally together. *Finally*. I couldn't be happier.

The bad news: Today was Toby's first at-home physical therapy session with Mom, and I was stuck in traffic, and I was more disappointed than I wanted to admit about missing out on time with him.

All day I'd fought to stay angry with Toby to avoid getting my hopes up. He'd hurt my mom, even if she didn't show it or talk about it. He'd hurt me. When he'd stood aside while Deke robot-voiced his way through icy statistics, Toby had lived down to my already-low expectations of men, and clinging to my negativity felt safer than opening up.

But now, when I thought of Toby, I remembered him standing outside my doorstep, clutching the world's biggest bouquet of mixed flowers, smiling hopefully at me. I thought of us standing in the parking lot of Better Movement, and how he ignored the cold air raising goose bumps on his skin so he could talk to me, how he'd caught me when I slipped. I thought of him standing at the registrar counter, leaning close, sliding his phone toward me, asking for my number.

Traffic inched along. Thankfully I'd put a key under the mat for Toby just in case this happened. I texted him while I sat behind a dozen other cars waiting to get on the exit ramp.

Ivy: Running late. Key's under the mat.

He replied immediately.

Toby - 10/10 Smile: You're giving me a key to your place before our first date? How forward of you.

My first genuine smile of the day spread across my face. I could almost hear the text in his voice, filling my mind with colors and my body with emotions. Joy and pleasure at having a piece of our game back for a moment. Frustration with Toby for his Better Movement mistake. Gratitude at his offer for pro bono, at-home sessions. Anticipation at the idea of seeing him again.

No place inside my head or heart was safe right now. It was all because of Toby, and somehow I liked him for it.

When I finally parked in my garage, I hesitated.

Usually I came home already dreading tomorrow's workday, wishing I could go anywhere other than back to the registrar's office in the morning.

Today was different. I felt…eager. Toby was just inside. What would he say? What would he do? Would he be happy to see me? What a silly question—he was always happy to see me. Was I happy to see him? The answer worried me.

Definitely a minefield.

When I opened the door from the garage into the kitchen, Toby's voice was the first sound I heard. The gloomy gray from office and traffic noise washed into brightness. My mood lifted instantly.

I slipped off my shoes and hung my purse by the door. Picking up Van and tucking him against my chest, I tiptoed closer to the living room, Toby's voice growing louder as I neared.

"There, see?" he spoke softly, adjusting his volume from his normal boisterousness to a tone that comforted and encouraged. Fabric shifted, and I sensed he was demonstrating something to Mom. "Here's your range of motion now. In a few weeks, we'll have it to right about"—another shift of fabric—"here."

Mom sighed. "I didn't have that range of motion even before I fell."

"Then, like moms always say, I'll leave you in a better place than I found you," he said.

I leaned my forehead against the edge of the doorframe, peering around to see Phyllis perched on the couch, raptly watching Mom and Toby. Mom sat on the edge of her recliner with her injured leg extended in front of her. Toby knelt before her in a tangle of resistance bands. He held her ankle in his hands.

I'd always known Toby was big. I could only guess at his height. But, unlike a football player I'd briefly dated in high school, Toby's size never intimidated me. His larger-than-life personality stood out more than his physical self. But now, with him kneeling in front of Mom, who looked more and more feeble and frail every time I turned around, he looked gigantic. And she looked waiflike. But the way he smiled up at her, with his large hands turning her ankle this way and that…my mom had nothing to fear from Toby.

I, on the other hand, had plenty to fear. I was supposed to be mad at him. But how could I, when he looked at Mom with bright-eyed humor?

What did he see when he looked at her? As an outside observer in this moment, I paused at how she seemed to revel in his attention despite her best efforts to dislike him. He was solely focused on her. And she was blossoming like a flower in sunlight.

Maybe all she needed was attention. She hadn't had much of it, come to think of it. She'd gotten pregnant with me in her mid-forties, when she'd been happy in her refusing-to-grow-old-partier lifestyle, in her brief and intense relationships, like what she'd had with my dad, whoever he was. We had very few pictures of her at that age, but in the photos we did have, she looked like someone fighting against middle age. She wore too much makeup and dyed her hair a shade too dark. A single mom in her forties didn't have time or energy for herself, and children don't tend to think of their parents as needing attention. Children are focused on themselves. *I* was focused on myself.

In moments like this, her overinvolvement in my life made sense. Looking back, without the haze of adolescence surrounding me, I could see the desperation in her choices. It'd been just the two of us. She'd thrown herself into being a mother like I threw myself into art—for the sheer rush of losing yourself in what you loved.

Toby must've felt me watching, because he turned to look at me. He smiled. I shoved away my smile that instinctively rose to answer his. I couldn't let myself feel so much, I couldn't—

"Another couple reps," he said to Mom, even though he looked at me. "Then we'll move to the next exercise."

"That's what you said a couple reps ago," she complained.

"I did?" His feigned innocence was charming enough, but it turned irresistible when he winked at me.

I grinned and rolled my eyes, retreating into the kitchen before his lethal charisma could pry back another chink of my armor.

Fine, I admitted it, I wasn't mad at Toby anymore. He'd shown his true colors in his interactions with Mom, proving the sincerity and humor I'd first noticed at the registrar's office wasn't a false first impression after all. But that didn't mean I would be naive. Fool me once, shame on you; fool me twice…

I opened the pantry and perused our dinner options. Maybe some pasta sauce. That was better than canned soup, right? Actually, where were my canned soup and pasta sauce? What were my cookie sheets doing in here? The pantry looked different.

Mom. She had moved everything. Had she really hobbled around to rearrange my kitchen?

Noticing a sticky note on the kitchen table, I tilted my head to read it.

Eggplant parmigiana is on the second shelf of the fridge. -T

He'd picked up dinner, just like he'd offered. Feeling oddly sentimental about the gesture, I tucked the note into my pocket.

"So, about that lunch date."

I turned to see Toby leaning against the doorframe, grinning at me like he'd been reading my mind a moment ago.

"What happened to 'no strings attached'?"

"Our lunch date doesn't qualify as strings. This is called rescheduling."

I turned back to the pantry so I could collect my thoughts without having to maintain eye contact. What had happened to flirty, indomitable Ivy? Since when did I avoid eye contact? Since Toby proved each of my assumptions wrong, starting with our flirtationship and ending with his apology last night.

No. Toby wouldn't change me. I was not a shrinking violet. I armored myself in red lipstick and gave as good as I got.

"How are you?" he asked.

I spun to face him. "I'm good. Sorry I was late."

"It's okay. I let myself in and made a lot of progress with your mom." He peeked into the living room to make sure she was still exercising.

"Thanks for bringing dinner." Since I didn't need to cook, putting my kitchen back in order could wait for another day. "Is she being a good patient?"

His low laugh smeared gold through my mind. "Probably better for me than she'd be for you. She mentioned you tried to take my place yesterday?" His voice lowered. "You know I'm irreplaceable, Ivy."

Of course Mom had told him about my ill-advised attempt. Late last night when I'd explained to her why I'd covered the kitchen in painter's tape, I didn't think she'd blab about it to Toby.

I leaned against the countertop behind me. My eyes roamed his body slowly, from head to toe and back again. I lowered my voice to match his. "I know."

This felt familiar, safe, returning to our game. Teasing. Flirting. Giving a little to see what he would give back. Relief washed away my too-deep emotions as we went back to our routine.

The floor creaked in the living room where Mom did whatever physical therapy Toby had just given her. The moment broke.

He cleared his throat. "How was your day?"

I shrugged. "It was okay. Nothing terrible, nothing great."

The great part would be later tonight, when I painted in my studio after Mom went to sleep. My fingers tapped a rhythm, itching for a pencil or brush to capture the angles of Toby's face as he'd worked with Mom.

"How was your day?" I asked.

He smiled. "It's a ten now that you're here."

I rolled my eyes. "Flatterer."

"You should give yourself more credit. Your greatest talent, other than your art, is sending my daily ratings skyrocketing to a ten."

The sincerity in his eyes had me wondering if I could curl up small enough to hide in the cabinet behind me, but I forced myself to stand tall. This conversation was a way to offer forgiveness, start over. He was trying his best. He was being the bigger person here.

I thought back to last night. He'd stood in the cold as long as I'd made him, petty as that was. The bouquet, brilliant and colorful and a testimony to his thoughtfulness, sat on the counter. All of that even after I'd jumped to conclusions about him.

I swallowed the boulder in my throat. "I'm sorry."

Was he holding his breath like I was? Because I couldn't breathe easily until he answered. It shouldn't matter so much whether he accepted my apology. I shouldn't feel any suspense as I watched him straighten away from the doorframe, looking at me like we were the only two people in the entire city.

He stepped closer. "What are you sorry for?"

I parsed my words carefully, picking and choosing from the thoughts circulating in my mind for the last twenty-four hours. "For overreacting. You couldn't do anything about your boss. We've all had bosses like that."

He shook his head. "You're stressed and exhausted. It's perfectly under-standable—"

"I know better than to take it out on you."

His chest moved on an exhale. "Thank you. I needed to hear that."

Watching him step closer, I regretted my apology. This was the opposite of our flirtationship. His forgiveness soothed the ache beneath my rib cage. I could breathe again. He'd handled me as gently as he'd handled Mom's injured ankle, and now I felt completely at the mercy of my emotions. How did I have so little control over my feelings?

"Don't get too comfortable," I quipped. "It takes more than a pretty face to earn a place around here."

He blinked but switched gears quickly enough. Grinning, he ran a hand along his jaw. "But have you tested that theory on a face *this* pretty?"

I rolled my eyes and moved to the fridge, digging out the eggplant parmigiana he'd brought for dinner, trying to ignore how uncomfortable I felt about free physical therapy *and* free dinner.

His voice held equal parts humor and hope. "Is it too soon to ask about that date after all?"

I laughed. My laughter wasn't one of my more attractive traits. I could keep it low and flirty if I focused, but my knee-jerk laugh at something that struck me as genuinely funny usually ended in a snort. Not exactly sexy.

Stifling the sound, I glanced over my shoulder at him. His head tilted at a smug angle, his expression delighted.

A voice called from the living room. "Ivy, did you know Toby is a wee baby?"

He coughed to cover his own chuckle. "I'm twenty-seven. My birthday was last month."

"Happy belated birthday," I said, noting I was a year older than he was.

"Your parents must be proud to have such a *young* physical therapist in the family." Mom's tone emphasized Toby being young, not his family being proud.

Ladies and gentlemen, my mother in all her meddlesome glory.

He shrugged. "I'm a little on the young side because I finished my degrees as quickly as possible."

"You must be very disciplined to manage that," I complimented, both because I liked to see Toby smile and because I wanted to counteract Mom's hints at his inexperience.

"I am," he agreed. "I'm unstoppable once I set my sights."

And his sights were on me.

I swallowed. Any residual anger I held against him since Better Movement evaporated. How could I hold a grudge when he looked at me like I was essential to him?

Mom's voice cut in. "What are you two doing in there?"

"If your session is over," Phyllis said, "we can start watching *Swamp People*."

"I think I'm more in the mood for *The Bachelorette*," Mom said.

"That's right, they left us on a cliffhanger last episode."

Toby gestured over his shoulder with his thumb. "I'd better—"

"Good idea." Hiding my smile, I pulled plates from the cabinet.

Being in Toby's sights felt very, very good.

CHAPTER 18

TOBY

Toby: Van puked in my shoe. I cleaned it up, and it's not a big deal, but I wanted to let you know in case he's sick.
Ivy: He keeps eating yarn from Mom's knitting in the middle of the night. No matter where I hide it, he finds it. I'll buy you new shoes.
Toby: Oh, I always imagined he slept in your room.
Ivy: So he can chew on my hair all night? No, thanks.

I sat in the kitchen, having just finished my third session with Ivy's mom. She and Phyllis were in the living room, the volume of their reality show turned up too loud. Ivy was upstairs somewhere, changing out of her business casual work clothes and into the leggings she preferred around home. Van curled in my lap, contentedly purring beneath my hands, while I made sure whatever Ivy had on the stovetop didn't boil over, per her instructions.

With a few moments alone, I answered Cameron's text from an hour ago.

Cameron: Video games tonight?
Toby: Can't. Working late.
Cameron: Again? You had evening hours last week too.

I smiled. I would never complain about extra time with Ivy.

Honestly, I hadn't thought he would notice the fewer evenings I had free lately. Now that Cameron and Mel were finally on the same page, they were always together. His place, her place, their families' places on weekends. I was thrilled for them. I was also thrilled I had Ivy and her mom to fill my time, or I would be the stereotypical lonely bachelor by now, with Cameron too busy being googly-eyed.

Cameron: I need evidence you're actually working. For all I know, you've been practicing Street Fighter all this time.

Toby: Here's your evidence.

I sent him a poorly taken selfie of me and Van. It was the worst kind of evidence to prove I was "working," but my duffel bag of equipment sat next to me, so I didn't look completely useless.

Cameron: That's Van! Are you at Ivy's house?!

My thoughts faltered for a moment.

Was I *where*? How did Cameron know this was Ivy's house? They worked at the same university, but the college was big. I'd wondered if they vaguely knew each other, like you do when you work at a big company, but that scenario didn't leave room for Cameron to know what Ivy's house looked like. The only coworker he talked about was Mel, since she'd been the only woman on his mind since his first day at the university. He never mentioned his other colleagues. Just Mel.

But Cameron knew this was Ivy's house. So what if…

It had never occurred to me that Cameron and Ivy might have been *together* together. It wasn't beyond reason that Cameron would have a casual relationship with another coworker while he waited five long years for Mel. But Ivy?

I swallowed.

I would need to tell Cameron. We would need to hash it out. Because I couldn't walk away from Ivy. She might not have much hope for us yet, but I was working on that, and I could work on Cameron at the same time. I just *knew* the four of us, Cameron and Mel and me and Ivy, would be great friends. The best of friends. I just needed to convince them, that was all. I refused to acknowledge any reality where Cameron and Ivy didn't get along.

He texted again before I could formulate a reply.

Cameron: Ivy is Mel's best friend. The three of us hang out all the time. Or used to, before her mom fell and Ivy got really busy.

What sweet relief. Ivy, Mel, and Cameron were friends. Only friends. This I could handle. I hadn't broken any bro codes after all.

Toby: Small world!

Cameron: I didn't realize you were her physical therapist. How's her mom coming along?

Toby: We're making good progress.

Cameron: Good. Isn't Ivy the best?

"The best" didn't begin to cover it. She was a dichotomy of confident flirtation and the inability to accept compliments. She was fiercely independent to the point of rarely asking for or accepting help. She was beautiful, from the way she rolled her eyes when I teased her to the way her blond hair caught the light when she tilted her head.

Some things I definitely wouldn't tell Cameron, and now wasn't the time to bring up the fact that Ivy had been my lunch date. But I could tell him other things.

Toby: Ivy's great. I asked her out for sushi. I haven't convinced her yet, but hopefully it's a matter of time.

Cameron: No way! I could see you two hitting it off.

Before I could reply, another message popped up.

Cameron: Let me know how the convincing goes. She's a bit standoffish, but she has a good heart. I can talk you up from my side.

Then another.

Cameron: The four of us should hang out. We would be the ultimate Trivia Tuesday team.

Another excuse to spend more time with Ivy? Where could I sign up?

Cameron: Or a Monday night. Mel, Ivy, and I hang out almost every Monday night after work. It's been more sporadic since her mom fell, but I think the next one is at Ivy's house. You in?

Toby: Of course!

Cameron wouldn't need to be won over after all.

I leaned back in my chair, mentally counting the days until Monday night with Cameron, Mel, and Ivy. Was this what love was like? Endless waiting? Because almost as soon as I finished waiting for the next time I'd get to be with Ivy, it seemed like I had to start waiting all over again.

But my patience would be worth it. I'd heard about these get-togethers, what with Cameron gushing over Mel, but I'd never been to one. I tapped my foot against the kitchen floor, thinking of sitting next to Ivy on Monday night, or staying late to help her clean up after Cameron and Mel left, or—

The steps creaked as Ivy made her way downstairs. "Do you realize what you've done?"

Van and I looked up, both of us blinking at her. She wore leggings and something long-sleeved that I barely noticed because I was busy watching how she held her body in one stiff line. Her eyes were guarded.

What I had done…um… "I've been making sure dinner didn't boil—"

"You told Cam about us."

Us. It had a nice ring to it. But she didn't look happy when she said it.

Van darted off my lap and out of the room. Coward.

All I'd done was text that selfie to Cameron, which was a bit juvenile, sure, but not a crime as far as I knew. Clearly I'd missed something.

Feeling uncertain, I stood. "I don't know what he said to you, but we were texting, and it came out that I'm your mom's physical therapist. Is that…okay?"

Whatever this situation was, it felt ridiculous. Did I need to ask her permission to talk to my best friend? I couldn't guess the conclusions her mind was jumping to.

I watched her. She shifted her weight on her feet. She crossed and uncrossed her arms. If anyone had ever embodied irritation, Ivy did.

"It's fine," she said.

Ah. *Fine.* Every man's favorite word to hear when a woman is mad at him.

My brain slowed, puzzling together pieces I hadn't thought of before. Not long ago, the university had published a profile article about Cameron, and the student writer had quoted me, so Ivy had to have known that I knew Cameron. She knew we were good friends. She'd had every opportunity to say, "Did you know I'm friends with Cam too?" Or "I work with Cam, and he mentioned you two are close. What a coincidence, right?"

Ivy had chosen to pass up every chance she'd had to draw a simple connect-the-dots line between me, Ivy, Cameron, and Mel. Why?

"I don't understand why you're mad at me," I said.

She didn't say anything at first. If there was one thing I knew about Ivy, it was that she always had a sarcastic quip waiting behind those red lips.

"I'm not mad at you."

I lifted my brows in a skeptical look. "So you were planning on hiding our mutual friendship with Cameron for…forever?"

She rolled her eyes. "No, I was planning on seeing how things played out between us before I told Cam and Mel."

Oh.

"Well…surprise?" I grinned sheepishly. "I take it Cam and Mel's texts were a little more over-involved than what Cam sent to me?"

"Cam and Mel are nosy," she said. "Well-meaning, but nosy."

Of course they were. I would be too. I'd been nosy about Cameron and Mel, and that was without knowing Mel personally.

Without saying anything, Ivy handed me her phone.

CHAPTER 19

IVY

Mel: It's just the two of us. Isn't Toby hot?
Ivy: I'm going to tell Cam you said that.
Mel: Cam agrees with me.
Ivy: Of course he does.
Mel: Just imagine how perfect it would be, the four of us together. Cam and me.
Toby and you.
Ivy: Put away your wedding planner, friend. I like my independence.

I'd been upstairs, digging through my stack of very nearly clean laundry for a pair of comfy leggings when my phone blew up with texts from Cameron and Mel.

Cameron: Ivy, you know Toby?! You chose him for your mom's physical therapy?

Mel: You know Toby?!

Cameron: My friend groups are uniting into a single superpower!

Mel: Does this mean Trivia Tuesdays are now a thing? Because, Ivy, I need some support out there.

Cameron: Absolutely. Trivia Tuesdays are now double date nights. Monday nights are now double date nights. Everything is now a double date, except for all those other nights I didn't name, which you're not invited to because I need to make up for years of NOT putting the moves on Mel.

Mel: Hold up. Are Toby and Ivy dating, or do they just know each other and you're playing matchmaker?

Cameron: He asked her out. For sushi.

Mel: Ivy, this is perfect! You love sushi! You and Toby will be great together.

It was overwhelming, to say the least. I'd gone from sniff-testing a pile of clothes to determine whether they were clean enough to wear, to feeling cornered into a relationship I was still struggling to accept for myself. A relationship that, if it failed, might make my friendship with Mel and Cameron awkward, to say the least. Now I stood in front of Toby, watching his reaction to the text thread between me, Mel, and Cameron.

Toby handed my phone back to me. "Yeah, this is much more than what Cam sent me."

"They're romantics like that." I hated my grumbly tone. But I didn't want whatever might go wrong between me and Toby to become a problem between the four of us. Because if anyone was immature about relationships, it was me, and I was self-aware enough to admit it.

A floorboard creaked behind me. Toby looked over my shoulder. His concerned expression changed to guarded amusement. I knew what I would see before I turned around.

Mom and Phyllis bent around the corner like schoolgirls eavesdropping outside the principal's office. Their eyes were wide, their faces drawn in concentration, their posture leaning forward as far as they could without toppling over. Noticing our gazes, they straightened.

"We just needed some fresh water," Phyllis explained, shuffling toward the kitchen sink.

"Yes, with lemon," Mom echoed.

I resisted the urge to point out Mom couldn't balance a glass of water while she walked with crutches.

Grabbing Toby's arm, I maneuvered him into the garage and closed the door behind us. It was cold, but we wouldn't be out here long.

"They just don't stop, do they?" Toby chuckled.

I didn't have the headspace to deal with Mom and Phyllis right now. I'd laugh about it later.

"It could get weird with Cam and Mel," I said.

Monday nights wouldn't be easy camaraderie if Toby and I didn't work out. Cameron would crunch too loudly on tortilla chips. Mel would light every vanilla candle in the city and still not feel zen. I would feel responsible for ruining the best friendships of my adult life.

He pushed his hands into his pockets and rocked on his heels. "I don't think it'll be awkward. I'd say our chances of the four of us getting along are pretty good since you and I get along, and you and the two—"

"I mean if you and I don't work out, and Cam and Mel are in the mix."

"If we date-divorce, I'm fighting you for custody of Cam. See me in court."

"I'm serious."

"This really isn't a big deal. We're going on a date. We're seeing what happens. If we break up, it just means we weren't a good fit for each other. We can still be friends with Cam and Mel, even if we can't be friends together."

I ran the scenario through my head, surprised by the ending he proposed. I thought we got along well enough that a relationship wasn't the only outcome possible. "You won't want to be just friends with me?"

Toby stepped closer. "Maybe this makes me an uncompromising jerk, but I'm not a masochist, so, no, I don't want to be just friends with you."

I wouldn't have believed it if it weren't for the way he was looking at me right now. I cleared my throat. "It's always all or nothing with you, isn't it?"

He didn't hesitate. "All or nothing."

The sincerity in his voice might look colorful in my mind, but it drew icy goose bumps down my spine. The vulnerability it took to jump with both feet was exactly the vulnerability I couldn't comprehend. I didn't want to comprehend it. I wanted to stay safe behind my thick walls.

But that same sincerity that drew goose bumps on my skin also inspired curiosity. What would it feel like, to go all or nothing with Toby? If I flung myself off that cliff, would he catch me?

He stood perfectly still, watching me.

Yes, he would catch me.

"I'm not good at this kind of thing," I whispered.

"What kind of thing?"

I hesitated. "Relationships."

"Tell me more." He spoke gently, coaxingly, like newcomers spoke to Van.

I sighed a partial laugh. "I've dated some real scumbags, and between their immaturity and my immaturity, we hurt each other. In my experience, men only want sex. And when they get what they want, they ditch me. That's the *Reader's Digest* version of my relationship track record."

I looked away then, unable to hold eye contact with a man who probably only did long-term relationships, with purpose and intentionality. We couldn't be more opposite.

When I peeked up at him, he hadn't moved. Had he even breathed? What was he thinking?

Chickening out and hoping to come across as indifferent, I shrugged. "I'm better at hooking up because it's straightforward. It's simple. I expect little, so I'm rarely disappointed. We're on the same page."

He frowned at that. "Are you worried you and I aren't on the same page?" He continued before I could answer, moving closer. "Because I want more than sex, Ivy. I plan on sticking around unless you outright tell me to get lost." Another half-step toward me. "Are you planning on telling me to get lost?"

The quiet rumble of his voice echoed through my mind and splashed gold against a cobalt and emerald background.

"Not at the moment."

There it went—my tough-girl façade shattered into splinters. I was falling off that cliff, and he stood at the bottom, arms outstretched.

"My last relationship was with someone who wanted to keep her options open," Toby said. "I was good enough for her to pass the time with but not to get serious with. So I try a little too hard. I come across a little too strong. But that's how I'm 'straightforward' about being on the same page as you."

Beneath the simmering moment between us, I spared some anger for his ex-girlfriend. I couldn't imagine someone leading on Toby, with his big smile and even bigger heart.

"So are we on the same page, Ivy?"

I shivered, and not from the cold. "We're on the same page."

He stood inches away now. His fingertip felt warm and teasing as he traced it from my temple to my cheek, then from my jawline to my chin, then at the edge of my bottom lip. I couldn't breathe. He didn't seem to be breathing either.

Maybe I was wrong about him catching me as I fell. Maybe we were both leaping over the cliff together.

A scuffling sound behind the garage door broke the moment. The kitchen light glowed through the seam at the bottom of the door, where I saw two shadows. Mom and Phyllis.

Toby took a step backward with a smile. "You're not allowed to use Cam and Mel as an excuse to keep turning me down. I already bought my tux for our sushi date."

“A tux?” My eyes widened. “You’re kidding, right?”
His only reply was an enigmatic smile.

CHAPTER 20

IVY

Mom: hi
Ivy: Mom? How did you learn how to text?
Mom: phyllis showed me
Ivy: Don't you have a flip phone? Texting is a pain on flip phones.
Mom: phyllis gave me her old smart phone

Not much rattles me. I tend to take life as it comes and then process it later in solitude. This trait is particularly useful at the registrar's office, at art gallery showings, and today, apparently, when I stepped into my own home and was greeted by half of a man's bare rear end pointed in my direction.

I stumbled backward, not fully comprehending what I was seeing.

Who was the man with his butt in the air? I'd seen Toby's car in the driveway, and I'd known he would already be here since I'd been stuck in traffic again, but this definitely wasn't Toby.

"Is that Ivy?" Mom called from the living room.

The man straightened, still kneeling at the foot of the steps, various tools spread around him, and a long, metal contraption leaning against the stairs. He removed a baseball cap to reveal a receding hairline.

"Hello," he said. "Am I in your way? Sorry about that." He moved to stand.

"It's okay; I'll go around," I mumbled, unsure where to look when I'd already seen too much of him.

He smiled good-naturedly and turned back to his work, bending again. Exposing again.

Fixing my eyes on the floor, I maneuvered around his feet and tools. Leaving the kitchen and the kneeling man as quickly as possible, I escaped to the living room.

When I next dared to look up, I met Toby's eyes. His mouth twitched with laughter, and I bit my lower lip to contain my own chuckle. His eyes followed the movement. My stomach dipped. I couldn't look at him when he watched me like that.

Glancing away, my eyes widened at what else was in my living room. Old-fashioned, outdated medical supplies. Everywhere. A wheelchair, a walker, a standalone raised toilet seat, an IV pole, and a dozen other gadgets and gizmos I couldn't name. They filled every flat surface and every corner.

"What is all this?" I asked.

Toby's brows snapped together. "Nobody asked you?"

"I'm so glad you're home," Mom said. "I was starting to worry about you."

"There was traffic." My voice was distant, my eyes still taking in the clutter filling my house.

Phyllis shuffled into the room. "I told some of the neighbors about your mom's injury, and they offered to let her borrow their supplies. Isn't that nice?"

"But we can't use all this." I pointed at the raised toilet seat. "Do you need that?"

She shrugged. "Well, you never know—"

I looked at Toby. "Does she need it?"

He shifted his feet. "Physically, she should be able to handle moving from sitting to standing without any assistance."

"We're not keeping that thing," I said.

"But what if—"

"No." This was nonnegotiable.

Phyllis decided to try anyway. "But the neighbors have been so kind—"

"Yes, they have, but Mom is only going to get better, not worse, so we don't need most of the supplies in here."

My gaze fixed on Toby. I willed him to read my mind. *Help me out here. I can't breathe with all the pressure of this clutter, and Mom being in my business, and Phyllis, and now some man in my house—*

He nodded. "Professionally speaking, you don't need this equipment."

Thank you, thank you, thank you. I could kiss you right now.

Speaking of which, what kind of kisser was Toby? Would he place his hands on my waist as he leaned closer? Maybe he would sift his fingers into my hair and against the back of my neck. Better yet, he might—

I realized he was still talking.

"...the walker would be useful, because your arms have to be sore from the crutches. The stair lift would be great, actually, since all the bedrooms are upstairs. But that's up to Ivy, since it'll mean some pretty serious changes to her house."

I closed my eyes and rubbed my temples, feeling a dull throb beginning behind my eyes. I imagined the holes we would need to drill into my walls for the stair lift. I imagined the peace of mind I would feel if I didn't need to worry about Mom wobbling up and down the steps.

"The stair lift can stay," I said. "Keep the walker too. Everything else needs to go."

Phyllis sighed. "I'll have to ask Chester to take it all back to the neighbors' houses then."

"Who's Chester?"

"That nice man you probably met when you first came in," Mom said. "He's already started on the stair lift. He offered to help us install everything else, too, if you change your mind."

"I won't change my mind."

"Did you get to meet Chester?" She didn't wait for my answer before raising her voice. "Chester, come meet my daughter!"

He ambled into the living room, adjusting his pants higher on his hips. "Nice to meet you."

"Chester is such a dear," Mom gushed.

"He offered to help with anything you might need," Phyllis said.

"He lives just a few houses down," Mom said, "so it's no hassle."

I smiled. "Thanks so much for your help, Chester. I really appreciate it."

He ran a hand through his thinning hair. "No problem. I'm about finished here for now, since I need to run to the hardware store for a few more things tonight."

"What a great idea!" Mom said. "Ivy can keep you company."

My head swiveled to stare at her. "What about dinner?"

She waved a hand. "Phyllis and I can manage."

Little red flags snapped to attention in my brain. To my right stood Chester, a man in his fifties, again hitching up his pants, again smiling at me with clueless good nature. To my left stood Toby, his arms crossed over his chest, one hand covering his mouth like he was hiding a grin. In front of me sat Mom and Phyllis, faux innocence plastered on their faces.

No. Way.

I turned to Chester and spoke in my registrar voice. "I've had a long day and can't go to the hardware store with you just now." Mom tried to interrupt, but I continued. "If you bring the receipts with you, I can reimburse you for any expenses. I'm happy to compensate you for your time too."

Toby cleared his throat and turned to Mom. "I see you," he joked, "trying to distract me from your session today. Let's get down to business. Did you practice your exercises from last time?"

Mom frowned at him. Phyllis divided her attention between the muted TV screen and me, ushering Chester to the kitchen, where I helped him gather his tools. I locked the front door behind him with a sigh.

Mom stopped mid-exercise to frown at me. "That was very rude, Ivy, throwing him out like that."

Internally, I rolled my eyes. Externally, I shrugged. "He said he was done for the night."

Claustrophobia, something I never thought I had, closed in. Equipment still filled my small house. My zen home, the safe haven I loved, felt foreign. My head was already filled with colors from every sound—I didn't need more visual clutter than necessary.

"Chester is a very nice man," Mom said.

Phyllis dipped her tea bag into her mug, in and out. "Not everyone would volunteer their time like he has."

"He's so good with his hands," Mom said.

A strangled sound burst out of Toby, a laugh he barely managed to smother with an obviously fake cough.

I scowled at him.

"That's the kind of man you need in your life," Mom said.

"A fifty-plus-year-old man?"

Phyllis nodded earnestly. "Older men take care of their women."

"Older men provide more stability," Mom picked up. Had they rehearsed this? "They know what they want, and they're not as easily distracted as"—she glanced at Toby, who rummaged in his duffel bag of equipment—"younger men."

Phyllis squeezed out her tea bag and then dropped it into the mug again, momentarily distracting me from her words. "You should give Chester a chance. He might surprise you."

"No." I couldn't get much clearer than that, right? I didn't over-explain or ramble with excuses. Just a firm, clear no.

"At least consider—" Mom started.

"My answer is no, and it's not changing."

Toby straightened from his duffel, gently pushing a curious Van away from his bag and dropping some resistance bands on the floor. He knelt in front of Mom.

"Why don't you let anyone in, Ivy?" Mom's plaintive voice smeared yellow inside my head.

Toby's movements paused. Phyllis slurped from her tea.

The claustrophobia of the supplies all around me and the frustrating, overwhelming conversation squeezed me further into an emotional corner. I forced some deep breaths into my lungs before I spoke again. "I don't want to be with a man who's probably twenty-five years older than I am," I explained.

Mom waved a dismissive hand. "Young men are unreliable."

Toby looked at her. "Am I unreliable?"

Ignoring him, she continued. "You need someone who can help you fix things around the house."

Phyllis squinted one eye at Toby. "Can you fix things around the house?"

All gazes turned to Toby, where he knelt in front of my mother, wrapping a resistance band around her foot. He glanced up at me. His face was serious, but I knew that gleam in his eyes far too well. "Not really, but I can fix bodies, and I can cook a mean ugali."

Genuinely curious, and also grateful he'd given me an out, I smiled. "What's ugali?"

"My family is from Kenya, and my mom—"

"Chester is a nice man," Mom pressed.

"I'm not having this conversation with you anymore. I'm not interested in Chester, and I never will be."

I strode to the kitchen and opened the fridge. My skin crawled with the urge to hide from the humiliation of the last few minutes. If it had been Mom and Phyllis, it would've been embarrassing enough. But Toby was here too. He'd seen and heard everything. As much as I appreciated his efforts to help me, knowing he'd been there ratcheted my embarrassment into abject humiliation.

Mom didn't know about my history with Toby. She'd only overheard some mild flirting. She didn't know how I felt about him—rather, *if* I had feelings for him. She'd jumped to conclusions and then decided he was too young for me.

He was one year younger. One. Year. Hardly worth throwing me to the wolves, or Chester, in this case, who was less like a wolf and more like a happy-go-lucky Saint Bernard, tongue happily lolling out of the side of his mouth.

Breathing deep in hopes my cheeks would stop burning, I tried to focus on dinner. I'd planned on stir-fry tonight. But the veggies weren't in the fridge. Why were my veggies gone? Why did Mom rearrange more of my house each day?

Needing the distraction, I turned to the sink and filled it with water, dumping in dirty dishes with clunks and splashes. I bent to find the dish soap in the bottom cabinet. My position reminded me of seeing Chester when I first walked through the door, and I couldn't help laughing to myself. Mom and Phyllis had made my life more interesting, if nothing else.

I was elbow-deep in sudsy water when Toby appeared.

He leaned back against the countertop next to me and grinned. "Looks like I have some competition."

I rolled my eyes.

"Maybe you'll let me take you to sushi if I can outshine Chester's glory. Or should I say out-moon?" Toby smirked, clearly pleased with himself.

This was why he was friends with Cameron. This ridiculous sense of humor.

"You never got to answer my question. What's ugali?"

He beamed, clearly delighted that I'd asked again. "It's a Kenyan side dish. It's almost like really dense porridge, only it's made with cornmeal and tastes vaguely like popcorn. My parents moved here from Kenya when Mama was pregnant with my oldest brother, but she still cooks Kenyan food almost every day. She taught all of us how to make it when we were young."

I nodded, imagining young Toby, standing on a stool so he could watch his mom make ugali. I liked the meaningfulness of it. I'd grown up learning to heat jars of spaghetti sauce; he'd grown up learning traditions important to his family.

"What do you eat it with?" I asked.

"Stew of some sort." He winked. "I think my ugali puts me ahead of Chester by at least ten points."

"Ignore them." I nodded toward the living room and lowered my voice. "Mom thinks of relationships in very traditional ways, like the man always being older than the woman."

"So what we have is a relationship now?" Not giving me a chance to answer, he said, "I never knew our one-year difference would be such a strike against me."

I rolled my eyes. "I'm halfway in the grave already, can't you tell?"

His shoulders shook with a silent laugh. He shifted, bringing his body closer to mine. "Contrary to popular opinion, younger men know what they want too."

I withdrew my hands from the dishwater, resting them on the edge of the sink. "And what's that?"

His hand inched toward mine, his fingertips drawing a slow, smooth pattern through the suds dripping off the back of my hand. "You already know," he whispered and then sauntered from the room like he hadn't just made washing dishes the sexiest household chore of all time.

Admittedly, I'm a noisy dishwasher, splashing everywhere and causing more of a mess as I clean. Plus my house is old, and the floorboards squeak at the slightest movement, so I generally know where everyone is at all times.

But I never heard the sound of medical supplies being moved. Only when I dried my hands and turned away from the sink did I notice cleared walkways through the tangle of outdated medical items.

Toby stood in the living room, lifting the last box to the top of a pyramid of other boxes. His shirt pulled across his arms and shoulders as he reached for the top of the stack. He smiled when he saw me. "I thought it might help if you had some breathing room."

Mom sat on her recliner. Phyllis sat on the couch. They looked around the room like we hadn't just witnessed the most thoughtful thing Toby could have done. He'd made space for me.

The overwhelming chaos was just regular chaos now. We could move easily between the upstairs, kitchen, garage, and living room. The boxes partially blocked the basement door, but I never went down there. Until Chester could take all these supplies back where he found them, this was doable.

Toby, shifting on his feet, tucked his hands into his pockets. His gaze turned uncertain the longer I didn't speak. "Or I can put it all back? I guess I should've asked—"

"No." I shook my head. "No, it's perfect. Thank you."

Not much rattled me, sure, but Toby's colorful voice and thoughtfulness did. This certainly felt like more than a flirtationship. But flirting was just, well, flirting, wasn't it? I wasn't looking for more right now. I had too much going on in my life as it was—I didn't need to throw man drama into the mix. I'd never liked the vulnerability of needing people, of my happiness depending on them in any way. And I'd never liked their vulnerability of needing me, either. It always felt too much like stepping close to a cliff's edge and peering over the side, debating whether to jump or remain firmly on the ground.

But this was different. Toby stood in front of me, a relieved smile on his face, and he looked at me with an expression like…caring?

What rattled me more than Toby's kindness, more than the warmth in his eyes right now, was the fact that I didn't mind peering over the cliff's edge with him. Not even a little.

CHAPTER 21

TOBY

Ivy: Thanks again for moving all those boxes a few days ago. Van is enjoying his new favorite view from the top of the pyramid.
Toby: Van is a regular sphinx!

After a long workday of Deke training us on new processes and procedures for the paperwork he loved so much, I was eager to get to Ivy's. I parked in her driveway, bounded up the steps, and nearly tripped over the biggest bag of sidewalk salt I'd ever seen.

Ivy stepped around the corner. "Are you okay? I thought I'd leaned it against the wall, not in front of the door."

"I'm fine."

I was more than fine. I was standing in Ivy's house, and I would spend the next few hours with her in one way or another. I loved that I got to do this multiple days each week. I loved that she'd gradually grown more comfortable around me over my last few visits. She might think I hadn't noticed how she conveniently watered her mom's African violets during my therapy sessions with Irena, or how she watched me working with her mom, or how she pretended she wasn't staring at me when I turned around and caught her gaze. But I noticed. I noticed everything.

I busied myself with removing my coat and shoes. "I'm impressed you even managed to carry that bag over here. Did you remember to lift with your knees?"

"I tried, but my knees were having trouble grasping on, so I had to use my hands after all." To placate my delicate physical therapist's sensibilities, she made a big, albeit sarcastic, show of keeping her back ramrod-straight and squatting to move the heavy bag. I laughed even as my eyes lingered on her long legs.

Phyllis spoke up from the sofa. "Chester will be here tomorrow. He can salt your sidewalk then."

"No need to strain your back," Irena said.

Turning toward the kitchen, Ivy sighed in exasperation even as she affectionately rested a hand on her mom's shoulder. "I've salted my own sidewalks for years. I can manage without Chester."

Chester. Did I feel threatened by him? Definitely not. But I was vaguely annoyed that Ivy's mom apparently thought a man twenty-some years older than Ivy would be a better fit for her than I was. Fortunately, I liked a challenge.

I worked my shoes back on my feet. "Do you remember your warmups?" I asked Irena.

"Of course I do."

"I'll remind her if she forgets anything," Phyllis said.

I was already pulling on my coat. "Great. Start on those first, and I'll be back in just a second."

I paused, watching Irena's unsteady motions. She moved with more fragility than I liked, and she relied on physical supports more than she should.

I'd been facing this dilemma for a few days now. I needed to tell Ivy her mom wasn't progressing like she should be with her physical therapy. We'd been meeting for a few weeks now. While her mom showed some progress, it was slow, and it was limited. All the signs pointed to vestibular, or balance, issues. If she had balance issues, the likelihood that she would move back to her own house and live self-sufficiently was slim at best.

Even being the eternal optimist, I knew this was not good news.

I also knew Ivy struggled with being a caretaker to her mom. I couldn't blame her. She handled the load better than I could have if I were in her position. But I knew one of the reasons she coped relatively well was because she was counting down to the day her mom moved out. I couldn't blame her for that either.

How could I tell Ivy her mom was unlikely to be well enough to live on her own again? At the least, she would need a medical alert necklace. At the next level, she would need a visiting nurse, then a live-in nurse. At the worst, a retirement facility. How could I break the news to her?

Feeling like the villain in this scenario, I kept putting it off. Ivy wouldn't blame me. She wasn't unfair like that. Still, I couldn't help feeling responsible. I recoiled at the thought of seeing Ivy's disappointment at the news.

But first, Ivy needed ice-free sidewalks, and I was the man for the job. Chester was not.

I stepped out Ivy's front door, the bag of salt tucked under my arm. The days had quickly grown short, so it was dark outside, just beams of light shining from porches and streetlamps. The silence of the neighborhood was only broken by the salt crunching under the soles of my shoes and the dogs barking next door.

I mentally rehearsed my lines. I could start with small talk about rating our days or jokes about buying suspenders for Chester. Maybe I could ask her how she felt her mom's physical therapy was going. Surely she had questions or concerns. Then I could mention I had some concerns, too. Or—

I made it to the end of the sidewalk, sprinkling salt as I went. Turning back toward the house, I noticed the living room drapes were open, affording a clear view indoors. Ivy stood in front of her mom and Phyllis, her hands on her hips. They gestured outside. She reached for her coat.

Once Ivy stood beside me, she said, "You knew I was planning to do that myself."

Getting busted had never been so much fun.

I smiled. "I'm happy to help. It's not a big deal."

If her body language said anything, it *was* a big deal. The outdoor light cast half of her in shadow, but it didn't hide how her hands twisted her coat's zipper pull. Maybe I hadn't made as much progress as I'd thought. She wasn't comfortable accepting my help just yet. She did like her independence, after all.

I answered by spreading another few handfuls of salt. I stepped along the sidewalk as slowly as possible, not eager to go back inside and work with Irena for the next hour. I much preferred Ivy's company, for obvious reasons.

"All day at the office, Clarice worried about the ice storm rolling in tonight." Ivy tilted her head conspiratorially. "Gotta love those coworkers who complain in advance about the weather because they think you'll fall for it when they call the next day to say they're iced in, you know? Anyway, I always worry about Mom, so I planned to salt the sidewalk just in case. I could've managed."

I paused in front of her. Lifting her chin with a finger, I frowned down at her, considering. "It's just salting a sidewalk. Why are you thinking so hard about this?"

Vulnerability blinked behind her eyes before she withdrew her chin from my touch. "I'm thinking so hard about all the slip and fall lawsuits you just saved me."

Normally I would laugh at a comment like that. Normally I would shift the conversation with a flirty quip. I wouldn't push Ivy's walls too hard or too fast. But tonight curiosity won.

"Has it always been you and your mom? Neither of you mention any other family."

She nodded. "It's just the two of us. She had me pretty late in life. I wasn't part of her plan, and my dad was basically a summer fling." She shifted her feet, salt crackling beneath her soles. "I went through a phase in school where I confronted Mom about my dad. She said, 'My love is enough for you. You don't need a father too.' And wrapped me in the biggest hug."

That sounded…unhealthy, to say the least. One human being, no matter how great they were, should never be everything to another human being. That kind of isolation and codependence wasn't good for either person. What if something happened to that one person? What would the one left behind do?

But Ivy definitely wasn't asking for my opinion about healthy relationships.

"How did you feel about that?" I asked. "I can't imagine not having my dad around."

"Growing up, that hug was one of my favorite memories. Once I was older, I saw it differently. It's always been me and Mom against the world. But that changed when her helicopter mothering became outright smothering. I moved out, and she started calling me multiple times a day." She stopped speaking, frowning up at me like she hadn't meant to say so much.

I didn't mind. I had time to peel back her onion layers, one at a time, until I reached the real Ivy behind all her walls. Her words already filled missing puzzle pieces in my mind, putting together a clearer picture of why she never wanted to need anyone.

A thumping sound drew me away from my next question. My gaze moved over her shoulder, and I grinned at the sight. "Don't look now," I whispered, "but your mom is throwing rocks."

Her posture stiffened. "Like…literal rocks?"

I nodded.

She turned.

We stared at her mom, who stood in front of the open door, leaning on one crutch. With her free hand, she took rocks from one of Ivy's flower pots and threw them toward the neighbor's property.

Was she…trying to stone someone? I couldn't see anything over there. Was she hallucinating?

Another rock thudded against the neighbor's low fence, her throw too short to clear the top of the boards.

"Mom! What are you doing?!"

"Those dogs never stop barking. I just want a moment's peace."

"Stop! You can't throw rocks at the neighbor's dogs."

"Why not? Their dogs bark night and day. You don't hear it because you're at work—"

"It doesn't matter," Ivy said. "This is not okay. Ignore the dogs, turn up the TV volume, whatever you need to do. Just stop throwing rocks."

Grumbling, Irena turned and hobbled back across the threshold. The indoor lights cast a halo around her curly white hair before the door closed behind her. Even though I couldn't hear her grumbling, something told me she'd thrown rocks at the neighbor's dogs before. Probably several times. We just hadn't been here to catch her. I imagined it all playing out, the harmless, happy neighbors looking out their window to see rocks mysteriously dropping from the top of their fence.

I tried not to laugh. Honestly, I did. But when Ivy turned back to me, her lips parted, eyes wide, brows furrowed, I couldn't help myself. I pressed a hand to my stomach.

"What's so funny?"

"Your mom…is trying to stone…dogs."

"It's not funny! My neighbors will hate me."

"Come on. Isn't it just a little funny? She's so feisty about it." *Just like you're feisty.* But comparisons between Ivy and her mom wouldn't be welcome right now.

She crossed her arms over her chest. "So happy to amuse you."

"I mean, they're small rocks, and she can't throw them hard. There's no way she'll do any actual damage. It's…it's farcical."

Her lips twitched against her best efforts.

"There!" I touched a fingertip to the corner of her mouth. "I knew you thought it was funny!"

"Maybe just a little." She batted my hand away, but I grasped her palm and wrapped our fingers together.

"Your mother is full of surprises."

"That's one way to look at it." Her gaze fixed on our hands.

Her fingers felt soft in mine, and I hoped my calluses weren't too rough against her skin. A current ran between us. Did she feel it too?

I didn't want her to pull away—not now, not ever—so I scrambled to keep talking and distract her. "And with Phyllis in the mix? Your life is like *Arsenic and Old Lace*. Minus the murders, as far as we know. That'll be their next scheme."

Her brows lifted. "You've seen *Arsenic and Old Lace*?"

I scoffed. "Of course I have. Give me some credit. I'm the complete package: a hunk of muscly manliness, and I'm cultured too."

Ignoring my self-aggrandizing, she tilted her head at me. "I wouldn't have pegged you for a classic movie aficionado."

"I haven't seen all the classics, but you can't beat *Arsenic and Old Lace*. Or *Casablanca*. Or *Charade*."

Honestly, those were the only classic movies I'd seen. Three total. But she didn't need to know the mental notes I took each time I learned something about her, like my new plans to go home and binge-watch classic movies tonight so we could talk about them tomorrow.

"Everybody has seen *Casablanca*," she said.

I'd watched it for the first time last week, actually, after she'd mentioned it in passing, but that was beside the point. The point was that I now had another piece of Ivy figured out, and I still held her hand. In the harsh porch light and snowy background, her blond hair looked almost white. With the shadows on her face and her blue eyes staring at me, the moment felt otherworldly.

"We should have a movie night," I said.

She smirked. "Have you given up on sushi so easily? That didn't take long."

"No, I'm just catching you up on the plan. Sushi for our first date. Pizza and movie night for our second. Then a live event for our third. Maybe the comedy theater in town? Or, since you're an artist, we could go to a gallery?"

Ivy nodded slowly. "Is this your dating template you use on all the girls?" Her hand started to withdraw from mine, belying her teasing tone as meaning more than she wanted to let on.

I tightened my fingers a fraction. I didn't dare hold on like I wanted, or she would spook, but I couldn't let go without trying to keep her just a little bit longer.

"There's no template," I said. "My plan is one hundred percent tailored to you. You like sushi, pizza, movies, live events, and other such human pastimes, don't you?"

Now she paused, her thumb drawing loops on the back of my hand. "You know, you don't have me figured out like you think you do." She paused and stepped back, our hands still joined, our arms outstretched between us. "But keep at it. Maybe you're on your way."

I watched her walk back inside, her hips swaying in those jeans, her blond hair iridescent in the night. I released the breath I'd been unconsciously holding.

No, maybe I didn't have her figured out completely. But I planned to.

CHAPTER 22

IVY

Mom: chester asked abt u 2day
Ivy: Tell him I have literal skeletons in my closet.
Mom: i told him u said hi and he has pretty eyes
Ivy: Don't tell him that.

Sliced cheese and crackers sat on the coffee table, a box of wine stood next to some glasses since I don't have Mel's love of mixing drinks, and the only candle I owned flickered next to the TV. I already had our movie for the night paused on the screen. Even Mom cooperated, opting to go to bed early with a novel.

A Monday night with my best friends? Life finally felt a little normal again. It would be a little different since this was the first Monday night with Cameron and Mel as a couple and not as friends, but I was relieved for the change. All those years of covert glances and shy maneuverings had driven me crazy. I was more than ready to feel like a third wheel.

The only thing that didn't feel normal? Toby.

I glanced at my phone, nervously reviewing my text conversation with Cameron and Mel.

Mel: On our way!
Cameron: Can't wait to finally bring my friend groups full circle.
Ivy: You and Toby sound way too dreamy about this.
Mel: They're bromantics.

Cameron: I've been outnumbered for too long. Toby will bring order back to the world.

To say I regretted Toby being here tonight would be an understatement. I'd been the only one who knew our mutual connections for so long, and I wasn't sure how I felt about my worlds colliding. Toby being friends with Cameron, and me being friends with Cameron and Mel, didn't make it a given that the four of us would mesh as a group.

I especially wasn't sure how I felt about Cameron and Mel knowing how much Toby was a part of my life. What if, as well-meaning as they were, they tried to push me and Toby into something more than I was ready for? Toby had already coaxed his way into my life in ways I hadn't expected. I wasn't sure how I felt about him coaxing his way into anything else.

Toby was already here, having stayed after his session with Mom, and I watched the oven clock as he chatted. He clearly had no worries about tonight, animatedly telling me about his parents and an ongoing joke where they hid a peanut, shell and all, around the house. The joke soured when one of the boys found the peanut, shelled it, and stuffed it up his nose in a classic kid move. Toby refused to reveal whether the culprit was him or one of his brothers.

I smiled more at his storytelling than I did at the story itself. Big gestures, imitations of his family's voices and actions, and unnecessarily detailed descriptions.

Toby ended his story and rubbed his palms together. "Are they on their way yet?"

I rolled my eyes. "You and Cameron are being over the top about this."

"What's wrong with that? We have big plans for the four of us at trivia night."

A loud bar with too many noises and too many people in one place at one time—no, thanks. In my teen and college years, I went to bars with my friends even though I knew I'd end the night with a migraine from all the excess noise and colors. Now I only went to bars for the occasional date, having matured enough to value being migraine-free over fitting in.

"Nothing could convince me to join trivia night."

He quirked an eyebrow at me. "Is that a challenge?"

A knock interrupted us.

I turned away to answer the door, wiping sweaty palms on my black jeans. "It's a statement."

Cameron and Mel smiled at me from my front stoop, his arm draped over her shoulders. They were absurdly cute together. Obviously smitten. Mushy in all the best mushy ways.

Cameron tilted his head down at me. "Ivy, I'm always happy to see you, so don't take this personally, but where's Toby?"

I opened the door farther. The three of us looked back at Toby, who stood in a superhero pose in the foyer. Legs braced, hands on hips, biggest smile I've ever seen.

Cameron moved forward for a side-hug, but Toby went all in. Of course.

Mel shook her head at them and stomped her feet on my doormat. "Thanks for hosting, Ivy. I know it's been awhile with how much you have going on. Feel free to kick us out whenever you need your space."

"You know my hermit ways too well. But I've missed hosting Monday nights." I took her offered plate of brownies and gestured toward the two men who were already involved in their own conversation. "Let's hope they don't talk about sports and video games all night. We might have to make our own fun."

Cameron focused on the food, claimed Mom's oversized recliner, and popped a piece of cheese into his mouth. He cleared his throat. "This is the perfect night. All my favorite people in one spot. The only thing that could make it better is some apple pie."

Mel put her hands on her hips. "You ate the last piece this morning. How can you already want more?"

"There's no such thing as enough pie."

Toby crunched on a carrot stick. "If everything Cameron says about your apple pie is true, I agree."

"You two need to learn to make your own pie," I said.

Mel smiled approvingly. "Thank you, Ivy."

"I am ever your eager student," Cameron teased Mel. He tugged her onto the recliner with him, but she pulled away with a laugh.

Leaving my friends to get settled, I took Mel's brownies into the kitchen. As I sliced the dessert into tidy squares, I listened to their conversation.

"You know," Toby said, "I was the one who finally convinced Cam to make a move."

Cameron scoffed. "I made that decision all on my own."

As their conversation continued, I closed my eyes and soaked up the colors of their voices and laughter. Mel's teal and Cameron's aquamarine, and Toby's multifaceted kaleidoscope, brighter than the others, filled gaps I hadn't noticed were there. Together, it was beautiful.

"I can help with dessert." Mel stepped next to me, opening a drawer. "Wait. Isn't this where you keep your serving spatulas?"

"Mom 'cleans' and moves all my stuff. I can't find anything."

She opened a few more drawers. "That sounds like the opposite of cleaning."

I cut another row of brownie squares. "Right? It's one of the few house rules I ask her to follow, and yet, here we are."

Finding a spatula, Mel hopped up onto the countertop and faced me. "How've you been doing?"

Her question felt too big to answer. Caretaking was the most impossible task I'd ever faced, and Mom only had a broken ankle. Imagine if she had dementia or cancer. How did nurses, doctors, and loved ones manage such a life of stress and fear and making do? All I wanted was to run upstairs, hide in my studio, and become a moody artist without any responsibilities. Instead, I was a moody artist with too many responsibilities. Where was the fun in that?

When I hesitated, Mel leaned closer, propped her chin on her hand, and used a mock therapist voice. "Tell me how you feel."

I smiled at her antics. "I feel stressed. Super stressed. Work, home, Mom, trying to still be myself, and everything in between. It's inevitable I'll drop something along the way. I just hope whatever I drop is a bouncy ball and not a crystal vase, you know?"

"It sounds overwhelming."

"It is. And, like that isn't enough, Mom meddles in everything." I glanced at the stair lift, grateful its motor sounded like a biplane so I couldn't miss Mom if she came downstairs unannounced. "I thought all her phone calls were bad before. I already told you about throwing rocks, and you know she learned how to text, but there's this handyman she's trying to set me up with."

Mel frowned. "You can't be with a handyman. You have Toby."

Ignoring the assumptions she was already making, I focused on Chester. "He's more than twenty-some years older than I am. He's just…" I thought of walking into my home, stumbling on all that pale skin that wasn't ready to see the world. "…not my type."

"I bet your mom is taking that with her usual good cheer."

I scoffed. "Right, she's cheerfully picking out wedding invitations."

She watched me cut the last square. I debated for exactly a millisecond before wiping the blade between my fingers, gathering the gooey chocolate crumbs, and shoving them into my mouth.

"Is Toby helpful?" Mel said casually. Too casually.

I feigned indifference. "Yeah, Toby is great at his job."

She shifted on the ledge. Mel was an open book, and right now, her cover page read, *How to Get Toby and Ivy Together Without Them Knowing: A Beginner's Manual.*

"He's here almost every night to work with your mom," she said, "so I'm sure he wouldn't leave you floundering if he knew you needed help with something."

My answer was to shove the biggest brownie square into my mouth before I said something I regretted.

She laughed. "Hungry there, Ivy?"

Toby popped around the corner. "You never told me we were watching *Arsenic and Old Lace* tonight!"

The movie had been pulled up on my TV long before Cameron and Mel arrived. He'd been too busy talking to notice. Talking to me, with all his attention.

He grinned at Mel. "Ivy tries to resist my charm and eye-candy good looks by telling herself I'm uncultured when it comes to classic movies."

Mel lifted a brow at me. "Eye candy? You said that?"

Why had I stuffed the biggest brownie into my mouth just before Toby walked in? I nearly choked in my haste to say, "No, I said—"

But Toby had already moved on, going back into the living room. I could hear him addressing Cameron. "Have you seen this movie?"

"It's black and white," came the reply. "Why would I have seen it?"

Toby's voice called back to me and Mel. "Let the record show the genius professor is the uncultured one, not the lowly eye candy."

I snorted a half-laugh before I could smother it with another brownie.

Mel stared at me, her own smile spreading across her face. She looked gleeful.

I rolled my eyes and strode to the living room, leaving Mel grinning smugly after me in the kitchen. She would've rather heard more about Toby, but I didn't have the vocabulary to explain how his voice colored my thoughts, how handsome and good he was, and how much all of that terrified me.

Cameron lounged in Mom's recliner, a purring Van on his lap. "How's the physical therapy going?"

Toby's focus stayed on his snack plate. "Fine. She's gaining back some good range of motion."

We waited for him to fill the silence with more details. He didn't.

My instincts pricked. "Is something wrong?"

"Nothing's wrong." But he still wouldn't look at me.

I'd asked him the other day, and he'd rambled a bunch of anatomy jargon I assumed related to the ankle bone. He could've been talking about outer space for all I knew. Maybe I should've listened more closely.

He sighed, bracing his hands on his knees and looking at me. "It's good. Honest."

"Then why do I feel like you're not telling me something?" I set down the brownie tray, which I hadn't realized I was still holding.

Toby stared at me, his dark eyes serious, his posture tense. Cameron stilled on the recliner, and Mel hovered by the kitchen doorway. We waited.

"Her progress is a little slow, but that's not unusual with patients in her age group. It's pretty normal, actually."

Mel cleared her throat. "Does this mean more physical therapy than you originally thought?"

"Possibly."

I felt three sets of eyes watching me closely, but frankly, I was too busy thinking to care. How much more physical therapy would Mom need? Did she need something I wasn't providing? How much more could I provide without burning out completely? I reached for a third brownie, biting into it even as my stomach churned with stress.

Cameron, his face serious, nodded at Toby. "I see. You're dragging out her physical therapy as long as possible for"—he glanced at me—"ulterior motives."

Toby leaned back into the couch, winking at me. "Maybe."

My worries temporarily defused, I sat on the opposite end of the couch from Toby and smiled back at him. "I believe it's pronounced 'definitely.'" I reached for the remote. "Who's ready for a movie?"

They mumbled their assent, Cameron still ribbing Toby, and I turned off the light as the opening scenes began. In the glow of the flickering black-and-white film, I glanced over at Cameron and Mel, who'd crammed themselves into Mom's recliner. Cameron's arm curled protectively around her, his hand twisting and untwisting the waves in her hair like it was an old habit. She leaned her head against his shoulder. Lovebirds.

I told myself to get it together. I wasn't a jealous third wheel. I was good at winging my way through life alone, no big deal. Curling up with a man in a recliner built for one wasn't something I wanted. I loved spreading out on the couch. And the gentle tug of fingers through hair, whispers and mushy smiles—no, I liked my space.

Later in the movie, Mel stood to refill her drink in the kitchen, and Cameron followed her out of the room. I nearly fell off my couch cushion when Toby moved from the opposite end of the sofa to the seat directly next to mine. He was so big that gravity tilted me in his direction, pressing our sides together.

Toby handed me another brownie—how had he known I was eyeing up my fourth?—and gestured to the screen. "This is my favorite part," he whispered.

I didn't look at the screen. I stared at his profile until he turned to look at me. He lifted a brow, daring me to call him out on his less-than-subtle moves.

Little did he know I never turned down a challenge. I could flirt no matter the audience. What was it I'd thought about strings? I was sitting next to a gorgeous man who clearly wanted to distract me. Maybe my curiosity was winning.

Holding eye contact, I took a bite from the brownie in his hand, making sure to nip a little at his thumb. That wiped the smug look from his face. His eyes focused on my mouth. When I licked a crumb from my lower lip, he blinked.

Satisfaction fluttered through me. I might be stressed, I might very likely be depressed and burnt out, but I could still make Toby's eyes darken.

Then he smiled, a triumphant spark in his eyes.

Maybe I hadn't won that challenge after all.

CHAPTER 23

IVY

Mom: watch 4 black ice 2day
Ivy: Thanks! Just got to work safe and sound.
Mom: gr8
Ivy: Why do you text like that?
Mom: this is how u text phyllis said so

When I first opened the door to Toby, I didn't see the takeout box he carried because I was too busy staring at his smiling face. Ugh, Toby already had me reduced to gushing when he rang the doorbell. I needed to get ahold of myself.

"I hope you don't mind that I brought dinner."

My eyes widened at his Take It Cheesy carryout box. "Did you buy the whole diner?"

"You wouldn't come on the date, so I brought the date to you."

Smiling, I stepped aside to let him into the foyer. Our fingers touched when I took the carryout box from him. I lingered when he shrugged from his winter coat.

This was ridiculous. I was ridiculous. So he was sweet. So what?

Get it together.

Mom and Phyllis watched us as we walked through the living room. They had a reality TV show turned on, the volume full blast, their hands busy with knitting needles and lime-green yarn. I wasn't sure what they were knitting, but I loved seeing them keep busy with something productive—aka not moving my things and not pestering me about Chester. That wasn't asking too much, was it?

Opening the carryout box on the kitchen table, I gaped at how much food was stuffed inside. Toby came to stand next to me, his arm touching mine, while he unloaded twelve sandwiches, sides of pickles, snack bags of chips, and packaged cookies.

"I've never ordered the party box before," I said, not minding the awe in my voice. This amount of delicious food was well worthy of awe.

"I usually get two of these boxes on the weekends I visit my family," he said, arranging the sandwiches in a row so their labels faced outward. "There's a lot of us, so it's just the appetizer before Mom's cooking steals the show."

A lot of us? Did he have an army or a family?

"Besides"—he shrugged—"I didn't know what kind of grilled cheese was your favorite."

I carefully read through each sandwich label, debating my pick while choosing one for Mom.

Toby stepped a little closer. "You know what else I don't know about you? Your sushi-eating habits."

After spending all day at a thankless job, then coming home to two meddlesome mother figures, I basked in his attention. How could I not? Like Van in a sunny spot on the floor, I couldn't resist Toby's warmth and attention. The similarities didn't stop there—my instincts also urged me to run from a potential relationship like Van bolted from a vacuum cleaner.

I rolled my eyes. "Maybe you need to take yourself on a date to the sushi place, because you seem pretty obsessed with it."

He ignored my comment. "I have very important questions. Do you use chopsticks or a fork?"

"Chopsticks."

"Ginger? Wasabi? Both?"

"I put a bit of wasabi in my soy sauce to give it some kick, and then I put a sliver of ginger on each sushi piece."

"See, this is crucial information. I'm on the proverbial edge of my seat." He turned to lean a hip against the table, staring down at me like he didn't have anything on his mind beyond our conversation.

I smiled up at him. "I just told you the answers."

He frowned, his lips twisted to one side. "What happened to our one shot, huh? Do we need to review our pros and cons list?"

I became aware of silence from the living room. When had Mom and Phyllis muted the TV? Soon they'd hold cups to the wall for fear of missing a single word.

Standing there, looking up at Toby, listening to him, *yes* to a sushi date felt so easy. I let myself imagine an evening together at any restaurant in the city, flirting and laughing and talking. We would probably stay until the waiter kicked us out. Conversation would flow easily. Being with Toby would feel natural. It would feel right.

My mind listed reasons to justify saying yes. The romantic, low lighting at the sushi restaurant would hardly be too personal since we saw each other every day. He'd seen me at some of my more vulnerable moments, specifically when I apologized for the Better Movement incident and when I'd walked in on Chester, and Toby was still standing in front of me.

But I didn't have room in my life for a relationship right now. Mom needed me, so anything more than this one date was out of the question. Surely one dinner together wouldn't hurt. All those weeks ago when I gave him my number at the registrar's office, he'd promised no strings attached.

So why not? What was the worst that could happen? Or, as he said, the best.

I opened my mouth to answer when Mom spoke loudly from the living room. "Ivy, remember that doctor you dated?"

I frowned. Not in vivid detail, but sure, I remembered. "What about him?"

"He was so nice. A well-paying job, an SUV, and a big house with lots of walls for all your art."

I still looked at Toby, waiting for Mom to make her point. The doctor had lasted all of four dates.

"He broke up with you because his family didn't like you, right?"

"I dumped him, Mom."

"Oh, right." Mom stage-whispered an aside to Phyllis. "She has commitment issues."

If only I could melt through the floor, through the concrete slab below my house, and into the earth's core. Sure, I had commitment issues—because I'd watched my mom avoid talking about my dad my whole life, and I'd seen her unable to pull herself together after her boyfriend dumped her when I was in high school. I'd watched her linger in depression for months. I didn't want that for myself.

I shook my head at Toby to protest, but I couldn't say the words.

"She went on a date with a nice kid when she was thirteen," Mom continued. "His family moved away, and she never heard from him after that."

Phyllis gasped.

"She was devastated. She's always been so sensitive."

No, I'd been devastated because I was thirteen. Everything is devastating when you're thirteen.

"On her second date, she went out with a high school football player." Mom's tone was conversational, like she was only talking to Phyllis, but she was loud enough that she obviously intended for us to overhear. "She came home with a scraped knee, and I called his mother."

Well, that had a simple explanation. We'd climbed the school bleachers so we could cover them with toilet paper as a classic stunt, and because it was dark, I'd fallen and scuffed my knee. Mom had freaked out like he'd assaulted me. She didn't need to know any details about the prank, or about how the football player was part of a long string of one-time dates. I'd never planned to live a saintly life like Mel had, with her handful of dull boyfriends before Cameron.

I stared at the door, listening to Mom loudly explain my dating choices to Phyllis, when we all knew she was trying to deter Toby.

"For years Ivy struggled with dating," Mom said. "She still does sometimes. She's on these dating apps now—"

"She'll be murdered!" Phyllis interrupted.

"—that's what I said! She needs to stop dating strangers." Here Mom's voice grew louder. "She should only date people she already knows."

"What a lucky coincidence you already know me," Toby whispered.

I looked up. He stared down at me, humor plainly on his face. The way he took Mom and Phyllis in stride, I saw with new clarity how ridiculous the four of us were: a mother and her friend standing in the way of our "one shot," Toby determined to go on a date, and me, unwilling to admit how scared I was to give him a chance because my time with him was already my favorite time with anyone.

My bad dates were my comfort zone, letting me prove myself right over and over again as loser after loser lived down to my low expectations. What a farce. Toby was nothing like that.

He kept his voice low to prevent Mom and Phyllis from eavesdropping. "I can bring some Neosporin on our date, just in case you scrape your knee."

I rolled my eyes. "I don't think I've ever had such an enticing offer."

Toby pulled his phone from his pocket and pretended to type as he narrated in a whisper, "Dear diary, Ivy prefers triple antibiotic to nude selfies." He looked up. "See? You think I don't know you, but I'm learning more about you every minute. I'll be an Ivy savant by next week."

"Easy, stalker."

"Is that a yes to sushi?"

I smiled at his persistence. I smiled at how much I looked forward to dinner with him.

"What time can you pick me up on Friday?"

CHAPTER 24

IVY

Ivy: Are you sure it's not a bother?
Mel: Of course not! We're thrilled to help out.
Cameron: We're thrilled to help you and Toby get married and make babies.
Ivy: I regret this so much.
Mel: Ignore him. Have fun tonight! Gorge yourself on sushi! Don't stress!
Cameron: When he proposes, make sure you act surprised.
Ivy: So much regret.

Just when I thought he couldn't get any better, Toby defied all expectations and put on a suit for our date.

Not just any suit. It was black, tailored like a dream, and did everything a suit was supposed to do for a man. Plus his crisp white shirt underneath, his cranberry-red tie, and his black dress shoes… My breath caught when I saw him.

He'd shown up in his work polo and khakis, helped Mom through her physical therapy session, and slipped into the bathroom with a garment bag. I'd underestimated the results. Now I stood in the kitchen, not yet dressed for our date, elbows deep in a vacuum full of Van's cat hair because Phyllis said she'd swept up her bracelet earlier today. And Toby strode out of the downstairs bathroom looking like a *GQ* photoshoot.

"It has to be in here somewhere," Phyllis insisted, poking through the pile of dirt while I stared at Toby.

He grinned and raised a brow. "Running late for our first date, Ivy Lunden?" His gaze flicked to my work clothes, now covered in grime.

How did this man always see me at my worst?

"If it's in the vacuum, it'll be in that pile somewhere," I said to Phyllis as I straightened. "I have plans tonight."

She remained stooped over the vacuum. "But I'm sure it's in here if you could help me a little longer."

I glanced at the clock. Cameron and Mel would be here soon to look after Mom. She'd insisted she didn't need "babysitters," but I remembered the night she traipsed up the stairs all on her own.

I cast a skeptical glance between Phyllis's clean hands and my dirty ones. "I believe in you," I said. Reaching into my back pocket, I paused. "Where's my phone?"

"In here," Mom called from the living room, holding out the phone to me from her end table.

"That's weird. I don't remember leaving it in here," I said, already moving upstairs and calling back to Toby, "I'll be ready in ten minutes!"

I took the world's fastest shower and slipped into a little black number I'd bought with Mel a few years ago. At the time, I'd bought it dreaming of an art gallery. Maybe someday. Instead, I'd worn it on a bunch of terrible dates. Tonight would be the first good date in this dress—or so I hoped. One pair of red heels, some red lipstick, and a little dry shampoo later, and I was ready.

At the bottom of the stairs, it felt a little like prom night all over again. Toby's reaction was everything. Toby, the man who never stopped moving for a moment, stilled completely. His eyes trailed down my body as his throat worked in a hard swallow.

In the background, Mom and Phyllis looked at me with equal parts pride ("Our beautiful girl!") and fear ("How late will you be out?"). It was all a bit overly dramatic.

Cameron and Mel must have arrived while I was upstairs, because they stood to the side, both nodding their approval.

"Are you sure this is a good idea?" Mom clasped her hands together. "What if something happens?"

Cameron tucked his hands into his pockets. "No curfew, kids. Stay out all night if you—"

Mel cut him off with an elbow to his side, rolling her eyes. I mentally rewarded her with some friend points, but I took them all back when she stepped forward with her phone. "Stand together so I can take a picture."

Grabbing Toby's elbow, I hurried past the peanut gallery. "No, Mother Mel, you can't take a picture, we're running late, bye, don't ever mention this again." And just as we were ducking out the door, I shouted, "Thank you for coming over tonight!"

Toby's laughter rolled around me as we made our way down the snow-lined sidewalk to his car. "Sometimes our friends get a little excited," he teased.

"Sometimes our friends get a little annoying," I grumbled, but I still smiled.

He held his car door open for me.

"So chivalrous," I said. "A suit *and* manners."

"It's our one shot. I need to make it count."

I watched as he walked around the hood of his car, taking in how his dark suit cut a perfect silhouette against the snowy backdrop. The bright streetlights cast long shadows around him in stark relief. I committed every detail to memory to paint later.

"How far is the restaurant?" I asked once he buckled his seat belt.

He narrowed his eyes at me. "Either you're already tired of me, or you're hungry."

I let my eyes linger on his suit again. "Definitely hungry."

Toby grinned. "Glad the dry cleaning was worth it."

We bickered about music as he drove down the street. He insisted acoustic rock was perfect for a date, pulling up a playlist he'd made called "One Shot." While I wasn't a fan of the songs he chose for our playlist, I was charmed he'd made one in the first place.

My phone vibrated with a call. Normally I would ignore it, but since Mom's fall, fear was always close by.

I dug around in my purse. "Sorry, do you mind if I check this? Just in case it's about Mom."

"Whatever you need to do."

My heart pattered at his words, the traitor. He was an open door, his generosity coming and going freely.

I answered as soon as I saw the caller ID. "Mom? Are you okay?"

"I fell again."

Panic slammed into me. I whispered for Toby to pull over. He stopped on the shoulder of the road, thankfully clear of snow.

I turned on my speakerphone. "Say again?"

"I fell. Right out of my recliner."

This time her cheerful tone registered.

I glanced at Toby, who still looked at me with worry. "Okay, tell me exactly what happened."

"Phyllis and I were watching TV," she said, "and the remote dropped to the floor. I thought I could get it without any problem. I was wrong."

Mom never sounded this happy to be wrong. No human being sounded this happy to be wrong.

"Are you okay?"

"Of course not. We should go to the ER."

Multiple feelings hit at once. Relief for Mom clearly being just fine. Frustration with her for behaving this way. Embarrassment. She didn't like Toby. I was well aware of this. But her behavior was uncalled for.

"Could you put Cam and Mel on?"

"Well, yes, but—"

I heard Phyllis whispering in the background.

I repeated myself. "Could you put Cam and Mel on, please?"

"I'm not a child," she huffed. "I thought you might be concerned…"

As she spoke, Toby unlocked his phone and tapped out a text to Cameron, angling toward me so I could read his screen.

Toby: Got a call from Ivy's mom. Everything okay?

Cameron: Everything is fine.

Toby: What happened?

Cameron: You missed the most melodramatic stage fall in the history of bad acting. If only you'd been here.

I took a deep, calming breath, wishing I could exhale the yellow she'd left staining my mind. "Mom, I think you sound fine. We can check for serious bruising tonight, but otherwise I'll defer to Cam and Mel, okay?"

"But—"

"Okay love you Mom bye," I rushed in one breath and hung up.

We sat in silence for a moment, both of us staring at my phone.

"I'm either the worst daughter ever or the worst date ever. Take your pick."

Toby laughed, his shoulders shaking inside his outrageously perfect suit. "You're not the worst anything. The night is still young."

· · ·

The server tucked us into a corner booth where the lighting was dim and the music was faint. A clear radius of empty tables surrounded us. The high backs on the seats featured decorative glass designs. It was just as romantic as I'd expected.

Toby stretched out his arms on his side of the booth, looking smug. "Remember that time you wanted a quick lunch date at Take It Cheesy just so you could run away from me?"

Of course he'd noticed my escape plan, but I hadn't expected him to call me out on it so blatantly.

"Remember that time you wanted to go to a romantic sushi restaurant to seduce me?" I countered.

"I'm not seducing you."

I twirled a finger at our surroundings. "What do you call this?" I gestured at his suit. "And this?"

He gave me a happy-go-lucky grin. "Wooing."

I snorted a laugh, which only made his smile brighter. "Wooing? Are you sure you're younger than I am? Because you sound ancient right now."

"You'll know when I'm seducing you."

That was the thing about Toby. He never gave up. Whether he was at work, salting my sidewalk, or "wooing" me, he kept at it. He knew what he wanted, and what he wanted was me.

I looked away. "Pride comes before a fall, you know."

He leaned forward in his seat, the picture of calm, laid-back confidence. "I'm still feeling good about my odds."

I pretended to look over the dinner options, my fingers softly drumming a rhythm on the corner of the fabric menu. I never chose my food before the server arrived to take orders. I liked the whim of choosing at the last minute, when the pressure felt greatest.

"Tell me about your art." Toby gestured to my tapping fingers. "You do that more when you don't have something you can doodle on."

Was I pleased or annoyed at how he'd not only noticed my habit but identified the cause? I wasn't sure.

He looked amused at the surprise on my face. "I'm not clueless. I've seen your sketches on all the napkins and envelopes you leave everywhere you go. You reach for them every time you start tapping like that."

He'd noticed?

I hesitated. My art wasn't first-date conversation material. Sure, I left doodles everywhere I went—it was all very public—but I didn't talk about it. Words were hard. They weren't my thing; they were Mel's thing. I couldn't just open my mouth and sound intelligent when I was passionate about something.

Fortunately, the server appeared, taking our orders and walking away with practiced efficiency. Unfortunately, he took my reason for stalling with him.

Toby watched me, patiently waiting for my reply.

I swallowed and fixed my eyes on my water glass. "I got lucky in the art world after college. I made some good connections, had some good showings. I loved it. Then some important people wanted commissioned pieces, and then their important friends wanted commissioned pieces. I made enough money that I was able to help Mom with some financial stuff, paid off student loans, bought my house. Then it just…stopped. I couldn't paint anymore. I couldn't create."

He cocked his head to the side. "Burnout?"

"Maybe more of a creative burnout, like an artist's version of writer's block? I'm not sure. It's sad, really. I was so eager to live the dream I thought I wanted that I didn't realize I was chasing the wrong thing."

"So what did you do?"

"I failed. I'd walk into my studio every day, waiting to feel that creative flow, but I felt nothing. Just…" I snapped my fingers, demonstrating how quickly I'd dropped that life, or maybe how quickly creativity had dropped me. All the fancy soirees, the sophisticated dinners, the galleries and shows, gone in an instant. I didn't miss those parts of my old career.

Toby frowned at me. "I wouldn't call it failure. You were making it."

"But I couldn't *keep* making it." I glanced away, looking around the restaurant for a reprieve from Toby's curious eyes. "I couldn't even manage the commissions, let alone anything more original that I actually wanted to do. It was like the creative well inside of me went dry, and I couldn't find a way to fill it back up again. The longer I went without painting, the more it slipped away."

He nodded. "I can understand that kind of drain on a person. But how come you can still sketch?"

"I didn't for a long time."

I thought of the dark years, which felt like centuries, of blank canvases and my abandoned studio. I'd kept the door closed so I wouldn't have to look at it. I would reach inside myself for colors, just like I always had, and there was simply nothing. I'd been terrified, not knowing if I could ever create again.

"The last few years, I've had a couple flashes here and there. Weirdly enough, I've been much more productive over the last few months." *Ever since you became part of my life.*

If anything, the last few months should have been barren, given all the stress, but instead, my studio was becoming the haven it used to be. It was therapy when life with Mom was particularly overwhelming. It was an outlet for all the vibrant colors from Toby's voice.

"You're painting again?"

"Sometimes. I have ideas. That's half the battle."

He reached for the drink menu. "Do you, well, make a plan or something? I don't know how art works."

"Some artists plan, and I used to a little bit, like when I made cohesive collections for a showing. But normally I just grab a brush and wing it."

Toby gasped, placing a hand on his chest. "You mean you don't have your next three to nine Fridays planned down to the minute?"

I smiled, biting my lower lip. Happiness thrummed in me when he watched the movement. "Lately my ideas have had a theme, I think. So I might try to tackle that and see what happens."

"What's the theme?"

I shouldn't have mentioned it. Why did I always end up saying more to him than I'd planned? Talking to Toby was like talking to a therapist. Not the physical kind, either. He listened, he asked the right questions, all without being so pushy that I instinctively put my guard up. There was no turning back now.

"I think the theme is community," I said. "Relationships. Compassion. Something along those lines." At his frown, I continued. "I have these particular images that strike me and stay in my head. Like that family over there."

We watched them for a moment. A man and woman juggled eating their own meals while also keeping their young daughter entertained and fed. They had impressive multitasking skills. But beneath the vague semi-chaos, I watched them simply be a family together.

"What about them?" he asked.

I looked back at the family, smiling at the girl's braids. One was still neatly plaited; the other was half undone. "The way the parents are interacting with their daughter, showing her how to use chopsticks, keeping the wasabi out of her reach so she doesn't scorch her tongue off."

"So…what would you paint from that? A fire-breathing dragon? Because the scorched tongue is the only thing I can imagine right now."

"Not a dragon. Probably something more conceptual." I listened to the restaurant around me, the background music, the quiet murmur of other voices. I focused on the cardinal red, tangerine, and amber. I watched a streak of blue spear through the middle. "I would paint red and orange colors across the background, and then I'd use a palette knife and matte black paint to make lines— only straight lines—to hint at hands holding chopsticks. Only hint. Then I would paint more of the background colors across the black lines, sort of layering the picture." The images were half-formed, the colors blurry, the sentiment just an inkling.

Toby smiled, clearly delighted. "Fascinating. I look at that family and think about how they all have the same neck angle, so they must use the same awful pillows that will take hours of therapy to correct. Not quite as inspirational as yours."

"Hey, neck pain is a serious problem in the world."

"Have you posted any of your art online?"

"I did earlier, before I stopped doing commissions," I said, "so I have a website and social media accounts I can go back to. I didn't disappear or turn anonymous like Banksy; I just stopped working. Once I have something worth posting, I'll start sharing again."

The server appeared, leaving our plates with quick motions and minimal questions.

Eager to talk about something else, I asked, "What about your family?"

His eyes lit up. "There's a lot of us."

"Give me the rundown."

Holding his chopsticks but too distracted to eat, he launched into his family tree. "So there's my mom and dad, whom we call Mama and Baba. They immigrated here from Kenya when Mama was pregnant with my oldest brother. They both worked really hard to make sure my brothers and I appreciated living in New England but still valued Kenya and our history. We go back to visit extended family once a year or so, as long as we can all get away."

"Do you speak Swahili?"

He winced. "A little, and not very well. I didn't appreciate learning it when I was younger and more worried about fitting in. I've been practicing Swahili with my brothers when I can. I'm hoping I'll improve enough that I can talk more with Bibi, my grandma, when we're next in Kenya.

"Both of my brothers are better at Swahili than I am. The one who rubs it in the most is the oldest, Silas, who likes to remind us he's the oldest all the time. He's married to Estelle, and they have four kids. Then there's my other brother,

Amos, who hardly talks, but he's brilliant. He's engaged to Annika, and she has two kids. He'll adopt them when they get married.

"Fun fact: Baba and Mama wanted to give us more American first names without leaving behind Kenya completely, so when we're at home, Silas, Amos, and I go by our Kenyan middle names: Feye, Tumaini, and Sokoro."

"Sokoro," I repeated, hearing the colors. "What does it mean?"

"Lucky one."

I smiled. "Let me guess. You're the lucky youngest?"

He laughed, a sushi roll raised halfway from his plate. "What gave me away?"

"Hm. Your need for attention, maybe?"

"I have *your* attention, so I'd say it worked."

It certainly did work. I could hardly look away from him tonight. I felt myself peering over the cliff's edge, considering how far the fall would be. He would be there with me, right?

CHAPTER 25

TOBY

Cameron: Look at you pulling out all the stops by wearing a suit.
Toby: Is the red tie too bold?
Cameron: It's perfect. It'll hide the bloodstains when her mother drops from the ceiling and stabs you with a chopstick.
Toby: Hilarious.

Tonight couldn't have gone any better.

Ever since I'd secured a date with Ivy, I'd been impatient. The days had lagged, with time moving so slowly, it was barely perceptible. It was all I had been able to think about, to the point of distraction. My physical therapy sessions had made my skin itch with impatience. My paperwork had felt more tedious than ever. I'd felt stretched taut, with little to no tolerance left over for Irena's rambling stories about people and things I didn't know—"My cousin's friend's brother's wife, who's been looking for a car that exact shade of orange," or "The neighborhood tree they cut down four years ago."

Whoever said patience was a virtue had never been waiting for a date with Ivy Lunden.

But Friday finally came, and here we were. Ivy's body language said she was relaxed. She ate her sushi exactly like she'd told me she would, with the wasabi in her soy sauce dish, a neat slice of ginger balanced on the top of each sushi roll.

Let's face it. Sushi isn't an attractive food to eat. The rolls are just big enough that you have to unhinge your jaw to eat a piece. Nobody cuts up a piece of sushi like you would a steak. That's just wrong.

So why couldn't I look away from Ivy eating sushi, of all things?

"Tell me about the first time you met Cameron," I said. "Please tell me it's an embarrassing story I can tease him with later."

She sat straighter, clearly delighted at the prospect of making Cameron squirm. "I wish it were more embarrassing. We met as new hires at an orientation staff meeting. He walked through the door, saw Mel, and practically tripped over himself trying to get the seat next to her."

"Sounds like what he told me himself. He texted me that night and couldn't stop gushing about her. That's when I realized my best friend was actually a thirteen-year-old girl."

She laughed. "I met Mel that day too, right before Cameron showed up. We were the only women not wearing heels, so we bonded over defying the fashion patriarchy."

"But you're wearing heels tonight."

I knew that for a fact. Like her dress wouldn't have gotten my attention on its own, she'd traipsed down the stairs in those red shoes, and my jaw dropped onto her living room floor with a loud *thunk*. In front of her mother.

Ivy added another lump of wasabi to her soy dish. "Heels are okay tonight because I know I'll be sitting the whole time."

"I've seen you wear heels at work before," I said, revealing how much I noticed and remembered from our past conversations at the registrar's office.

Ivy, because she's the opposite of my cards-on-the-table approach, innocently said, "Have you?"

How much should I give away? Actually, why was I even asking myself—I was a cards-on-the-table kind of guy, and I couldn't play this any other way with Ivy.

"I noticed everything about you from the moment we met."

Her lips twitched into a curve. "I'm anti-heels, with very rare exceptions that seem to have *you* as the common theme."

I leaned back in my seat, healthy male ego about to bust apart my ribs. Ivy kept track of when I would be coming to the registrar's office. She'd anticipated me just as much as I'd anticipated her.

Ivy looked as smug as I felt. She leaned forward and rested her chin on her thumb, leaving her fingers to trace the edge of her red lipstick.

The gentlemanly thing to do was look away. I was pretty sure she didn't want a gentleman.

She teased that *I* was seducing *her*? Listen here, kettle.

But seduction wasn't part of the agenda for tonight. I'd thought this through well ahead of time. There were two scenarios for our date. First, if I moved too close too quickly, she would try to push us back to safe flirting ground. There was a certain safety in superficial relationships. I could understand that. Second, if she was so stressed from life at home that she wanted a quick escape, hooking up with me would be her best bet.

I couldn't let either of those things happen. Ivy meant too much to me. She'd said men only wanted her for sex, and I was determined to avoid anything that put me in that category. I meant what I'd said. I played the long game, and I played for keeps. Especially for her.

But there weren't any rules saying I couldn't play along for a little while.

I was so busy staring at Ivy, I didn't notice the table two places away from us where the server seated new patrons. My first clue of an oncoming disaster was when Ivy's hazy eyes widened in horror.

"Mom?!"

If I was ever in danger of giving myself whiplash, this was it. My head spun toward our new neighbors.

Irena and Phyllis sat at their own table, perusing their menus. At the sound of Ivy's voice, they looked up with feigned disbelief. They both squinted in the dim lighting.

"Oh, what a surprise!" Ivy's mom said.

"What a coincidence!" Phyllis echoed.

Cameron was right. They were terrible actors.

Ivy wasn't acting. Her voice rose. "What are you doing here?"

Her mom tugged her reading glasses out of her purse, making a show of putting them on and studying the menu. "Having a nice dinner out."

Phyllis beamed. "We felt spontaneous."

Ivy's gaze was still focused on her mom. "You don't eat sushi."

"Surely I can find something on the menu that isn't full of parasites," her mom said.

"Maybe we can ask them to fry the sushi," Phyllis said helpfully. "I've heard they do that sometimes. It kills any bacteria—"

"How did you find us?" Ivy's gaze turned to me, narrowed in suspicion. "Did you tell them the name of the restaurant?"

I shook my head and lifted my hands in surrender.

Ivy refocused on her mom. "Where are Cam and Mel?"

I pulled my phone from my pocket, where I'd put it on silent. No missed texts. Ivy showed me her phone screen. No missed texts there either.

Maybe Irena and Phyllis had threatened Cameron and Mel with that crutch Phyllis brandished the first time I met her.

"What did you do to Cam and Mel?" Ivy repeated.

"Nothing at all," Phyllis said.

"They went to find a video I wanted to watch," her mom said.

"A video." Ivy groaned. "You sent them to the basement for one of those awful home video VHS tapes. You locked them down there, didn't you?"

Her mom and Phyllis glanced guiltily at each other. If I ever needed someone to cover for me so I could get away with a crime, these two would not be at the top of my list. They wouldn't even make the list.

"Well," I muttered to Ivy, "I'm sure Cam and Mel will find something to do with their time. At least we know they're not suffering."

Her mom sighed dramatically. "Stop assuming the worst of us and tell us what you ordered. It looks good. Do you think we can ask them to fry it?"

Ivy's pretty mouth thinned into a single line. Her cheeks were almost as red as her lipstick. The glare she leveled at our intruders could have cut their table in two. They didn't seem to notice.

As our evening unraveled, I pictured our one shot Ivy had agreed to. It was disappearing before my eyes. There was nothing I could do to stop it. Even if we left the restaurant, there was no coming back from this.

I reached across the table, offering her my hands. "Hey. It's okay."

"I don't understand how they knew," Ivy whispered more to herself than to me, her eyes focused on a middle distance I couldn't see.

"It doesn't matter," I said. "Let's—"

"It does matter," she whispered. "Because wherever we go and whatever we do, we'll never have a moment of peace."

The human brain can be irrational, and speaking from experience, the male brain can be even more irrational when a beautiful woman is the topic. So the biggest takeaway I got from her words was that she'd already made space in her mind for us to go out again.

Maybe distracting Ivy would help. "Does this mean you want to go on a second date?"

Ivy chewed at her lower lip, frowning at her mom. She wasn't listening.

Now was probably a bad time. I'd circle back later.

Ivy gasped and pointed an accusing finger at Phyllis. "My phone. You're always watching YouTube videos, so you could figure out how to turn on 'find my phone.'" The finger moved to her mom. "You had my phone earlier tonight, even though I don't remember leaving it near you. That's how you followed us."

Phyllis unwrapped her straw. "Technology isn't that difficult once you watch a little YouTube."

"The bracelet in the vacuum was just a distraction too." Ivy focused her anger on her mom. "I can't believe you did this. No, actually, I *can* believe you did this."

Her mom closed the menu and waved a dismissive hand in our direction. "There's no need for theatrics. Now that we're all here, we can enjoy a nice dinner, and then we can take you home to save Toby the trip, and—"

"I'm still taking Ivy home," I said. That wasn't up for debate. This was my one shot, and I would do it right. These meddlesome two wouldn't take that away from me.

"That's not how this is going to work," Ivy told them.

Her mom smiled. "Why not? We're all here."

If Ivy hadn't been angry with her mom, her next words would've been my favorite of the night so far. "You don't like Toby, but maybe I do. All we wanted was a nice date with just the two of us."

My brain, again being irrational, snagged on her words. She liked me? No, she *maybe* liked me. But it was a starting point.

Reason kicked back in. Ivy's grip on her chopsticks turned brutal. The flush on her cheeks spread to her hairline, and while I'd enjoyed making her blush before, this was different, and not in a good way.

I took both her hands in mine, chopsticks and all. Her fingers felt terribly small in my large palms, so I used minimal pressure to try to get her attention. I kept my voice soothing. "Ivy, let's get some takeout boxes and finish our food somewhere else. We can go to your place or mine, and—"

"I need to ask about the parasites." Phyllis craned her neck to look around the restaurant. "Where's the server?"

"We can ask where they get the fish from too," Ivy's mom said. "Best not to take chances."

Ivy's seething whisper didn't bode well for our first date. It didn't bode well for any of us.

"I can't wait for you to move back to your own house," she growled, "and just leave me alone."

I held my breath. Ivy's anger was justifiable, but moments like these were when we said things that weren't easy to forgive or forget. Both Lunden women were under a lot of pressure—one to heal, one to cope—and they'd managed a tenuous peace. Until now.

To my surprise, her mom shrugged, unfazed. "That will never happen. I sold my house."

Silence.

I held my breath, my gaze instantly going to Ivy. With the stress of juggling work and caretaking, I couldn't imagine how much she'd been looking forward to her mom moving out. I hadn't brought up the vestibular issues, but we would've made time to discuss options. Do some research. Think it through.

This? This was a hand grenade, gleefully flung from the foxhole of two lonely women into our romantic little dugout.

Ivy's stunned face showed it too. Lips parted, brows drawn down, throat working to speak.

I pressed her hands more tightly with my own.

Her voice was hoarse when she spoke. "What did you just say?"

"I sold my house," her mom said. "Fully furnished, so you don't need to worry about moving any of my furniture. The sale closes in a few weeks. Anyway, you need me to stay with you. I help you clean—"

"You move my things so I can't find them."

"—I help you cook—"

"You sit in the living room and narrate what's happening on the TV while I do the cooking."

"—I know my medical bills have been expensive, and I don't have much in savings. The money from my house will help to cover expenses."

Phyllis smiled at Ivy. "It's such a thoughtful thing for your mom to do—"

"The two of you teamed up on this, didn't you?" Ivy accused. "You did all of this without consulting me."

I frantically wished for a way to defuse the situation before their tempers got any worse, but how was I supposed to handle two elderly women and feisty Ivy?

Phyllis frowned. "What a rude thing to say."

"We did what we thought was best for you," Ivy's mom said.

"You did what was best for *you*!" Ivy glared.

Phyllis stirred the lemon slice in her ice water. "We met with realtors and banks and sellers. The home is going to a good family who will take care of it nicely."

Irena smiled. "I couldn't have asked for better buyers. And now you and I have more time together." She turned more fully toward Ivy. "Living alone isn't good for you. You need me."

Ivy shook her head slowly, her eyes still dazed with anger and hurt. "No. I can't deal with this right now. You two are leaving."

"But I already ordered the spring roll appetizer when the waiter seated us," Phyllis said.

Ivy stared at her plate, not even looking at them anymore. "No, you are both going, because I won't let you force me to leave. Phyllis, please drop off my mother and then go back to your house. You are no longer welcome in my home."

Irena and Phyllis must have sensed now wasn't the time to cross Ivy any further. They picked up their oversized purses—how much did they possibly need to carry?—and meandered back to the door, returning their unused menus, paying their bill for the spring roll appetizer, and picking up two complimentary fortune cookies. They unhappily shuffled out the door.

I stood, meaning to slide into Ivy's side of the booth and put an arm around her, but she was already out of her seat and reaching for her purse. When she thought of our one shot, I hoped she remembered more than just the last few minutes.

"I can get the check and take you home," I said. "Or we can finish our date. Or we can take the next flight to Mongolia."

She sounded dazed. "Mongolia?"

"It's the first faraway place that came to mind."

"I choose Mongolia." She nodded, thought about it, and then nodded again. "Definitely Mongolia."

I helped her into her coat, my knuckles grazing the warm skin of her neck when I untucked her hair from the collar. I'd never felt anything as silky as her hair. It sifted through my fingers, frictionless like water. I tried not to think about it, knowing Ivy had to be feeling anything other than romantic right now. But maybe I could still make her smile.

I cleared my throat. "Well, by Mongolia, I actually mean a spontaneous road trip to Florida for the weekend."

Her mouth curved into a half-smile, still not looking at me.

We left the restaurant, disappointment turning my stomach sour. It'd taken me weeks to convince her that one date was all it would take. I'd been short-sighted. One night would not be enough to win her over, especially with meddlesome Phyllis and Irena in the mix.

There went our one shot. More like a complete misfire.

CHAPTER 26

IVY

Mom: heres the final sale price of the house in case ur curious
Mom: its good news, isn't it

Toby drove us home in silence. Thick snowflakes floated toward the ground. Everything looked black and white with our headlights bleaching the snow and night darkening the world beyond.

He seemed to sense my need for space, and his response was to hold my hand as he drove. His palm warmed mine. His fingers twined us closer. Old habits told me I should find his grasp suffocating; the present moment told me this was exactly where I belonged.

Feelings warred within me—pleasure over my time with Toby, anger with Mom, guilt for feeling like my best efforts blew up in my face, regret over our date.

Toby let his car idle in the driveway. We stared at my house. I didn't want to go inside. I didn't want to face Mom after everything that happened tonight. I dreaded the conversation we needed to have; I hated thinking about how she'd sold her house, my childhood home.

"I'm just a call away if you need me," Toby murmured.

"Thank you." I swiped my thumb over his skin, sensation spiraling up my arm. I didn't want to let go. My hand felt permanently attached to his, my self-control shattered by his kindness.

"I almost forgot." He reached into the center console. "Our fortune cookies."

We cracked our cookies open, unfurling the small pieces of paper.

He grinned. "Mine says *Your fortune lies in another cookie.* Hope yours is better than that."

He leaned closer under the pretense of reading the fortune over my shoulder. I turned toward him, enjoying our closeness.

I read the scrap of paper. "*The man on top of the mountain did not fall there alone.* Whatever that means."

"I think it means it took a team for the man to reach the top of the mountain. Your fortune is telling us to stick together."

With our eyes fixed on one another, without the usual distractions of daylight and Mom and Phyllis, I could take in everything that made Toby who he was. His broad shoulders, slightly stooped to accommodate the size of his car. The way his eyes creased as if he was about to smile at any moment, even now. His expressive face that gave away his every thought.

"I'm sorry about tonight. It turned into a disaster of epic proportions."

"It's not your fault," he said. "We can always try again."

I hesitated, stuck on my frustration with Mom and Phyllis.

"Whenever you're ready."

I nodded. "I should go." I forced myself into motion, unbuckling my seat belt and tucking the paper fortune into my coat pocket. "Thank you for being here for me tonight."

After the briefest hesitation, he leaned across the console and pressed a soft kiss against the corner of my mouth. It was as close to kissing my lips as he could get without actually kissing my lips. We both paused, staying close to one another, skin grazing skin.

My hand acted on its own, fumbling for the door handle. The sincerity in his gaze was magnetic, but I found myself moving away instead of toward him. I knew I was locking him out. I knew withdrawing was not a healthy way to cope. But I needed to be alone.

"Goodnight," I said.

"See you soon." He didn't drive away until I closed the front door behind me.

Cameron and Mel were waiting for me in the foyer. They explained how they escaped the basement on their own by picking the lock from the inside. They said goodbye and apologized as they made their way to their car, both of them looking mildly embarrassed, either because Irena and Phyllis outsmarted them, or because of their messy hair and red lips. Toby had totally called it. I would have to text him about it later.

Still standing in my foyer, I reread Mom's texts. The final sale price was impressive. Mel had been right all those weeks ago; Mom's home was worth a lot. Maybe it was enough to buy a small condo or patio home for her to live in, and we'd still have some left over for medical expenses. Maybe a live-in or visiting nurse would be enough. Tension melted from my shoulders at the thought of finding a professional to care for her the way she needed, of not feeling like I was solely responsible for her wellbeing.

I closed my eyes and mentally toured the home I grew up in. That doorframe still had the pencil lines marking every inch of my growth spurts. That oven had the ancient electric burners that Mom insisted on cleaning within an inch of their pitiful lives instead of replacing them. That kitchen table, decorated with an empty vase, was where I first started to draw on napkins, much to Mom's frustration with my messy table habits.

To me, that house was the only home I'd ever known. To my mom, that house was the home she'd created. A single mom, on her own, working long hours to stretch a few pennies, raising a wild daughter all on her own. It took a kind of strength I couldn't fully understand without living it in her shoes.

I set aside any sour memories and chose to remember the look on Mom's face when she bought thrift store sheets and made curtains out of them. The pride tinting her voice when she shared tomatoes from her garden with her neighbors. When she haggled with the tree trimmers, forcing them to give her a discount because they backed over the mailbox, she'd strutted away like a victorious Napoleon. The precision and determination she used to make a threadbare house into a home for herself and her daughter when she didn't have anyone to lean on.

Selling her home must have broken her heart. I needed to remember that when I walked inside, tempted to shout at her instead of solving this problem together. What mattered most, long-term, was setting up Mom in a safe place. We could deal with the issue of a visiting nurse or nursing home later. One step at a time.

Rubbing my arms, I left the foyer. I absently picked up a pencil from the side table where I'd left a sketch on an envelope. I twisted the eraser between my fingers.

Mom sat in her recliner, her permed hair a little frizzy from her exciting night out.

"Mom, we need to talk."

"Did you get my text?"

"I did, but—"

She lightly clapped her hands together. "Think of how much better this is." She began ticking items off on her fingers. "We can pay off my medical bills, and we can put some in savings. Then maybe we can make some changes around here. We could paint these walls some colors. I love your artwork, but it doesn't need to be on *white* walls, does it?"

Yes, my artwork did need to be on white walls. Because I liked my home like this. Because my days were spent with colors spinning in my head, and I needed all-white walls and all-black clothes to give myself a mental break.

Sitting down, I willed myself to be calm. I could figure out a way to reconcile this. Harsh words wouldn't help, but honesty would.

"We can't live together."

Her tone was a forced, cheerful yellow. "We lived together until you moved out for college. We can do it again."

"No, Mom, we can't. When your ankle is healed, we'll find a little place or apartment or condo, and we'll use the money from your house, and we'll move you in there. You can have your independence back."

Didn't parents want their own space without their kids? There were books and movies about how moms and dads could encourage their kids to launch into the world. Why didn't she want the same?

She blinked but quickly recovered. "But imagine how much more time we'll have together. We need each other."

Time together, the unspoken fear for both of us. It fueled most of my decisions when it came to Mom. We might have a few years; we might have dozens —who could know?—but fear of losing her couldn't be the driving force behind everything else in my life.

"I want time with you," I said. "I do. But it's not healthy for two adults to be so codependent. You taught me to be strong because that's how you are. I realize health issues might make you feel less independent than before, but please don't give that up."

Her lower lip quivered.

Great. Now I'd made her cry.

"I'm trying to be understanding," I said, my tone gentle. "I really am. But, Mom, if you keep moving all my stuff—"

"Is that what all this is about? Fine! I'll stop cleaning!"

"—and calling me sixteen times a day—"

Mom gasped. "I've never called you sixteen times in a day!"

"—and sabotaging whatever it is that's growing between me and Toby—"

She scoffed. "I don't like him. He's too young for you."

Anger simmered inside me. I'd pictured myself as the calm one in this conversation, the one who kept a cool head and logical reasoning. Instead, she remained indifferent, and I wrestled against mounting frustration.

I cleared my throat, trying to regain self-control. "He's barely a year younger than I am. It doesn't bother me or Toby."

Her reply was instant. "He won't be steady for you."

"Mom, he's been nothing *but* steady. Every day, without fail, he comes here for your physical therapy sessions, encouraging you." I gestured toward her ankle and the resistance bands stowed beneath the coffee table. "He helps me and supports me in a million different ways. He's a wonderful person."

"Most young people don't know what they want in life. He'll figure it out too late and then change his mind." She shook her head as if to say *and then where will that leave you?*

But Toby knew exactly what he wanted, and he was very clear about it. He wanted me.

I held up a hand in a stopping gesture. "Look, whether Toby is a good fit for me isn't even up for discussion. We're dating. I'm asking you to respect that."

"I don't think—"

"Respecting me and Toby means no more embarrassing stories about my dating life." I began numbering with my fingers. "No more eavesdropping. No more talking about Chester. Ever. No more showing up wherever Toby and I go on a date."

Her hands fluttered helplessly in her lap.

Mom and Phyllis had thrown plenty of proverbial wrenches into my life lately. Their behavior had become a normal, albeit exasperating, part of my life. But they'd gone too far when they sabotaged my date with Toby. It was one thing to be ornery. It was another to be manipulative.

"What you and Phyllis did tonight was completely inappropriate. It cannot happen again. Okay?"

With her lips compressed into a thin line, Mom's determination bordered on grumpy.

"Please," I said. "I'm doing my best to respect you. I need you to respect me and my life too."

Mom sniffed and looked down at her hands, now clasped together on her lap. "I didn't realize I was such a burden to you. My apologies. I'll be out of your life as soon as I can walk again."

The pencil in my fist broke into three pieces.

"That's not what I said. Don't you dare turn my words back on me."

"That's exactly what you said."

Mom had always been a force of nature, a boulder the rest of the ocean had to find a way around, because she wouldn't move for anyone, even her own daughter. She got her way, or she made it happen at any cost. But she had grown old without me fully realizing it at first, and now that I knew, I didn't want to spend our remaining time frustrated with each other. She was my only family; she wouldn't be around forever.

I took a deep breath. "You're the only family I have in this world, and I want what's best for you. Why don't you want the same for me? Why can't you see that Toby could be what's best for me?"

The silence was the worst thing yet. Van watched us from his seat on the windowsill. I stared at her, and she stared at me, her eyes unblinking, her mouth compressed into a straight line.

I swallowed. "You're clearly looking for something to fulfill you. I don't know what it is, and I don't know how to help you, I just know that *I'm* not what you need. I would never ask that of you, and it's not right for you to ask that of me. It's not right for you to ask me not to give Toby a chance. I can't live up to being your everything."

Even as my heart stuck in my throat like a cactus, I knew I was right. My words hurt her; I knew that too, but I hoped she felt the love behind them. I simply didn't know how to get through to her.

"All the years I sacrificed because of my love for you—"

"Yes, you gave up everything for me; I've heard it a million times. News-flash—this isn't love. This is suffocation. Love is letting people go, letting people grow, and you've never done that with me. You just need and need and *need*, and I don't have anything left to give!"

The tsunami of words stopped. My anger stopped with them.

Shame stuck so thickly in my veins that I wondered if I would turn to concrete. Maybe spontaneous combustion from shame would be a less painful way to go than this moment, because I couldn't believe I'd just said—no, *yelled* my emotional vomit all over my mom.

She looked at me like I was a stranger. Her eyes were wide, her lips curving downward, and her brows pulled together to add more creases to her forehead. But her shoulders, always so straight and formal, slumped forward.

Too late to take back the words, too angry to think my stance wasn't valid, but too ashamed of my failure to take care of her, I stared down at the pieces of my pencil curled in my fist. Shame mingled with my anger until I couldn't separate the two. Our roles were reversed now. I was the mother who needed to take care of the vulnerable one, and I was burnt out.

Dropping my broken pencil pieces to the carpet, I turned to the kitchen. Caught between guilt, embarrassment, rage, and self-doubt, I felt exposed like never before. I needed to walk away before I said even more I would regret.

I needed to run to my bedroom and hide under my covers for a little while. But not in a childish way. In a cool, defiant way.

Instead, I came face to face with Toby.

CHAPTER 27

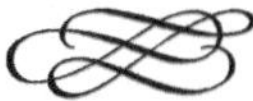

TOBY

Cameron: Sorry your night got cut short. How did the first half of the date go?
Toby: The first half was good. As for the rest, let's just say Arsenic and Old Lace *is my life right now.*
Cameron: Need any help burying a body in Ivy's basement?

I'd felt this level of helplessness only a few times in my life, and I had to say, I wasn't a fan. I also wasn't a fan when the shock in Ivy's eyes changed to shame. Her expression said it all. She wished I hadn't been there to see the argument—okay, I wish I hadn't been there either—and she feared my judgment of her.

Judging Ivy was the last thing on my mind. Helping her, holding her, convincing her she could be strong and flawed at the same time and that was perfectly okay—those were on my mind. The fact she thought I would judge her at a moment like this cut me open.

I raised my hand, her purse dangling from my fingers. "I noticed you forgot this in my car, and I thought you might need it, so I brought it back…"

She hesitated before reaching for the small leather bag. "Thank you."

I watched her face flush to her hairline. Her thoughts were clearly painted on her face: Toby overheard every word of that fight.

Maybe not every word, but most of it. I wished that their mother-daughter relationship could be better, that there didn't need to be these hard conversations.

I hated how she had to be feeling right now. But Ivy had stood up for me, for us. Maybe tonight hadn't been a misfire after all.

Ivy looked away, blinking rapidly to hold back tears. "I'm about to tuck Mom in. If you—"

"I can do that."

She let her blond hair fall in a curtain between us, shielding her face from my sight. "You've already done so much—"

I stepped a little closer. I tucked her hair back and tried to make eye contact. "You need a few moments. I can give them to you."

She didn't need any more encouragement to leave the room. I waited there for a few moments, watching her mom stare at the floor.

Irena stood, only a little wobbly. "I can help myself to my room tonight, thank you."

Nodding, I stepped out of her way, watching her carefully as she walked to the stair lift. I listened for any sounds of distress, but the house remained relatively quiet, the creaks in the old floors allowing me to hear Irena's progress until she settled into bed.

Only when I heard silence did I make my way upstairs. I'd noticed Ivy always left a hallway light turned on for her mom at night, so I did the same, noting the way Irena's bedroom door was cracked just enough for the light to seep through.

I walked slowly through the house. Each creaky floorboard in the upstairs hall sounded deafening, announcing to Irena that I was going to Ivy's bedroom. So be it.

I hadn't been this far down the upstairs hallway before. Like the rest of the house, the walls were white, and the old wooden floorboards were sanded and polished to a soft sheen. Original Ivy artwork hung on the walls. If I hadn't been so worried about her, I might have paused to take in the colors. Maybe next time I would enjoy her personal art gallery. Just not tonight.

I opened a couple of doors—a bathroom, a closet—before I found her bedroom. It was just as dark as the other rooms, and at first it appeared empty, but headlights from a passing car beamed through the window and caught on the shine of her hair. She was sitting in the fetal position on the floor on the far side of the bed. Her shoulders shook with sobs.

It took some maneuvering on my part, but I squeezed between the wall and her body, wrapping my arms around her. She stiffened and faced away from me. I didn't mind. I could hold her and still give her privacy. Her upper back, pressed against my chest, trembled with silent sobs. Silky hair slipped in front of her face and brushed my cheek. It took some time, but eventually she relaxed a little against me.

Her voice sounded confessional when she spoke. "She needs so much. All the time. It never stops. And I'm empty. I've given her everything I can, and still she wants more. You see how she is. It's an endless cycle that I can't break. I can't do this anymore."

The self-reproach in her voice was something I could understand to a lesser scale. Not all of my patients were out-of-this-world successes like Cameron. Sometimes they didn't get better quickly. Sometimes they didn't get better at all. I struggled with letting go of the responsibility I felt each time I let them down. I couldn't imagine trying to let go of that responsibility if my mom were a patient.

If I asked questions, she would feel defensive. If I gave my opinion about us always expecting too much from the ones we love most, she would withdraw. Actions were stronger than words, right? So I tightened my hold on her.

"There's no shame in your feelings," I said.

She shifted in my arms, leaning more fully against me. My chest warmed at the motion. Apparently my ego didn't know this was a bad time to feel flattered by her trust. I told it to savor this moment later, at a more appropriate time.

"I feel so guilty that I can't give her whatever it is she's looking for."

"There's no shame in that either," I whispered. "Maybe her answers lie somewhere else, and none of us know it yet."

She made a scoffing sound.

I lightly rested my chin on her shoulder. "I know she's very demanding. You've already done everything you can to help her. She's at a loss because she feels fear about her future, or disappointment about her health, or grief for losing her independence."

"Grief?"

I shrugged. "It comes in lots of forms, for lots of different things."

Silence settled around us. I debated saying more—that her mom needing other people wasn't necessarily a bad thing, it was just that she should spread the need around so it didn't rest squarely on her daughter. The Ivy curled against me now was an Ivy without her walls. This might be my only chance to say something more.

I wrapped my arms a little tighter. "I also think your mom is scared of needing other people, so she's focused all of her need on you. But, you know, it's okay to need other people too. It isn't weakness to need people in our lives.

Strength can be found in community. It's natural and right. Phyllis can be a nuisance, but she's actually an important part of your mom's life right now, giving her friendship and easing a little of her loneliness."

She sighed. "You think I shouldn't have told Phyllis not to come back."

"No, I think you can leave that decision for tomorrow." In the pause that followed, I saw her hesitation. "What is it?"

She wiped at the tears running down her cheeks. "When I was in high school, Mom had this boyfriend who broke her heart when he left. She was devastated. I work so hard to be strong, first because she was so strong to raise me on her own, and then because I never wanted to be at someone's mercy the way she was at his. But what if that strength makes me too jaded, too hard to love?"

You're not hard to love. Don't worry.

I nuzzled closer to her shoulder. "That's for the people in your life to decide, not you."

It's for me to decide. And I already made that call.

We sat in silence for a long while, curled together, her back against my chest, my arms around her. Van's eyes glowed for a moment in the doorway, and then he was gone again. A car's headlights slanted through her window as it drove past. When I brushed aside her hair to see her eyelids drooping, I allowed myself several long moments to enjoy that she trusted me enough to fall asleep against me.

I lifted her onto the bed, careful not to disturb her when I knelt on the mattress to arrange the pillow under her head. Her hand sleepily gripped mine.

I smiled. This was Ivy without her prickly walls.

I couldn't have resisted if I'd wanted to. I pulled the comforter over us and settled as close to her as I dared without waking her. In the darkness, I watched her face relax in sleep. Pretty red lips, fair skin, blond hair coiled around her. Best of all, the way she kept my hand firmly tucked under her chin, like she would never let me go.

If she needed me to be her friend right now, that was what I would be. For now, anyway. Because I could feel her pulse, and if my eyes wandered to her collarbone, and then lower, where her dress gaped just enough for the slightest sweet curve to glimpse through—could you honestly blame me? I'd been pining after the ice queen for so long.

She kept me at a distance, kept me wanting to know what she thought and felt and wanted. She held her real self close to her chest like I would blackmail her for simply being human. She'd melted a little tonight, and I'd been lucky enough to see a glimpse underneath her frosty crown. If only I could thaw her out the rest of the way, and press my lips to her neck, then her collarbone, then that slight, sweet curve—

A snore erupted from her pretty face.

I grinned.

Now that was definitely blackmail material.

CHAPTER 28

IVY

Mel: Did you talk to your mom? Are you okay?

If someone had told me I would sob on Toby's shoulder, wake up beside him the next morning, and still be able to make eye contact with him, I would've laughed in their face. But I should've known better. There was a unique piece of the puzzle in that scenario. It was named Toby.

As usual, he was unwavering.

I woke slowly, groggily, struggling into awareness. We were wrapped around one another. Our legs were tangled, his hands at my back, my arms around his waist. My face rested against his chest. It was a cocoon of warmth and delicious Toby scents, and I would've given all of my designer paints to stay there forever.

There's no shame in your feelings, he'd said. Shame was my biggest feeling of all. I'd said the truth, the necessary, hurtful truth, to Mom, but I wished I had used my words as tools instead of weapons. Imagining myself from Mom's and Toby's perspectives, I wouldn't want to hear those words from my daughter or my girlfriend.

Wait. *Girlfriend?* Feeling how entwined we were, yes, I realized. Definitely yes. I may not like labels, but I had no doubt about his intentions, and he'd made it clear he wanted this label.

What if I'm hard to love? I'd opened the floodgates. I took pushing people away to another level. Add that emotional baggage to my relationship cargo, and

I needed my own landing strip of loneliness. All that luggage would crush any chance we had at a relationship. If Toby were smart, he'd run away screaming like he was a Stephen King character. If I became serious with Toby, someday he might be on the receiving end of an outburst. I wasn't sure I could wrap my mind around that with a clear conscience.

But last night, when Toby said my feelings were okay, I believed him. He'd told me it wasn't for me to decide whether I was lovable. Through all my blubbering, he listened. Held me as I cried, and then held me all night as I slept. He could've said so many things after seeing our fight last night. But he didn't. He set aside all judgments and just…loved me?

Whoa. Slow down. Apparently waking up surrounded by delicious Toby scents was messing with my brain.

"Morning." His voice was foggy with sleep.

I swallowed. Hard. Sensations overwhelmed me—the colors in my head, his forearm across my waist, his soft shirt against my face. With the sensations came feelings I wasn't ready to acknowledge, not yet. Maybe not ever, even though they felt incredible coasting through my body. I shoved them away.

"How did you know I was awake?" I kept my face against his chest, avoiding eye contact, both because I was embarrassed about last night and because I hadn't washed off my makeup or brushed my teeth before I fell asleep. I didn't want him to get an eyeful.

"You stiffened up like concrete." His fingers absently rubbed into my back, relaxing muscles I hadn't realized were tense. His touch felt natural. He was so good at this. "You're loose when you sleep."

"Loose?" I squeaked, mentally scrambling to rebuild my walls as I reeled inside. I tried to cover how exposed I felt by saying in a mock British accent, "Are you questioning my virtue?"

"You wrapped yourself around me of your own free will." His voice was so smug, I didn't need to look up to see his smirk.

Sabotaged by my unconscious self. What was a girl to do when she was snoozy and faced with Toby's teddy bear kindness and beautiful smile and muscled arms?

I frowned. "What I do in my sleep shouldn't be held against me."

"Hm, but it should definitely be held against *me*," he whispered, further tightening his arms around me.

Images arose in my mind, of all the ways I could wrap myself around him now that I was awake. I pushed the thoughts away. They drifted back.

Recklessness taunted me. Sensibility argued back. Toby wasn't the type for casual sex. I wouldn't use him like that. He was my mother's physical therapist. It was probably a breach of, well, professionalism. Or something.

Unfortunately my sensible half was so much more persuasive.

"I also knew you were awake," he continued, "because you stopped snoring."

"I don't snore!"

"Yes, you do. Like a geriatric with sleep apnea."

I pushed at his chest, but he laughed and shifted so his face nuzzled into my neck. He breathed deeply, as if he planned to stay there. "Don't worry; it was very sexy snoring."

Heat spread from my chest to the rest of my body. His lips brushed against my collarbone now, his stubble scratchy in the best possible way. What if he found my pulse next? Then he would know how much I fought myself when we were together. The game would be up.

Even as I worried, my neck angled instinctively, giving him more access. *Please,* my body begged, *please,* even as I lectured myself.

The raspberry he blew against my neck was loud and obnoxious. I squealed and pulled away, but he drew me back into his chest for a final, laughing embrace.

"Morning, Ivy. Let's make breakfast."

And then he was gone, bounding out of my bed as if he'd bounded out of my bed a million times before, giving me a saucy wink over his shoulder as he walked out my door. I struggled to reorient myself. I couldn't keep up with him this morning, and he was using it against me. The nerve.

So why couldn't I stop smiling?

CHAPTER 29

TOBY

Toby: Very early this morning, your mom texted me an apology for ruining our sushi date. She included emojis.
Ivy: Sorry. Did you enjoy the abundance of snowmen and heart bubbles?
Toby: No, it was the multiple eggplants that drew me in.
Ivy: Please tell me you're joking.
Toby: It's okay. I'm sure she doesn't know what it means. I only wish her daughter would objectify me like she does.
Ivy: Maybe I do.

Time to woo Ivy Lunden. Time for pancakes.

I'd already been wooing Ivy. I was pretty certain it was working. But I still had a ways to go. I could do it, one day at a time.

It took some work to find the ingredients—who stored their flour on top of their plates?—but soon I had pancake batter standing at the ready. She didn't have any blueberries, but she did have chocolate chips, and those were the next best thing for pancakes. Butter sizzled in the pan, eggs frothed into a thick mixture just waiting to be slid into the skillet, and coffee percolated.

Not that all this food was completely charitable, my stomach reminded me with a growl. Normally I would've been up for a few hours by now. Cameron and I would've gone for a Saturday morning run and then had brunch somewhere, stuffing our faces with French toast and telling ourselves we'd preemptively burned off the calories that morning.

But this, with Ivy, was better. No offense, Cameron.

I flipped a pancake. Perfectly golden brown, with perfectly melted chocolate. The only thing missing was music, which I fixed with a quick tap on my phone, keeping the volume low in case her mom was still sleeping.

I heard Ivy's ambling footsteps just as I removed the last skillet from the burner. Grinning, I watched her groggy progress. She must have showered quickly, because her long hair was still damp against her shoulders. Black leggings, black top, but no lipstick. Her lack of makeup only made her eyes bluer.

Then I noticed the red patch on her skin, where I'd deliberately rubbed my stubbly chin earlier this morning. I swallowed.

Ivy shuffled straight toward the coffee pot, pouring and sipping eagerly. "It smells good in here."

I fanned my hand over the food like a gameshow host. "Scrambled eggs, chocolate chip pancakes, and fresh coffee. All still warm."

She looked at me, not the food. She could probably see straight through me, to the nerves I tried to hide. I couldn't help reevaluating the last several hours as I tried to guess at her thoughts. Maybe she didn't see last night like I did. What if she didn't want me to stick around this morning? I could go home, I supposed, but I hoped she wanted me to stay. I hoped to spend the day with her.

Her eyes flicked toward the food but quickly returned to me. "Thanks for breakfast. I'm sure it's great. But I need to wake up a bit more before I eat. Don't wait for me."

I couldn't help grinning. "Not a morning person?"

She shook her head in answer, her eyes fixing on my phone as it played the next song.

"I can change the music if you want," I said, already reaching for it.

Another headshake. "No, I like it."

"You don't usually have music on."

It was more of an observation than a question. I assumed her house was already filled with enough noise, between her mom and Phyllis and their disregard for normal TV volumes. My apartment, on the other hand, was stone silent, so music was a relief.

She shrugged, staring into the dark depths of her coffee. "My mind is a busy place. I usually don't need music added to the mix, but this is nice. It sounds…"

I tilted my head. "It sounds…?"

Ivy rolled her eyes like she didn't care about this conversation topic, but the intensity of her gaze on mine told me something else. "Purple."

"Um…purple?" Maybe I'd heard her wrong.

"Have you heard of synesthesia?"

Purple music, I didn't understand. Synesthesia, I did. This I could talk about.

"Sure. It's where sensory inputs cross over, like someone experiences specific tastes when they hear a sound, or sees a color when they…hear a sound. Are you…?"

She watched me closely. "I see colors when I hear sounds. Your music sounds purple to me, almost lavender."

My mind quickly ran through everything I knew about synesthesia, which was very little. "Is it all sounds, or just certain sounds?"

"All sounds."

"Do the colors associated with a sound change over time?"

"Not so far. I've heard it happens sometimes. Maybe it will for me someday."

I thought of all the times she'd come home from work to a house full of noise —her mom, Phyllis, me. Even just traffic noises had to be overwhelming. I would be prickly, too, if I had to deal with so much overstimulation day in and day out. Maybe the Ivy onion wasn't so complicated after all.

"Do you get headaches?" I asked.

"It has to be a really bad day for that to happen. Airports, amusement parks, concerts, and sporting events are the worst. So are confined spaces, where I can't get out to clear my head if I need to." Her fingertips traced the bottom edge of her mug, tapping out an anxious rhythm.

"What about the TV? Your mom has it on all the time."

"Unless it's a show with really jarring sounds, it can fade into background noise, or colors, for me." She shrugged. "I tried to explain it to Mom when I was younger, but she didn't understand. I don't blame her. It's strange enough to live it, let alone try to put it into words. Maybe my dad had it, I don't know."

I thought it over a little more, my growling stomach completely forgotten. "How—"

Ivy laughed. "So many questions."

"I'm just curious. I've never met anyone like you before." In more ways than this, but thinking of how that sounded, I added, "If you don't want to talk about it, I'll stop."

She sipped more coffee and shifted her feet until she leaned against the counter edge. "I haven't told many people. But I figured after last night, I have nothing left to hide. Maybe this is what will scare you off."

I could've made my answer flirty or cocky, but I didn't. "Ivy, it'll take more than genetics to scare me away. Leaving you over something like this would be as logical as breaking up with someone because you find out they're left-handed. In fact, knowing this about you makes me even more in awe of you." I let the words, vulnerable in their sincerity, linger between us.

"I thought this bit of weirdness on top of all the other baggage in my life would be the last straw, and you might think I'm not worth all the drama. There are much easier people to be with."

"No. If anything, I wish I could see the world through your eyes."

She stared at me, cheeks slowly blushing to match the scruff mark I'd left on her neck.

The song changed to a smooth, sweet melody. Acting on instinct, I placed my hands on her hips and drew her into a dance. It was more of a swaying hug, what with her coffee mug held to the side, but I didn't mind. When her free hand spread on my chest, I soared.

"What are you doing?" she asked stiffly.

"Dancing with you." I nudged her into motion.

Her knuckles whitened on her coffee mug. "It's too early for dancing."

I fitted myself closer to her. "You don't really expect me to believe that."

Her words might protest, but her mouth was parted, and her eyes fixed on my lips. I'd bet she tasted like coffee.

The eggs and pancakes were cold by now. I didn't care. The music changed. Our dance didn't. We swayed in circles around her kitchen floor, each rotation drawing us closer together. I pretended to dip her dramatically, keeping her coffee mug level and unspilled, and when I swept her upright again, she laughed. I could've sworn I grew taller at the sound.

I moved a little closer. All it would take was the slightest lift of her chin, the slightest dip of mine, and we would kiss. Just the slightest…

A whirring sound broke the moment. We both blinked, looking behind us to see a shadow looming in the staircase. The whirring grew louder, the shadow stretched into warped shapes, and after several long, agonizing moments, Ivy's mom appeared on the world's slowest stair lift. Her mechanical chair inched downward, the fluffy corner of her flowered robe dropping from the edge of one stair to the next, step by step.

Chester's stair lift might've been free, but it certainly came at a high cost. One that I begrudgingly paid in the form of a ruined kiss that very well could have been perfect.

Ivy's mom smiled hesitantly at us.

Tension corded between mother and daughter as they stared at one another. I gently pressed my hands on Ivy's hips in a gesture I hoped Ivy would take as reassuring and not overstepping. *I'm here,* my hands said, *and I'm staying.*

Ivy glanced at me, sipped some coffee, and looked back at her mom. "I thought about what I said to Phyllis yesterday. She can come over."

Her mom's face was bright enough to power the neighborhood. "I'm so happy to hear that."

"All I ask," Ivy said, "is that you both please respect me as an adult human being from now on. And Toby too."

This was better than I could've hoped. She saw both the importance of Phyllis in Irena's life and the importance of setting boundaries. Whether they listened was another matter, but this was a start. This was Ivy granting Irena a friend who filled some of her need, and in the process, Ivy took a little piece of her own life back too.

As Irena glanced between me and Ivy, I hoped she understood that no amount of shenanigans could get rid of me.

"We'll do our best," Irena finally conceded.

Ivy nodded. "We'll figure it out together. I'm sure it'll be an ongoing conversation. But right now, it's too early, I'm too sleepy, and Toby made us breakfast. Want some?"

Her mom nodded. "It smells good."

The melody changed to an upbeat hip-hop song. Music like this seeped into my bones and made me move; there was no stopping it. I danced over to Ivy's mom, who looked at me warily from her stair lift perch.

"Let's dance, Irena."

She clung to the armrests. "I'd rather not."

"I know you're in a fluffy robe, but I'm sure you still have some killer moves."

I coaxed her into standing, always making sure she had a firm grip on her crutches. We half-shuffled, half-hopped, half-danced a few steps in Ivy's kitchen.

"See? I knew you were groovy!"

This marked the first time I ever heard Irena laugh. She giggled like a teenager. I laughed too, thrilled I'd finally cracked her, even if it was short-lived.

Quickly fed up with my goofiness, Ivy's mom shooed me away and moved toward the kitchen table. "Where did you ever find him, Ivy?"

I hadn't expected Ivy's expression, but once I saw it, I couldn't look away. Warmth, maybe even affection, lit her face.

"I didn't find him," she said. "He found me, and I'm glad he did."

CHAPTER 30

IVY

Mel: Ivy, your mom just texted me. Is this how the apocalypse begins?
Ivy: You mean the apocalypse of my sanity? Yes. Yes, it is.
Cameron: Hey! She didn't text me!
Mel: Her texts are mostly emojis. She's bringing back hieroglyphics.
Ivy: Half the time I have to guess at what she's saying. It's a mystery.
Cameron: I feel left out. Please forward screenshots of the latest developments.
Ivy: Please don't.
Mel: Okay, Ivy, I won't. (Cam, I totally will.)

Mom retreated to the living room as soon as she finished breakfast, eager to call Phyllis and tell her she was welcome to come over and watch the latest episode of *The Bachelorette*. Or maybe it was *Swamp People*. I wasn't sure. As much as my shoulders tensed at the thought (thanks for that, Sushi Incident), I knew Toby was right. Phyllis was an important part of Mom's life right now—a very necessary part of her life.

I pictured the rest of the weekend unfolding before us: Mom and Phyllis would watch TV; Toby would go home; I would paint in my studio as long as possible; Van would watch the snow fall from his vantage point among the African violets.

For now, I stood in front of the kitchen sink, my hands in the frothy water, and Toby stood in front of the dishwasher, barely restraining himself from helping me clean up the kitchen.

Being alone in the kitchen with Toby felt good, natural. When I'd first woken up this morning, I dreaded the awkward discomfort of a "morning after" situation. Toby had defused it right away. The anxiety hadn't resurfaced.

I pretended to scowl at Toby as he reached for a dirty skillet on the counter. "Don't you dare touch that."

His hand hovered. Guilty. His voice coaxed me. "It's just a skillet."

"It's only fair that I clean up after you made breakfast."

He started to protest and then stopped. "Fine. But I'm still keeping you company." Instead of moving away, he brushed his arm against mine, bringing warm friction. "Let's do something random."

"Such as?"

"Let's go to a thrift store."

My brows lifted. "Your idea of random is thrift shopping? We need to work on your creativity."

"I'm extremely creative." His gaze met mine. "Phyllis will be here any minute. We'll keep our phones on, so there's no need to worry about your mom. Don't you want to see what random treasures we'll find?"

I glanced toward the living room, frowning. What if Mom needed something, and we were too far away? What if Mom and Phyllis got themselves into a bind that they couldn't get out of?

"Come on, it'll be fun," he coaxed. His expression was full of boyish mischief and fun.

If I were honest with myself, maybe it wasn't Mom I was truly worried for. Maybe I worried about Toby, and the dozens of ways he'd hopped over my barriers, one by one. Maybe I worried for myself, and who I was without my walls, or, more importantly, the fact that what I'd wanted before didn't quite match what I wanted now.

In the end, the colors made me do it. The way his voice painted inside my head was irresistible—it always had been—but now combine that with his skin touching mine, and I didn't stand a chance.

Persuasion, meet your master, Tobias Azumah.

"Let's go thrifting."

. . .

Toby stood just inside the entrance of the thrift store, his hands on his hips. "Can't you feel the possibilities just waiting to happen?"

I glanced around. "Possibilities like…a rusty toaster?"

He glanced at the endcap display of hodgepodge items, including a toaster that had seen much better days, probably in the 1970s, if the wooden paneling and tangerine-orange knobs were any indication. "It just needs a good clean," he said. "Wait, look at that! A spinning wheel!"

I followed him slowly, watching his long strides carry him toward a corner display, complete with a life-sized spinning wheel. I tried to picture his big frame balancing on the wooden stool, his fingers plying fibers into string. I didn't doubt his abilities, but the mental image was ridiculous, to say the least. "Do you… make yarn?"

He laughed. "No, but I've never seen a spinning wheel that's not a Disney cartoon. This thing is huge." He ran his fingers along the wooden spokes. "Your mom knits, right?"

Of course he thought of my mom and her hobbies instead of himself. "If you're asking me to buy her a spinning wheel, my answer is no. If you're asking me to send her a picture, I'm okay with that."

I couldn't help smiling when Toby grinned and rubbed his hands together. "Do you want to pretend to spin yarn, and I'll take a picture? So she can have a size reference?"

"Sure." I handed him my phone and perched on the wooden stool next to the spinning wheel.

"Pretend you're pricking your finger on it."

Laughing and shaking my head at his antics, I mimicked Sleeping Beauty pricking her finger.

He took several photos, overly dramatic as he perfected the angle of my phone. "Work it, work it."

That had me outright laughing. Not my flirty laugh, my snorting laugh, which made him laugh, and then we were caught in a fit of hysterical laughter. It was ridiculous. It was so much fun. What were we laughing about again?

Still stifling his laughter, he handed my phone back to me. "Okay. Let's focus. I'll pick your outfit; you pick mine. Then we wear our new duds to the next phase."

"You've got to be kidding. People actually do this? It's not just a meme?"

He shrugged. "I've always wanted to try it. Now we can try it together."

I cast a skeptical glance at some of the eccentric clothing on display. I kept my clothes simple and black. It helped with my busy mind. "I don't know about this. Do I have the right to veto your pick?"

"Only if you give me solid reasons against my choice."

"What qualifies as a solid reason?"

"Well, like, wedgies."

I was on the brink of more hysterical laughter. "What?"

"I won't make you wear something that makes you uncomfortable. That includes wedgies, itching, chafing, what have you. I'm not a masochist." He lifted an eyebrow at me. "But I do expect you to be honest and not make up imaginary wedgies because you don't like what I've picked."

I shook my head. "This is…so weird."

He stepped closer, his eyes silently challenging me. "I can't help that I'm more adventurous than you are."

I sensed the dare. I rose to meet it anyway. "You're on."

We spent the next several minutes searching for outfits. I felt pleased with my selection for him. I checked the seams and fabrics for softness, so I doubted he could veto any of my choices.

We met in front of the changing rooms, exchanging items.

I winced. "I'm pretty sure the outfit I chose for you is much worse."

"I can handle anything but wedgies."

It took some effort to wiggle into the flared pants he'd chosen for me. They were electric red. The ugly sweater he'd found was too big, slipping off my shoulder. My black jeans and top cried in the corner.

I stepped out of the fitting room to see Toby standing in front of the three-way mirror, his face serious as he surveyed his powder-blue suit with its faint plaid design. Personally, I didn't mind at all that the suit was definitely too small. Much too small. The leopard button-down and paisley tie clashed just as horribly as I'd hoped. Then there was the crowning achievement: a men's dress vest covered with badly embroidered cats.

He noticed me in the mirror's reflection. "You're right. I was much kinder to you than you were to me."

"Remember the rules," I quoted. "Wedgie, itching, chafing."

His eyes were fixed on my red bell-bottoms. "All good here. You?"

"Same. I guess this is it." I stepped close enough to him that our toes touched.

But his gaze was still considering my outfit, now moving on to the sweater. He frowned. "That's not enough for you."

I blinked. Logically, I knew he was talking about the mashed-up outfit, but his words struck a chord that I preferred to keep hidden. Something wasn't enough for me? Normally it was me that was the problem, me that wasn't enough, so I covered it with black clothes and bold lipstick and hoped nobody noticed. But for Toby to say something wasn't enough for me?

Looking over the clothing rack next to us, he plucked out a furry hot-pink coat. "There. It's too cold to go without a jacket."

Collecting myself, I pulled on the coat, untucking my long hair from beneath the collar. "What's the next phase?"

He grinned. "Wax."

Surely I'd heard him wrong. I hustled to keep up with him as we collected our regular clothes and walked toward the register. "Like…we're going to a salon? Could we opt for a couple's massage instead?"

He laughed. "That does sound appealing, but the point of these outfits is to keep them *on*."

My reckless side from this morning sighed in disappointment, but no matter. I'd figure out what this clue meant. Wax. Waxing cars? Wax candles—a candle-making workshop? There was a museum that—

"Oh, no." I groaned. "You want to go to that horrible wax museum."

He pulled his wallet from his pocket. "Who says it's horrible?"

"It's the stuff of nightmares, okay? I've seen the pictures. I've heard the stories. The warped faces, the bad lighting. It's disturbing."

"But it's so bad, it's hilarious, right? Kind of like a cringey movie?"

"Or it's so bad, it's just bad."

"Now you're in the spirit." Toby grinned down at me. "The wax museum is just one room in the Alaric Mansion. I personally think it'll be the highlight of the entire tour, but maybe there's some famous architecture too."

"You know it's elegant, right?" I gestured at our clothes, imagining us wearing these terrible costumes as we strolled through a fancy mansion and a wax museum bad enough to rival Louis Tussaud's House of Wax in England.

"How am I not elegant?" He posed with a hand on his hip, the suit jacket pulled aside to show off the badly embroidered cats.

Toby insisted on paying for our clothes, placing his warm hand over mine when I reached for my purse. As we drove across town to the Alaric Mansion, he made a game of naming the cats on his embroidered vest. My cheeks ached from laughter by the time we parked in the visitors lot.

We both leaned forward to peer out the windshield. Calling it "elegant" was an understatement—the historical home dwarfed the others in the neighborhood, with its stone archway over the door, stained-glass windows, and ironwork making it stand out. Judging from the look of the empty parking lot, we'd be the only visitors here today.

I glanced at Toby. "Are Clawdia and Catzilla ready for their big debut?"

He looked down at his vest in feigned seriousness. "Oh, they're ready. Kitty Purry is a little nervous though."

"It's not too late to change our minds and go to that couple's massage."

"I wouldn't miss this for anything." He pocketed his car keys. "We're making memories, Ivy."

At the main entrance, we were greeted by a very small, very serious man sitting behind a plexiglass window. With a monotone voice and expressionless face, he gave a brief history of the mansion and slid a brochure across the counter. He didn't give our outfits a second glance and happily returned to his paperback as soon as we stepped away.

Toby pulled me toward the wax room first. It was a large space, and wax figures stood, leaned, and towered in every corner, flat surface, and not-so-flat surface. The crooked lines of their faces and their poorly done wigs resulted in a vague, spooky familiarity to their real-life inspiration. It was horrifying. It was mesmerizing.

"Who do you think that is?" Toby took my hand and tugged me toward a brunette wax figure in a flouncy dress.

I studied her for a moment, taking in the crooked line of her pink lips. "Maybe Scarlett O'Hara?"

He considered her hair. "Scarlett O'Hara with a perm?"

"Let's call it creative license."

We moved on, meandering through the next few rooms. Up each set of sweeping stairs, across plush carpeting and glossy hardwood floors, his fingers stayed folded around mine. It was bewitching. I didn't register anything I saw.

We paused on the top floor. A large picture window overlooked the city, and even though I should have been appreciating the skyline, I was watching him look at our clasped hands. His thumb grazed my palm, and my fingers tightened against his.

His eyes followed the movements, his voice low when he spoke. "Every place I touch you, you answer me."

I waited for panic to make me restless, to force my hand away, but instead of fear, I felt...cherished.

Cherished. Had that word ever been part of my vocabulary before?

Experimentally, he circled his thumb again. Instinctively, my fingers flexed. He hummed deep in his chest, adding new textures in my mind.

As good as his touch felt, I needed to put a stop to it, didn't I? These feelings were getting out of control, and my old habits weren't kicking in as strongly anymore, and without those habits, what would keep me safe? I couldn't let this continue, but I also couldn't stop him. Nobody had ever looked at me like this before.

Sighing, he released my hand, only to wrap an arm around my shoulders, tucking me close under his arm, something most men weren't tall enough to do with me. Being this close to him reminded me of earlier this morning, when I'd woken up surrounded in warm sheets and Toby and—

I looked up to see him staring down at me with satisfaction, but also with wonder. He felt it too? This awed sense that we had always been seeking this connection and only just now found it?

Feelings rose, pushing at some boundary I set years ago, only now I was too enraptured to care. I wrapped my arm around his waist, reciprocating his movements, wondering if—

We moved into the kiss simultaneously. My hand rested on his shoulder, his fingers curved around the back of my neck. Our lips brushed together first with curiosity, then with boldness. His other hand moved to my lower back, tugging me against him with decisive pressure. My arms mirrored his actions as we sought to be as close as possible.

Somehow I'd known he would be an excellent kisser, and now, as he sipped at my lower lip, I reveled in the fact that he kissed like he flirted. Thoroughly, with his hand at my neck using the gentlest pressure to angle me. Playfully, his slow movements making each touch a moment of anticipation, which kept me waiting on the edge, kept me wanting more. This felt so good, and so new, and so completely unlike anything—

In short, Toby kissed like he did everything else: he was all in. He was so all in that he didn't notice when his phone started to vibrate in his pocket.

"Toby…" I could only manage that one word before he kissed me again.

"Hm."

"Your phone…" Another kiss.

"Ignore it." He didn't give me time to answer. His phone silenced for a moment, but then it began again. Sighing, he released me and checked the screen. "It's my brother. He never calls, only texts, so I need to answer this."

I nodded. "Sure. Right. Do whatever you need."

I stepped away, but he tugged me back to him, keeping me close as he answered the phone. "Hey, Silas." He frowned at the voice on the other end. "M-hm." He touched my smudged lipstick. A mischievous grin curved his lips. "I'm in the middle of something, but I'll be there as soon as I can."

I tried to keep my expression clear. Showing disappointment would only make Toby feel bad, not helping either of us. He was always sacrificing for my family. I could give up a little of Toby for his.

He ended the call, smiling when I bit at his thumb still tracing my lipstick.

"I'm sorry I have to cut our date short," he said. "Silas and his wife both have food poisoning, but their daughter is at a sleepover, so I need to pick her up and take her home. I'll probably take the other kids off their hands for the rest of the weekend too."

I grimaced. "Poor Silas. That makes for a rough weekend."

"They have four kids under the age of seven, so taking care of them would be the most helpful thing, I think." He sighed. "Any chance you want to come with?"

Mom and Phyllis had already been home alone for several hours, and the thought of meeting Toby's family in the throes of food poisoning sounded less than ideal. The thought of meeting Toby's family at all made my defensive walls rise again. No need to add bodily functions into the mix.

"I'd better go back home," I said. "I don't trust Mom and Phyllis being alone together for too long."

Toby kissed me briefly, deeply. "I'm especially sorry about cutting this part short. Maybe we can sneak a few more on our way out."

I already stood on tiptoe, drawing his face toward mine. "Exactly how many is a few?"

CHAPTER 31

IVY

Mel: Ivy, is your mom on social media now?
Ivy: What gave it away? How she spent all morning liking and commenting on my pictures from ten years ago?
Mel: I know, they're popping up on my feed.
Cameron: THAT was your hair ten years ago, Ivy?
Ivy: I bet you didn't look so hot back then either.
Cameron: My shag cut was very much en vogue that year. I regret nothing.

After our unconventional night sleeping together—literally *sleeping*, my recklessness raged—and a weekend of missing Toby every minute that passed without him, I felt light. Breathless. Happy.

It was terrifying.

One moment, my feelings peaked in elation: Toby was more wonderful than I'd thought when I first met him; he was right about our chemistry—we now had dozens of kisses to prove his point; he'd held me Friday night like he would hold me forever if I only asked, and wasn't that what I really wanted after all?

The next moment, my emotions would crash into horror: Toby had finagled his way through my barriers and would leave when I needed him most; I felt too good when I spent time with him, or touched him, or thought of him; nothing this good came without a cost, because that was how the world worked.

But if I didn't think, if I just let myself flow through the day, I felt, more than anything else, awe. Like this morning, for example. Mom had been extra "helpful" since dropping the bomb about her house, and she'd made me coffee today. Coffee that tasted like tar. But I didn't tell her it tasted like tar, and I didn't sneakily dump it down the drain when she wasn't looking. I choked it down, waited for the caffeine to jolt me from zombie into human, and thanked her for thinking of me this morning. That was not the normal way Ivy Lunden, perpetually late and not a morning person, behaved before noon.

My phone vibrated with a text notification.

Mel: I'm sorry your sushi date with Toby was so awful. I'm sorry for the ways Cam and I contributed to the awfulness. But I heard he made up for it?

Of course Toby had told Cameron about our thrift store date.

Ivy: He more than made up for it.

Mel: I knew he would!

She knew he would make up for a ruined date because Toby was kind. Because he made you feel special, no matter who you were.

I wondered if I did the same for him. Probably not, because Toby was sweet, and I was cynical, and sweetness wasn't my thing. But maybe I could do something nice for him. Cookies? Take It Cheesy takeout? A do-over of our sushi date?

I knew these ideas were nothing compared to his generosity toward me—at-home physical therapy for Mom, rearranging medical equipment—but I felt compelled to do something. Anything.

Ivy: Okay, now get back to work. I know you're at the tutoring center.

Mel: Work can wait. Tell me how you feel about Toby.

My thumbs hovered over the digital letters on my screen. I thought of how I'd felt all day. Content. Purring with satisfaction. Eager to see him again tonight. I was, essentially, my cat, emotionally preening against Toby like he was an integral part of my happiness.

He didn't make me feel alternately used or cornered like other men. He made me feel like an optimized version of myself. With his attention focused on me, I could even paint a Picasso or chisel a David. Anything was possible.

Ivy: He's amazing, and he makes me feel amazing. Not sure what that means, but there it is.

Mel: I know what it means, but I'll wait for you to figure it out.

Ivy: Yeah, yeah, calm down.

Mel: I just really love you and want you to be happy.

Only when my cheeks ached did I realize I was grinning at my phone beneath my desk. My brain told me this was pathetic. My heart frolicked through meadows and told my brain to get lost.

Ivy: I am happy. For the first time in a long, long time.

I was supposed to be processing the new catalog for next semester. Instead, I doodled some of the images that had been floating through my mind the last few weeks. My mechanical pencil hovered over the computer copy paper, snapshots taking shape.

In the upper left, two hands reached out to touch an African violet.

In the upper right was the exact picture I'd told Toby about at the sushi restaurant, with sets of hands and chopsticks.

The last snapshot taking shape was Toby's hands as they unrolled Mom's sock to inspect her ankle. His fingers were mid-motion, gently rolling the top of her sock toward her heel, his other hand cradling her lower calf so he didn't put any stress on her injured joint. I could see it in color now—bright, bold splashes of cobalt and ruby and violet.

The sketches littered the page. My pencil moved. Later I might turn them into paintings, complete with all the colors in my mind.

Toby had asked if my art ever had themes. Typically not. None of the commissions I'd done had been thematic or unique. They'd been for wealthy people wanting art to show off their money, not art to make a statement or stir a feeling.

I would have to be incredibly dense not to see the pattern in these sketches. I hadn't planned to capture moments in relationships. But there it was. People needing other people, giving and accepting help, loving one another in the smallest of ways. Each image showed a way people were better together than apart.

With Toby, my life was undoubtedly better. A matter of weeks ago, I'd looked forward to going home to an empty house with Van, silence, and boxed wine. Normally I was eager for quiet after my workdays, exhausted from dealing with colors and with people—because *people*, right?

Now I saw a dangerous cliff's edge approaching. Thanks to Toby, my home was different. It was lighter. *I* was lighter. He filled my life with spontaneity and laughter and flirty quips, a brush of his shoulder when he walked past, a finger tucking my hair out of my face when I made dinner. Going home to Toby meant excitement in the midst of my humdrum routines.

My phone vibrated.

Toby - 10/10 Smile: Sitting in an endless meeting. Wishing our date hadn't ended so soon.

I smiled at my phone.

Ivy: Same.

Toby - 10/10 Smile: I think Deke's greatest love in life is himself.

Ivy: After one very bad first impression of him, I agree.

Toby - 10/10 Smile: Too bad you couldn't have met Hudson that day. He's my boss, and he's amazing. He's the opposite of Deke.

Since I wasn't feeling like myself in the best possible way, apparently I wasn't texting like myself either.

Ivy: Maybe that's why Hudson hired him. Their opposites complement.

His texts paused for a moment before popping back up.

Toby - 10/10 Smile: What happened to the Ivy who found just as much joy as I did in judging Deke?

Ivy: Still here.

Toby - 10/10 Smile: I don't believe you. What did you do with my Ivy?

My thumbs paused. *My Ivy.*

Were Toby and I better together than apart? I told hope to crawl back under the rock I usually trapped it under, but it kept tapping at the door, and I'd never before felt so tempted to let it in. What could it hurt? I reached for the doorknob.

CHAPTER 32

IVY

Toby - 10/10 Smile: Looking forward to seeing you tonight.

After work on Monday, I had to run errands, so when I got home, Toby already stood in the living room, chatting with Mom. He still wore his coat, so he must've just arrived. He looked over his shoulder when he heard me thump through the doorway with my armload of groceries. His face spread into a slow smile.

So this is why Cameron and Mel melt into gooey puddles when they smile at one another.

"Hi," he said.

All day I'd looked forward to seeing Toby. I'd waited for this moment. I'd thought of walking toward him, reaching up for a kiss, and—

And now…I panicked. It was one thing to be confident at work and text Toby from a distance. It was another to confront him, and my growing feelings for him, face to face.

"Hi," I said, then I rushed back outside. Groceries were still in the car, a completely legitimate reason to run away from Toby.

His footsteps crunched in the snow behind me. "Want some help?"

"No, I got it." I sped up.

"Um, Ivy?" The crunching of his footsteps stopped. "Didn't you park in the garage?"

I blinked. The driveway stood empty in front of me. How embarrassing.

Rolling my eyes at myself, I turned back to the house.

He stood on the sidewalk, hands in the pockets of his coat, a huge grin on his face, clearly feeling good about himself.

I strode closer, the narrow sidewalk walled in with several inches of snow on both sides, forcing me to walk directly up to him. I stopped in front of him.

He didn't move. "Do I fluster you, Ivy?"

Do not melt, do not melt, do not melt.

Instead of answering, I touched my fingertips to his mouth, my barely there touch tracing his lips. His grin faded.

"Don't mind me," I whispered. "You had a little smugness there."

His surprised laugh shimmered in my mind.

Now we were even. Now, with level terrain between us, it felt natural to pull him down for a kiss. Let Mom and Phyllis and the whole neighborhood see us, I didn't care. He was my Toby, and I'd waited all day to kiss him.

"That's more like it." He took my hand and walked with me to the garage. He grabbed all of the groceries with his free hand before I could wrestle a single shopping bag from him, and he offered to help unload everything in the kitchen.

"I got it," I repeated.

He ignored me. Unpacking each item and handing it to me one by one, he told me about his day, which rated at a seven. He asked me about mine, which I rated at a six, mostly because I'd missed him so much, but I couldn't force the words past the lump in my throat just yet.

Our conversation devolved into his impersonations of his coworkers. I'd never met any of his coworkers other than Deke, but Toby's imitations were pure entertainment. Our laughter echoed in my kitchen, splashing bubblegum pink into the margins of my mind.

Toby paused his antics, crouching until he was eye-level with a puddle of red juice on my kitchen counter. In the middle of it sat a soggy lump of fiber. It was disgusting.

"Are you…breeding aliens?" He moved to poke it and then thought better of it, retracting his hand.

I cringed and answered in a whisper. "You don't want to know."

"I do too want to know."

"It's a tomato."

Toby studied the blob, tilting his head at a comic angle. "It can't be. I've never seen a tomato look like that."

I bent next to him until I also stood eye-level with the goop, our shoulders meeting between us. It brought a sense of deja vu from school days in a science lab. "Mom doesn't like the skins, and she doesn't like the seeds. So she sort of"—I wrinkled my nose and gestured vaguely—"tears it apart."

His lip curled. "And then she doesn't eat it? She massacres the poor tomato for nothing?"

I smiled a little despite myself. "She eats part of it. She leaves the rest for later."

"Just…out on the counter like this?" His eyes darted around like he expected pink globs to drop from the ceiling or sprout from the top of the refrigerator.

"It's gross, I know. But I'm learning to pick my battles when it comes to sharing a house with Mom. And Phyllis." I sighed and straightened, moving back toward the groceries. "I share my house with both of them at this point."

He laughed quietly, glancing toward the living room. "So you trade desiccated tomatoes for them to…what, not desiccate something worse?"

"For them to stop rearranging my kitchen. But, to be fair, they haven't done that since sushi night." I hadn't made time to put my kitchen completely back in order, but I found it reassuring to know my canned goods wouldn't move without my say-so.

"What about for them to treat your house like a home and not a medical storage unit?"

I grinned. "For them to stop mentioning Chester."

He crossed his arms over his chest and leaned against the countertop. "That's right. My competition."

"He's not your competition."

"I won already? Yes!" His victorious smile would become my personal sunshine if I kept revolving around him.

I smiled and stepped toward the living room. "Hey, Mom, what sounds good for dinner? I have some chicken and…"

My voice drifted off. I'd thought the medical equipment was bad. And it was bad, and I was so happy it was gone the day after the Chester Incident. But now my living room was strewn with open boxes and Styrofoam molds. A knife rested on the coffee table, sticky from slicing through packaging tape. Phyllis sat on the couch, and Mom lounged in her recliner, her hands clutching a gun.

That's right. A gun.

I didn't have the wherewithal to keep my voice calm. "What are you doing?!"

Mom looked up, her face radiant like a child who'd finished a finger painting. "I shopped online."

I choked. "And you bought a rifle?"

"It's a BB gun," Toby said helpfully.

"It's a BB gun," Phyllis echoed, just as helpfully.

My head slowly swiveled toward Toby, my lips in a thin line. My nostrils flared, too, by the way his eyebrows rose. But then he grinned and winked at me. Winked. Like this was funny! Fine, it was a little funny. But the thought of my mother wielding BB guns, or weapons of any kind, was not a comforting one.

"Mom, what are you going to do with a BB gun?"

"Your neighbor's dogs are always barking, so I thought—"

"No."

She smiled at me, the picture of patience. "Of course they don't bother you, because you're at work all day, but I have to listen to them twenty-four seven. You should stay home with me sometime and try it."

"I'm home on the weekends," I said. "The dogs don't bother me then. You're not shooting at the neighbor's dogs."

Bending, I picked my way around the packaging and boxes and tape. A giant box of BBs was wedged between the floor and Mom's recliner. A manufacturer's warranty sprawled on the coffee table, with an instruction manual next to it. The pages were open to the French directions.

"The neighbors should have better control over their dogs in the first place," Phyllis said.

"Precisely," Mom said.

"You will not be shooting anything," I said.

Phyllis sighed. "It's only a BB gun. It doesn't do any actual damage."

"What if you hit an eyeball?" I barely managed to keep my volume at an inside-voice level. How could they have thought this was a good idea? What would my neighbors have thought? In what world was something like this okay?

"Ivy has a point," Toby said supportively.

"I'll be careful," Mom insisted.

"No." Taking the BB gun from her, I stuffed it into the box with the rest of the packaging around it and fumbled the cardboard lid into place. I strode toward the door, planning to put the gun in my trunk so I could mail it back on my way home from work tomorrow.

Then I stopped, horrified at a new thought. "Wait a second. You bought the BB gun online. What else did you buy?"

"Nothing." Mom's answer was too fast to be true.

Mom and Phyllis looked innocent as could be even as they exchanged conspiratorial glances.

Innocent my foot.

Toby covered his mouth with his hand, his laugh poorly covered with a cough. He moved away, speaking to Mom. "I'll be back for your session in a minute. I'm going to get a glass of water. Anybody else need anything from the kitchen?"

I followed him into the kitchen, meaning to go to the garage with the BB gun box, but he grabbed my upper arms and leaned his forehead against my shoulder, shaking with silent laughter. I felt the warmth of his palms even through my thick sweater.

"I can't believe you took it away from her," he whispered and wheezed. "What if your mom is the next Annie Oakley?"

I bit my lip so I wouldn't laugh. "The gun is bigger than she is."

"You're right. I'm glad you confiscated it. She already hates me. I don't want her to have weapons within reach." He straightened and sighed, clearly trying to compose himself.

"She doesn't hate you that much." Even as I took a half-step back, I felt a pull to move toward him and not away.

He scoffed and whispered, "She chooses Chester over me. What do you call that?"

I smiled. "Okay, you're right. She hates you." I moved toward the door to the garage, saying over my shoulder, "Better go keep her busy before she buys a Samurai sword next."

CHAPTER 33

TOBY

Toby: Did I hear you're buying pizza as a thank-you? Do you know how much pizza my brothers eat?
Ivy: I've got it covered. Mel warned me you all eat like locusts.
Toby: That mental image is a bit disturbing. I prefer to think we eat like an army.
Ivy: Isn't a large group of locusts called an army of locusts?
Toby: Actually, the internet says a large group of locusts is called a cloud, swarm, or plague.
Ivy: I pick plague. The Azumah men will descend upon my pizza like a plague.
Toby: Flattering.

It took a little convincing, but eventually Ivy agreed to a moving party. Her mom's house was closing soon, and even though leaving the furniture was part of the contract, Irena still had a decent amount of belongings there.

Our plan was for Mel to go to Ivy's so they could collect boxes, Cameron and I would pick up some coffee, and the four of us would meet at Irena's house. My brothers would show up within the next hour or "as soon as possible." With six kids between Silas and Amos's families, punctuality wasn't always a given. We would all drive separately so we could pack as much as possible.

I had mixed feelings about my brothers joining our little moving party. What if the extra pressure would make Ivy bolt? We were finally in a good place, with her starting to open up to me, and now my brothers would descend like a plague? It was funny, sure, but not exactly how I wanted my next step with her to go.

Tired of living with my own thoughts, I joined Cameron in his car while we waited for Mel and Ivy.

He rubbed his hands together for some added warmth. "Did you tell your brothers about Ivy?"

"You mean do I want my brothers to razz me about her nonstop all day? Of course not. I said a friend needed help, and they said they'd make it happen."

"They'll know she's more than a friend as soon as they see you two together."

"But," I countered, "at least this way they won't be preparing their lines hours in advance."

He paused to give me a long look. "You're really into her."

Somewhere between her sarcasm and tender heart, I'd found the real Ivy I'd known was there all along. Her pretty face helped, but it was more than that.

I gave Cameron a long look in return. "I am."

"You two are good together." He sipped his coffee. The steam fogged up his glasses, so I couldn't read his eyes, but I knew that tilt of his mouth and line in his shoulders.

"What aren't you saying?"

He sipped more coffee but wouldn't look at me. "I just always think of Ivy as a little, you know, prickly."

While my instincts rose to defend Ivy, common sense and my own experience nodded in agreement with Cameron. She was prickly. She was difficult to get to know. But the challenge was half the fun.

"She's the opposite of Yvonne," Cameron continued, "and I think that's a good thing. I never liked what she did to you."

"You mean when she led me on only to break up with me? I didn't like it either."

"It was more than that," he said. "I didn't like how she kind of...subdued you."

"Thanks for making me sound pathetic." I silently promised my ego it would live to see another day.

Cameron's fingers began tugging at his coat sleeves, tucking them tighter around his wrists and beneath his gloves. "Look, you two brought out the worst in each other. She was always irritated with you because you didn't behave the way she thought you should. You were always frustrated with trying to meet her standards. You two weren't a good fit."

I thought of how Mel encouraged Cameron to take more chances, and Cameron encouraged Mel to chase after her dreams. That kind of symbiosis was something I hadn't had in a relationship. What I'd had with Yvonne wasn't a matter of her inspiring me to become a better person. She'd wanted me to squeeze into a mental picture she'd dreamed up long before she met me.

"Now Ivy, I can see how she could bring out the best in you," Cameron said. "When you get too over the top—"

"It doesn't happen *that* often."

"—she could make some kind of sarcastic quip that pokes fun at you just enough to show that she's on to you but not so much that she belittles you. She does that sometimes with Mel. It's like a teasing way of keeping each other in check. And your optimism could be great for Ivy. I bet she's softer when she's with you."

Ivy the ice queen, with a weak spot just for me.

I smiled. "Less porcupine, more hedgehog."

Less prickly, more Ivy. Porcupines hurt no matter how I touched those quills, but once I learned how to handle a hedgehog, I could, well, go on dates with Ivy and hold hands and kiss, more kisses than I could count, and now I'd mixed the imagery of a hedgehog and a human, but I loved it anyway.

Mel and Ivy pulled into the driveway, parking as best they could on the narrow strip of pavement. Our footsteps crunched on the snowy driveway as Cameron and I climbed out of his car with coffee thermoses in hand.

I handed Ivy her coffee, ducking for a kiss on her cheek. "Morning. How are you feeling about today?"

It would be natural for her to be emotional. We were clearing all signs of her mom's life and Ivy's childhood from the home where she grew up. I would be emotional if I were her.

"I'm nervous we won't get everything done." She looked over the house with a cool detachment.

Never mind then.

"We'll have six people with five vehicles," I said. "We'll make it happen."

Over the rim of her thermos, Ivy cast a skeptical look my way. "You're way too cheery for how early it is."

Mel grimaced. "They willingly get up early to run on weekends."

Grinning, I slung my arm around Ivy just as my brothers parked on the street.

I felt her stiffen in my loose grip, so I pulled her a little closer. "Don't worry. They're going to love you."

"What's not to love, right?"

Another piece of the Ivy puzzle: she covered nervousness with false bravado. But I saw the truth in her lips, drawn into a taut line, and her expression, carefully blank.

Introductions were made. Silas gave Ivy a quick once-over and then focused on the logistics of the move. Amos inspected her with all of his quiet focus. Both responses were typical for my brothers. Neither would be good for Ivy's nervousness.

Nodding toward the house, Cameron tucked his hands deeper into his pockets. "Ready to go inside?"

We marched behind Ivy, who led the way with the key. Activity erupted all at once: Silas answered his phone, his big voice echoing through the quiet house; Amos rapped a knuckle on the wall to test whatever he was thinking in his genius brain; Cameron found a collection of windchimes tacked to a closed window and ran his finger through all of them at once; Mel stood with Ivy, talking through what still needed to be packed.

What did all this noise look like inside Ivy's head?

I gently pressed my hand on her lower back, steering her toward the first door I saw. "I have some questions about the drapes in here."

She balked. "The what?"

"You know, the drapes in here."

"But—"

I closed the door behind us, leaning against it.

"What was that for?" She crossed her arms over her chest.

I hedged. "My brothers can be too much."

"I don't think Amos has said a single word yet."

"Well, Silas is loud. And Cam was messing with those windchimes." I shrugged, hesitating to explain any further and come across like a jerk.

"I still don't understand why we're hiding in my mom's bathroom." She gestured at the room around us. "Which doesn't have any drapes, by the way."

I glanced around us for the first time. We were wedged into a small half-bath that fit under the stairs. My head would touch the slanted ceiling if I straightened all the way. There wasn't a single window in sight.

I rocked on my heels. "Well, it was really noisy, so I thought…"

She frowned. "So you thought, because I have synesthesia, I needed to be saved from all the ruckus out there?"

Now that she said it out loud, I felt like an idiot. Ivy was a grown woman. She didn't need me to drag her into tiny half-baths when she'd lived her life just fine without my interference. Maybe the hero complex she teased me about wasn't so far off.

She had every right to be full-on porcupine prickly with me now.

I backpedaled. "Sorry. I overstepped. I didn't think…I thought…"

Ivy moved closer to me. "You did overstep, but I understand. You don't need to intervene for me. I've been navigating a noisy world my whole life. I put on my big-girl panties this morning, like I do every morning."

Feeling put in my place and more than a little ridiculous, I decided to focus where my mind naturally wanted to go. "What color do these big-girl panties happen to be?"

"That's on a need-to-know basis."

We stood so close. Just another few breaths, and we would kiss. I spent an embarrassing amount of time dreaming about all of our kisses up to this point, and all the ways she felt incredible against me. The half-bath might not be romantic, and we might have an audience right outside the door, but the less-than-ideal setting wasn't stopping her from staring at my lips, either.

I moved closer, eyes fixed on her mouth. Just another breath and—

The door opened behind me.

"Is there anything in here we need to pack—oh." Silas's voice was deafening in this small space.

I froze, eyes closed, lips pursed in annoyance. Brothers.

A stifled sound had me opening my eyes. Ivy's eyes shone with restrained laughter.

I didn't need to turn around to see Silas crossing his arms over his chest.

"So. Drapes, huh?"

CHAPTER 34

IVY

Toby - 10/10 Smile: Your mom just tried to force-feed me one of those aliens
you've been breeding.
Ivy: The tomato slime? I'm so sorry.
Toby - 10/10 Smile: It didn't taste half bad.
Ivy: Please tell me you're kidding.
Toby - 10/10 Smile: The texture was only a bit off.

At the most superficial level, I'd figured out Toby's brothers. Silas was the bossy grump, and he enjoyed taking care of everyone around him. Amos was the quiet genius, half of his brain always calculating some impossible equation while the other half kept up with regular life.

What threw me off was how they weren't hazing me; they were just studying from a distance that could only be called coolly friendly. Silas peppered me with small talk about my work and my mom's health, while Amos silently watched me try to lift a too-heavy box until I accepted defeat and left it for him to do.

All that watching made me jumpy; Mel walked into a room behind me, and I nearly screamed. But I didn't care what Toby's brothers thought of me. I had plenty of worries keeping me up at night already. No need to add Silas and Amos to the mix.

I put together a box, popping the sides out and taping the seams.

Silas came to stand next to me. "My wife's a nurse."

Even though I'd told Toby I didn't need his intervention, I wished he were here to screen the small talk for me. The tearing sound of the tape screeched through my mind in fluorescent green, and Silas's wife's career didn't impact me at the moment, and I had too little emotional bandwidth for everything demanding my attention today.

I opened another box. "She and Toby must get along well with their medical backgrounds."

He nodded. "A lot of days are really emotional for her, but she says she has it easy compared to caretakers like you."

Oh, this wasn't small talk after all. Did all the Azumah men feel a need to talk to me like a therapist? I'd gotten used to it with Toby, realizing it was part of his sincerity, but apparently it was a family trait.

"It hasn't been easy." I shrugged, gesturing that was the end of it, but then the words kept coming, as if my lack of emotional wherewithal today also meant I lacked a filter. "I never would've thought my mom would be in this state when she's only seventy-three, but she had a hard life and never took care of herself."

Because she was too busy taking care of me, pouring everything she had into the daughter she'd never planned on, and now...now I heard an audible clock counting down our time together.

"Toby has helped tremendously."

"That sounds like him." Silas stood straighter with pride over his little brother. The same little brother he'd teased mercilessly about the drapes in the bathroom, but that was already water under the sibling bridge, something that mystified me as an only child.

Silas grinned. "He's always been a both-feet-first kind of guy."

"I gathered."

"It gets him into trouble more often than not."

I smiled at the brotherly tone in Silas's merlot voice. "I can imagine."

He glanced toward the door, clearly checking for Toby before fixing his eyes back on me. "Good thing you're not trouble, right?"

Maybe he was teasing. Maybe he wasn't. But if the Azumah family was anything like Toby, they would be worried about him. So I answered his question seriously, regardless of whether that was how he meant it.

"I'm not sure whether I'm trouble for Toby." I set aside the tape dispenser and looked directly at Silas. "What I feel for Toby, mixed in with everything else in my life right now, is...complicated. I don't want to get hurt, and I don't want to hurt him. That's the best answer I can give you right now."

Toss together two human beings, regardless of emotional baggage and crazy lives, and hurts were inevitable, weren't they? But Toby and I were adults about this, and we could handle our own relationship, couldn't we?

Between Mom, Phyllis, Cameron, Mel, and now Toby's brothers, my life was maxed out on busybodies.

Silas mulled over my words before he broke into a smile. "Sounds like exactly the kind of grounded common sense Toby needs in his life."

We sprawled in my living room, exhausted from a long day of hauling boxes from Mom's house to mine. Mom sat on her recliner, and Phyllis shared the couch with Cameron and Mel. Silas and Amos balanced their broad bodies on chairs we'd brought in from the kitchen. All of us held paper plates of pizza and plastic Solo cups, because Phyllis had casually mentioned—about four times— she didn't want to wash the dishes from so many people. My only thought was, when had Phyllis ever washed the dishes?

Toby and I sat on the floor, side by side. Like the best kind of shadow, all day he'd asked me where I wanted to stack boxes, where I wanted to pile thrift store donations, what arrangement left things most out of my way so my small house could still be functional despite being stuffed to the max. He'd taken every opportunity to touch me in little ways, brushing my arm when he moved a box out of my way, or grazing our fingers when he passed me a glass of water.

His brothers saw it all. They hadn't said a word. I almost wished they would tease him about me. As it was, I felt like the proverbial elephant in the room everyone carefully ignored.

Toby spoke quietly to me while the others continued talking. "Are you happy with where we put everything?"

I nodded. "I think this will work until Mom and I can sort through more of it."

"If you change your mind, I can come over and move boxes any time this week."

"You just want to show off your muscles."

He winked.

Mom spoke over the rest of the living room noise. "I shouldn't eat any more of this pizza. I'll get indigestion. Ivy, do you still get indigestion? Maybe you shouldn't eat any more pizza either."

I looked down at my plate. "This is only my second slice, and I never get indigestion."

"No, no," she insisted, "you used to get it all the time as a baby. Don't you remember?"

I answered as patiently as I could. "I was a baby, so no, not really." I lifted my cup as a hopeful distraction. "Refill, anyone?"

She wasn't listening. "I'll never forget when you hadn't pooped for a week, and I was so worried I took you to the doctor. He stuck a thermometer in you, and you exploded like an overripe banana."

Mel set down her pizza slice mid-chew, edging her plate away.

I glanced toward the kitchen, eyeing where Van crouched over his food dish. Maybe Mel and I could join him for dinner instead.

Toby shifted, propping himself up on an arm that he braced behind me. His forearm rested against my lower back in silent solidarity.

"When I first started dating," he said, "I thought I'd use science to outsmart the popularity system at school."

Cameron grinned. "I hope this is the story I think it is."

"What did you do?" Mel asked.

"I saw a commercial for a cologne that had pheromones in it. I saved up for a few months before I could afford it. The day I got the cologne, I doused myself in it and went to school expecting all the girls to fall in love with me. None of them did."

Silas's laugh boomed at us. "Because you stank too badly for anyone to come near you."

Toby shrugged. "Probably."

"You also ate dirt," Amos said, saying more words at once than I'd heard from him the entire day.

Toby cringed. "We don't need to talk about that one."

Silas laughed again. "Just dirt? He ate everything. Grass, tree bark, the stuffing from inside throw pillows."

"And worms," Amos added.

Mel choked on her drink. "Worms?"

"I forgot about that," Silas said. "The cutest girl in the neighborhood dared him to eat a worm, and he wanted to impress her. So he ate several, because why go an inch when you can go a mile?"

Toby focused his mischievous gaze on me. "I've always liked a challenge."

"And you've always liked strong women," Silas added.

Toby answered him but looked at me. "Still do."

I swallowed. My feelings ranged from heart-pounding joy at Toby so blatantly stating his feelings for me, to discomfort that he'd done this in front of his family I'd just met. Fortunately, everyone else stayed focused on the worms.

Grimacing, Mel moved her plate off her lap and onto the coffee table. "I'm completely disgusted, but I have so many questions. What did the worms taste like?"

Toby shrugged, his arm against my back shifting with the motion. "I swallowed them whole so I wouldn't have to find out."

She frowned. "Are we talking about earthworms or caterpillars?"

"Earthworms."

"Would you have eaten a caterpillar?" I asked.

His face turned sheepish for a moment. "Probably."

Mel was still stuck on the earthworms. "The texture had to be terrible."

"It wasn't great," he admitted.

Cameron addressed Toby but glanced at me. "Did you have any indigestion after?"

I pulled a face at him, and Mel elbowed him, but Toby patted his abdomen. "My stomach is made of steel. Nothing hurts me."

Mom lifted her brows at him. "I'm sure your mother would disagree."

Amos tugged at his lower lip, his gaze thoughtful. "Back to the pheromones. Weren't you sent home early that day?"

Silas nodded. "You smelled so bad your teacher got a headache."

Toby scoffed. "That wasn't it."

"Then why did you get sent home?" Cameron asked, transferring Mel's pizza onto his own plate and taking an enormous bite.

"I wanted my money back from the cologne, so I was selling it to other boys."

I laughed. "No way."

He wiggled his brows at me. "Three bucks per spray. I made a killing."

Amos nodded approvingly. "Very industrious."

Silas shook his head. "I hope you made enough to buy regular Axe like the rest of us."

The conversation continued around us. Toby and I lapsed into silence. To spare me some minor humiliation, he'd thrown himself in front of the conversational bus. He willingly looked silly for my sake, making fun of himself for pheromone cologne and earthworm snacks. And he'd managed to flirt through it too.

"You've always liked strong women."

"Still do."

Cozy warmth swelled from my chest outward, warming me down to my toes. I braced my arm behind myself, purposely resting my hand over his and drawing lazy, swirling loops across his skin.

CHAPTER 35

TOBY

Cameron: Enjoy your night. But not too much.
Toby: Is this payback for all those years I ribbed you about Mel?
Cameron: You knew it'd come around eventually.

Stuffing the last empty pizza boxes into garbage bags, I listened to Ivy's quiet house. Silas and Amos had gone home, and Cameron and Mel had driven away with promises to come over next Monday night. Phyllis had crossed her snowy lawn to her own house. An hour ago, Ivy's mom had gone to bed, whirring her way up the steps in her stair lift chariot. Even Van had retreated to his windowsill of African violets.

Maybe now Ivy would relax. She'd been tense all day, but her version of tense looked different than the stereotypical image of someone rubbing their temples all day. Instead, Ivy cracked sarcastic jokes, bought three extra pizzas so nobody went home hungry, and tucked Van under her arm every chance she had. But by the end of the day, she'd stopped looking at my brothers with trepidation and started smiling with a bit more ease. I couldn't have been happier.

The simple truth was, as much as Ivy could charm and flirt with the best of the best, crowds were hard for her. I understood that better now that I knew about her synesthesia.

I hauled the garbage bag outside, my skin tingling with cold until I returned

"

to the kitchen. Ivy stood at the cabinet, putting away some of the nonperishables we'd moved from her mom's.

I found two Solo cups with our names written in Sharpie and retrieved her box of wine from the fridge. "I'm going to sit on your couch and drink your sangria for the next hour or so, if you want to join me."

Ivy turned to follow me at the word "sangria." Good to know for future reference.

I sat on the middle cushion.

"Really? You have to sit there?" She frowned at the empty cushions on either side of me.

"What's wrong with here? I'm leaving you two perfect options." I patted the seats next to me.

She curled herself into the space to my right. "If you would've sat on one end or the other, then I could've stretched out."

"I'm not in your way." Not giving her a chance to react, I pulled her socked feet toward me until her calves rested across my lap. I placed my forearm over her shins to stop her from wiggling away. "See? You're stretching out."

She tried to hide her smile behind the Solo cup I handed her. I saw it. I always saw her.

"We haven't played our game in a while," I said. "Rate your day."

After a healthy gulp of wine, she said, "Seven."

Given all the chaos of the day, the noise of five extra people in and out of her house, I'd expected much lower.

Ivy grinned at my surprised expression. "Maybe your eternal optimism is corrupting me."

I pinched her calf in retaliation, and she laughed.

"Why a seven?" I asked.

She began numbering items on her fingers as she spoke. "We ordered more than enough pizza. Cam and Mel are adorable to watch. Did you see them bickering over how many boxes fit in the trunk?"

I chuckled at the memory of Cameron trying to wrestle a box from Mel's arms.

Ivy lifted another finger as she listed, "I got to meet your brothers."

Remembering the story about earthworms, I groaned and dropped my head against the back of her couch. "That's a good thing?"

"Definitely." She continued listing. "We got a lot done."

Wariness crossed her face, drawing her brows closer together before she smoothed them into practiced indifference. "And I got to spend the whole day with you. I don't think we've ever spent an entire day together."

I smiled. "You're right. How have we never done that before?"

I watched her sip her wine, the smooth lines of her throat working in a swallow. A few wisps of blond had teased loose from her ponytail, and now they coiled in translucent swirls along her black top.

I looked back to my Solo cup. "What would it take to make your day a ten?"

She wiggled her feet. "A foot rub. Pretty please?"

"That's all? Consider it done."

She sighed and closed her eyes at the feel of my thumb on her arch. The blond curls on her shirt twisted into new shapes as she leaned her head back against the cushioned armrest. It would take very little effort for me to lean over and kiss her, but she had to be worn out, and I wanted our kisses to be mutual, not obligatory.

"What about your day?" she asked.

I thought for a moment before saying, "Nine."

"Why?"

"Spending time with you, of course. I always have fun with Cam and Mel. And I like physical work. The paperwork side of my job is a pain, and I love the days when I can move nonstop."

"That's why you love your job so much."

I nodded and moved my thumb to a different pressure point. "I hate sitting still, and I love helping people. Deke is obnoxious, and paperwork is terrible, but overall, those aren't deal breakers."

Her eyes opened at that. "You could always open your own physical therapy facility and push your paperwork off on an assistant."

"No way," I scoffed. "My boss spends all day on the phone, or managing employees, or dealing with maintenance and insurance. I would hate that."

She smiled. "You *would* hate that."

Our conversation paused, and we listened to the sounds of her home settling into the cold night. A few disjointed creaks from different rooms, Van purring loudly as he leapt from the windowsill to curl in front of a heat vent on the floor.

Ivy's voice was barely above a whisper. "And to get to a ten?"

I sighed dramatically. "I would need to turn back time so my brothers didn't tell you those stories."

She laughed, her legs shifting on my lap as she did. "Eating dirt. And tree bark. And those worms? You must've been such an adorable, terrible child."

"You'll have to ask my mother." I shook my head. "Don't bother asking my dad; he gets his stories about the three of us boys confused."

I could do without the embarrassing stories, but when my family met Ivy, they would love her. Mama would stuff her with Kenyan food, insisting she was too skinny for healthy grandbabies, because that was instantly where Mama's mind would go. Baba would ask her well-intended but clueless questions about art and have no idea what her answers meant.

Picturing the scenario play out, I glanced over to see her watching me. She quickly looked away. I fought the idiotic grin threatening to spread across my face. Ivy Lunden, ice queen, didn't want to get caught staring at me.

Her body stiffened, and her cheeks turned pink. "Thanks for helping today."

"Of course." I glanced at the clock on her wall. "I'd better go."

"What? Why?"

I patted her feet in a gesture meant to be dismissive, but really, I didn't want to stop touching her. "You look half asleep. I don't want to keep you up." I moved her legs off my lap and onto the couch. "Call me if you need anything."

I was partway through shifting to stand when she went from stretched out, to kneeling, to straddling my lap in one fluid motion. My hands acted without my awareness, palms settling on the outside of her thighs. I stilled. My heart did not still. It jerked to attention.

"Anything?" she whispered. She placed her hands on the center of my chest. "Anything at all?"

Absolutely anything. And then even more after that.

"Yeah," I managed. "Anything."

"Even this?"

Especially this. But that would be a stupid thing to say, so I nodded.

Slowly, Ivy moved forward and closed that last fraction of an inch, her gaze dancing between my lips and eyes.

Every kiss with Ivy was the best kiss of my life.

Even as I kissed her back, I fought to focus on the most important thing. She would not walk away from this moment, as unnamed as it may be, feeling less than special. Not as long as she was with me.

I refused to look away when she drew back. It was a battle, but I fought to keep my eyes on hers. I would not let them wander. I would not do a single thing that would leave her feeling less than human, discarded, or used, like other men had done to her. I would not ask her for more than she was offering.

I *would* show her I'd been waiting for this moment with her, because she was Ivy, and she meant more to me than I was brave enough to say aloud just yet. I'd promised Ivy anything. This was anything.

She leaned in for another kiss, threading her fingers into my hair.

Whatever she needed, whatever she wanted, I was her man.

CHAPTER 36

TOBY

Toby: Your mom just sent me a peach emoji. Am I being propositioned?
Ivy: Sorry to disappoint you, but no. She's asking you about dessert tomorrow
night. Your options are peach cobbler or applesauce cake. (I recommend the
peach cobbler.)
Toby: You Lunden women are bad for my ego. Thanks for the pro tip. Does the
dessert offer mean she likes me now?

Mary Poppins had nothing on me. I floated through the day. No, I didn't care how ridiculous that sounded.

At work, Hudson clapped me on the back with a jolly "Beautiful day today!" and interns surrounded the box of donuts I brought. That's right. I brought everyone donuts. Normally I was a happy guy. Now I was overjoyed.

Not even Deke and his clipboard could dampen my mood. He pulled me aside to ask me some questions about updating the employee handbook, and I sailed through his interrogation with a smile. I even offered to read through the revisions he'd made and give him my thoughts.

He stood a little straighter, as impossible as it seemed. "If you're not opposed to it, we could team up on this."

Team up? Deke didn't team up for anything. This had Hudson's fingerprints all over it.

His eyes moved around the room. He probably wished he could be anywhere else right now. Then again, so did I. I didn't want to work with the management team. I wanted to work with clients. I wanted the people, not the paperwork.

A mental image swam before me: Deke sitting rigidly straight at the table in the break room, droning on about the latest OSHA standards, and me sitting across from him, daydreaming about setting his clipboard on fire. The mental image vastly improved when I imagined leaving work that day to see Ivy. Much better.

I held in my sigh. "I can help a few hours a week if you need."

He gave a single, jerky nod. "Good."

I'd already mentally moved on, planning my next pass by my locker so I could check my phone and text Ivy, but I looked down to see Deke's hand extended toward me.

"To our new team," he said.

What…?

I shook Deke's clammy hand, echoing, "To our new team." Did I come across as reluctant as I felt in that moment?

Now, pulling into Ivy's driveway, I told myself to slow down. It was one thing to glow at work. It was another to glow around Ivy. I hadn't seen her since this morning. While I'd been floating Mary Poppins-style through my day, she might've been doubting and second-guessing. Ivy's mind had labyrinths I didn't fully understand. I just hoped she hadn't lost sight of what last night meant to both of us.

We had chemistry. We were compatible. We had fun together. As an added bonus, we complemented each other. She would need more time to adjust than I did. I was okay with that. I would bide my time until she was ready. This time, I knew when to stop.

I climbed out of my car, slung my duffel bag over my shoulder, and strode the sidewalk toward her house. Another ice storm was predicted for tonight. I should salt the driveway and sidewalk before our session just in case. It would be a nice gesture for Ivy, who wouldn't be home from work yet.

Home. Stepping up to the front porch felt like home in a way that would be dangerous to admit aloud, but I loved it anyway.

As usual, I knocked to give a heads-up to Irena and Phyllis, and then I used my key to get in. The TV cast a cold glow in the empty living room.

"Hello?"

Phyllis hustled around the corner from the kitchen, her hands fluttering. "In here! Hurry!"

In a few quick strides, I stood in the kitchen, towering over a mess on the floor. A mess that included a crumpled Irena Lunden.

Ivy's mom looked up at me sheepishly. "It was a simple accident. It could've happened to anyone."

Ignoring the broken bags of flour, sugar, and other baking supplies strewn across the floor, I noted there was no blood and no sign of serious injuries. She flinched when she moved, but that was probably just bruising. I would need to be sure.

I knelt next to her, not bothering to step around the mess. "Tell me what hurts."

Thirty minutes later, Irena sat safely on her recliner, watching TV. Phyllis and I, armed with vacuums and brooms and dustpans, attacked the kitchen.

They'd wanted to put Ivy's kitchen back the way it had been, Phyllis explained. Irena realized she'd crossed the line when she'd sold her house without talking to Ivy. She also knew her "cleaning," aka rearranging all of Ivy's belongings, frustrated her daughter to no end, so she thought putting the kitchen back to rights would help their relationship. She and Phyllis had descended on cabinets and drawers in all their paisley-print glory until a wave of dizziness sent Irena to the floor. Phyllis hadn't been strong enough to help her up.

As Phyllis and I cleaned, regret started to gnaw at me. Irena fell because of dizziness, because of vestibular issues. Vestibular issues I had suspected but hadn't mentioned to Ivy. I had hidden the truth from her because she was already overwhelmed and stressed. I'd hated the thought of making her burden heavier. So I'd said nothing. Now there were consequences.

"We thought we could do it before Ivy came home," Phyllis said.

"You did your best."

"Please don't tell Ivy," Irena called from the living room.

I stepped around the corner. "You know I need to tell her."

"It can be our secret," she said. "We don't need to upset her."

Every warning in my brain flashed to life. I might have laughed at Irena's antics when it came to Chester and throwing rocks and buying BB guns, but I would never laugh at the truly meddlesome ways she interfered in Ivy's life, like our sushi date or selling her house. These things weren't just ornery shenanigans; they were selfish schemes that hurt Ivy. That was where I drew the line.

There was harmless and overbearing, and there was manipulation. Keeping secrets from Ivy fell definitively into the latter category.

And *I'd* been keeping a secret from Ivy too.

Guilt stripped me bare from the inside out. Ivy and I were building a relation-ship, and I'd manipulated her. *Unacceptable, Tobias Azumah.*

I shook my head. "I can't keep this from her."

Irena's voice took on a wheedling tone. "Of course you can. Phyllis can run to the grocery store to replace what we broke, can't you, Phyllis? Ivy will never know."

I crossed my arms over my chest. Maybe my body language would convey the point more clearly. "You're right, I misspoke. I *won't* do that to Ivy."

Ivy's mom huffed. "It's not like I tell white lies for the fun of it. I only keep secrets from Ivy to protect her. She has enough to worry about right now."

Her words sounded like an echo from my own mind. How had I found myself in the same category as Irena? How could I have messed this up so badly?

I willed myself to stand taller, to hide any signs of weakness. "I'll never keep secrets from Ivy." *Again. I'll never keep secrets from her* again.

We stared at one another in our own game of chicken. The first to look away would lose. It wouldn't be me.

She glanced away to stare at the throw blanket tucked around her legs.

"She won't be upset with you," I said.

"You don't know that."

Was she more worried about herself or about Ivy? The two of them had been on unsteady ground since Irena and Phyllis crashed our sushi date. This uneasy mother-daughter truce was still in its early stages.

"You're right, I don't. But I know she loves you, and I know she would appreciate that you were trying to put her kitchen back the way it was."

Even as I turned back to the kitchen, I knew I wasn't being completely honest. Ivy would freak out about her mom falling. As much as their relationship was a source of stress, their whole family was just the two of them, and Ivy worried about her mom as much as Irena worried about her daughter.

Irena's voice, so quiet that I almost missed her words, made me pause. "Thank you. For helping me tonight. For being good for Ivy."

Glancing over my shoulder, I studied her face for a tell. If ever there was a moment in my life when I didn't want someone to be pulling my leg, this was it.

She still wouldn't look at me. "I'm sorry I haven't always treated you the best."

If my feelings weren't so crowded with guilt right now, I would be elated. Her words might not sound significant to an outsider, but I'd finally won over

Ivy's mom. Or at least we'd taken the first step. If only the timing were better. If only I didn't feel the need to earn Ivy's trust all over again.

"Thank you," I said.

Clearly uncomfortable with apologizing, her reply was a simple nod.

I returned to the kitchen. Plastic crinkled loudly as I took the trash bag, full of broken bags of flour, sugar, and other ingredients, to Ivy's garbage can outside. I paused, letting the chilled air cool the worries firing through my head.

I wouldn't keep Irena's second fall a secret, but I dreaded telling Ivy.

What I dreaded even more was telling Ivy about her mom's balance issues. Clearly my hunch was right. Clearly I was at least partially responsible for Irena's second fall, because if I'd said something earlier, if I'd insisted on making an appointment with a specialist, if—

Ifs didn't matter right now. I needed to come clean about my feelings for Ivy affecting my work. I had tried to give her all the support she could want. Instead, I'd moved too quickly, let my feelings take me too far, not putting on the brakes when I should. Again. Yvonne was right about me after all.

Earlier today I'd imagined a future with Ivy one way: the two of us, Ivy's house, someday a few little kiddos—or another way: the two of us, Ivy's house, a meddlesome woman creating obstacles at every turn. Earlier today my biggest concern was making peace with Irena's meddling so I could be part of either future Ivy chose.

Now my biggest concern was the irrefutable fact that I'd betrayed Ivy's trust. She had every right to be furious with me. *I* was furious with me.

Reaching into my pocket for my phone, I rehearsed what I needed to say. *Hey, Ivy. Everyone here is fine. Your mom fell. Phyllis was with her. I've checked on her, and she'll have a couple bruises, but otherwise she's fine, and by the way, I'm partially responsible for her fall because I knew she had balance issues, but I didn't say anything. Let's face it, we can't be distracted and risk your mom's health, so let's agree to put a pause on us until your mom is fully recovered, okay?*

Assuming she wanted to pause. Assuming she wouldn't want to call it quits entirely.

I needed to do the right thing: reevaluate a situation where I clearly couldn't stay professional anymore. I needed to start from the beginning again—if Ivy was willing to give me another chance at all.

CHAPTER 37

IVY

Mom: can u pick up milk
Ivy: Sure. Skim, 2%, or whole?
Mom: yes
Ivy: Which one?
Mom: whole

All day I counted the minutes to seeing Toby again. This morning, he'd bounced into the kitchen and cheerfully kissed me, and I'd groggily handed him an English muffin as I slouched out the door. Even knowing he was a morning person didn't ruin him for me.

I'd woken when it was still dark outside. Toby and I had been wrapped up together beneath my comforter like the last time he'd spent the night, only now he'd been deeply asleep, his breaths puffing softly against the top of my head. His warmth had seeped into me.

Now, sitting at my desk at work, I knew I had it bad. And it felt so good.

Nothing about this was simple. Toby played the long game; he'd said so himself. He pursued actual relationships. He generously gave of himself and probably fell in love, and I felt far out of my normal depths right now. Somehow, I didn't mind.

He was rubbing off on me. Superficial relationships didn't sound fun and carefree anymore. They sounded laughable. What a waste, two people giving the bare minimum to get what they wanted, then moving on. It would lack the connection I had with Toby, how he flung himself into whatever he pursued. His way sounded uninhibited and wonderful and worthwhile.

That was what I wanted now, not freedom in the form of meaningless Tinder dates. Of course, I was assuming last night had meant something to him—because what if he stuck around just long enough for sex before he left me like all the others had? Did he like me, or did he like last night?

The question had struck me more viscerally this morning, when Toby had been sprawled beside me. I'd always been tall, but I was built like a telephone pole, so his hulk had dwarfed me. I was completely vulnerable to his physical size and even more vulnerable to my feelings for him. If he was here for the physical benefits, if he wasn't actually here for *me*...

Pulling a Clarice move, I hid in the stairwell and called Mel.

She answered on the first ring. "Hey. Thank you for rescuing me from our scheduling software. It's sabotaging my life today."

"I'm not sure this is much of a rescue since I'm calling to talk about my feelings."

"The day has finally come. I can hardly believe it."

I knew she couldn't see me, but I still rolled my eyes. "I'm hanging up now."

"No! I'm sorry. I'll be serious. Tell me everything. I'm alone in the tutoring center, so I'm all yours."

I paused for a deep breath before I spoke. "I'm not scared of a relationship with Toby anymore. I mean, I'm a little scared. But I think I'm mostly...excited?"

"Okay, keep talking."

"I...don't have anything more than that."

Her tone became teasing. "You do too. Tell me your whys. Why doesn't Toby scare you anymore?"

"Because..." I considered her question. I thought about going back to life without Toby, life with just me and Van and our shared dinners while watching Netflix. It felt empty. The same freedom I'd always craved didn't feel like freedom now. When I thought about a future with Toby, a future with sushi nights and teasing texts and his warm touch, I felt a little trepidation, but mostly I felt thrilled.

Our flirtationship had grown into much more. Somewhere between meeting Toby at the university and last night, we'd grown beyond anything I'd expected.

"Because being alone isn't the same as being strong and independent. Because I feel like myself even when I'm with him."

"Good."

"But, Mel, am I really doing this? What is Ivy Lunden, Team Keep Things Casual, doing with Toby Azumah, Team Happily Ever After? I have more emotional luggage than the airport baggage claim, and he's all happy-go-lucky."

"First of all, he has his baggage, too, he just carries it differently than you do."

Was it wrong to be relieved at her words? Right now the biggest emotion in my life revolved around Mom and how to best enjoy whatever years we had left as a family. She might tell me Toby was too young, he was unsteady, he didn't know what he wanted, but she couldn't deny he made our lives better. These excuses were what she used to cover the truth: Mom was afraid to share me with anyone else.

If anyone could be understanding about the complications in my life, it was Toby. With him, we had fun despite Mom and Phyllis, and maybe even a little because of them.

But what if…

"Secondly," Mel drew me back into the conversation, "I know your dating experience has soured your opinion of love, but if there's anyone you can trust, it's Toby. Do you see that too?"

Fear and excitement twined together, pressing me closer to that cliff I'd been alternately edging toward and steering away from. If there was anyone safe to need in my life, if anyone was safe to trust, it was this gentle giant. If there was any man who wanted more with me, like I wanted with him, it was Toby.

I smiled. "I see it. Thanks, Mel."

She hesitated. "That's it?"

"I thought you'd be happy to talk about my feelings."

"I'm overjoyed to talk about your feelings." She laughed. "When you want to talk about the *rest* of your feelings, give me a call."

"It'll be awhile."

"I'm not so sure."

Staring at my phone, where a new text notification from Mom lit up my screen, I thought of her as I'd left her this morning, eating breakfast in the kitchen. Her injured ankle was propped on the chair in front of her, one hand gripping her mug and another absently scratching Van's head. She'd been alone her whole life, except for me. She'd poured everything she had into raising me, and she'd always struggled to let me go. Was she happy with the way she had only one person, her daughter, in her life? Did she regret it?

The truth was clear: Toby was a pivotal point in my life, opening a door to a future more like my mom's or a future entirely my own.

After texting Toby all day, and knowing I'd see him as soon as I got home, a phone call from him was the last thing I expected as I left the office.

Unlocking my car and tossing my purse onto the passenger seat, I buckled in and put him on speakerphone at the same time. "Hey, handsome."

"Hey. How are you?"

As usual, the gray of my workday vanished, and washes of paprika, indigo, and sunshine filled my head. I would never grow tired of this.

"I'm good, just leaving work." I adjusted the air vents and tucked my mittens beneath my sleeves as far as I could.

"Are you driving?"

Red flags lifted in my mind. "Why? What happened?"

A million scenarios flashed in front of me. Toby in a car accident. Toby getting fired, which was ridiculous, because who didn't like Toby? My mom finally driving Toby over the edge, so he was calling to cancel any further physical therapy. Phyllis and Mom found a new weapon to wage war against the neighbor's dogs.

"Everything is fine. I promise. We're all okay." His voice sounded too calm for a normal conversation. It was a voice I'd heard him use with my mom when she was being particularly stubborn about an exercise.

Fear wrapped its clammy fingers around my throat until I couldn't breathe.

His voice kept that annoyingly calm tone. "Your mom fell moments before I got here. Literal moments. Phyllis was with her when it happened. I've checked her, and she'll have a few bruises, but otherwise she's fine."

My mind flashed back to the night she broke her ankle. The house had been eerily silent. She'd felt so cold. I'd felt so scared and guilty.

"Ivy?"

I hadn't been there for her when she needed me. Again. How many more times could I fail her like this? How much more could her body take? If she had a serious fall, and I wasn't there, and Phyllis wasn't nearby, and Toby didn't show up, what would happen?

His voice broke into my thoughts, coating my worries in bright colors. "Talk to me, Ivy."

"I'm okay." I sounded robotic.

"Take a few deep breaths, okay?"

My body listened before I had a chance to consciously follow his directions. Just a few weeks ago, I would have been annoyed at how quickly he took the lead. But now, more than annoyance, I felt relief. I didn't have to be strong right now, because Toby was willing to do that for me. I would be strong later, but for now, he had my back. Even if my inner feminist cringed, I felt confident this was the right decision. This was what love did to people, how dependency stopped being a flaw and became a form of inner strength, how I could be strong for him, too, when he needed me.

Wait. Love?

"Tell me how you're feeling," he said, unaware of the epiphany I was having.

I couldn't put my emotions into words yet, but I knew Toby would never lie to me. If he said Mom was okay, I believed him. I managed to say another quiet, "I'm okay."

"I promise you we're good here. Your mom is sitting in the living room with Phyllis right now, watching *The Bachelorette*."

Relief loosened my death grip on my phone. Mom was just fine without me. My fears were unfounded, I told myself, even as they continued sticking in my throat.

If it were possible, Toby's voice softened even more. "Please don't worry about her. I'm here. Phyllis is here. Take a few minutes before you start driving."

I rested my head against the cold glass of my car window and closed my eyes. My cheeks felt wet before I registered the tears. Why was I crying? Everything was okay; everything was more than okay, all because I had amazing people in my life. Toby, who always came through for me. Cameron and Mel, who were always just a call away. Even Phyllis, with her nosiness and terrible timing.

Great. I wasn't even thirty, and I was already turning into one of those weepy women I'd always made fun of. Next thing I knew, I'd be crying over that *Better Together* billboard on my drive home.

Better Together. It didn't sound half bad.

"Thank you," I whispered.

As long as Mom was around, I'd always be living my life a little on edge, waiting for the next round of bad news. While at work, I'd always have my phone on me, and while at home, I'd always listen for any sounds of distress. In many ways, I'd be a mother to Mom for the rest of her life.

We paused. I took a few more deep breaths and listened to the sounds of Toby on the other end of the line: a dish clinking, a floorboard squeaking, a door closing softly and deadening the sound of the TV in the living room.

He spoke in a whisper, his words soft in my mind. "I'll be here when you get home tonight. Take your time and drive safe, okay?"

I waited for the old, familiar rush of panic. His words, so similar to something said in an actual relationship, would have sent me running in the past. It was one of the many reasons one-night stands were my favorite mode of connection—or lack thereof. I'd seek out another man to self-sabotage any current guy who seemed to feel too friendly toward me, or I'd drive aimlessly all night for "a change of scene" and not explain where I'd gone, or I'd call in sick and obsessively paint for twenty-four hours straight. With Toby, I'd been waiting to see if he was like all the others. Somehow the steadiness of loneliness had always felt more comforting than companionship.

But now the panic never came. The walls never slid back into place. Did a niggling doubt insist the walls would come back later? Of course. Change doesn't happen overnight. But for this moment, knowing Toby was with me, I felt okay. Talk was cheap, but Toby was rich with action.

"I know you're not going anywhere," I said.

His exhale whistled through my phone. "So you're not freaking out?"

No. Because of you. Thank you.

Here came those tears again.

I let my eyes close. "She's the only family I have."

"She is."

My voice caught in my throat. "She needs to stay with me, doesn't she?"

He hesitated. I could sense him weighing his words, slipping back into healthcare professional mode. "We can talk about this more when you get home, but yes. It doesn't seem likely that she can live alone again."

I tried to process his words. They painted a picture of my future that looked very different from the daydreams that buoyed me through Mom and Phyllis's antics. The old daydreams showed my art career taking off, so I could quit the registrar's office. The new picture showed me searching for a serving spatula in my own kitchen, but good luck with that.

Guilt stung at me. How could I be thinking of my stupid serving spatula right now?

"Any chance we could get lucky and she's faking it?" I quipped.

He chuckled. "If only it were that simple."

Gripping the steering wheel, I took a deep breath. "I'm going to do this. I'm going to do this. How am I going to do this?"

"With me." All signs of hesitation were gone, replaced with absolute certainty. "With Cam and Mel. With Phyllis, as much as she might cause trouble sometimes. We can take turns, or we can find a visiting nurse. Chester can help sometimes, too, as long as you don't marry him."

I couldn't laugh at his joke when all I felt was immense gratitude. Well, I had other feelings, like that pesky guilt, but mostly gratitude. These people in my life. How did I ever get so lucky?

A realization struck me. From the beginning of his call, except for one brief moment, I never once doubted him. My fears were focused on Mom. With any other man, I would've interpreted his call as a breakup conversation. With any other man, I would've assumed he'd gotten what he wanted last night, and now he was done. During this entire conversation, the thought had never even crossed my mind.

Better Together indeed.

"Thank you," I whispered. "I'm good to drive home now. See you soon."

CHAPTER 38

IVY

Ivy: Mom fell again, but she's okay. Toby was there to help.
Cameron: That's my man! Are you okay?
Mel: We can stop by tonight if you need us.
Ivy: Thanks, but I'm okay for now. I'll let you know if I need anything.
Cameron: She has Toby now. We've been demoted, Mel.
Mel: Being demoted has never made me so giddy. Ivy's in looooove!
Ivy: Ugh. Kill me now.

As soon as I pulled into the garage, Toby was there, closing the door to the kitchen behind him. I left my work bag in my car, barely managing to park and unbuckle before I darted out of the car.

"She's still watching TV, so there's nothing to worry—"

I flung myself at him, off that cliff's edge. He caught me.

It'd been mere hours since we'd kissed, but I missed him like it'd been years. He kissed me the same way, long and deep, his hands spread across my back like he couldn't touch enough of me. I pressed closer to him, my anticipation fraying into impatience.

Falling couldn't get any better than this.

Toby hummed against my lips. "My day is a solid ten after that."

I laughed. "Same."

He tucked a strand of hair behind my ear. "I thought you'd be stressed out when you got here."

When he started to move away, I pressed closer to him. "I had a realization."

He paused, his brows lifting. "Realizations are good. Care to share?"

How did I begin to tell him that I now knew my supposed strength was just a façade? How could I explain that the independence I'd been so proud of my entire life was simply a way to keep others distant and myself safe? More like theoretically safe, because that distance hadn't actually done much good, now that I looked back at it.

The words lingered at the front of my mind, tinted with Toby's bright colors. The bottom of the cliff rushed closer, faster, bigger. Instead of turning away from it, I leaned in for a faster fall.

I took a deep breath. "It's okay for me to need people."

Toby paused, frowning more than I would've expected, before he nodded. "Okay."

I needed to do better than that, say more than that. There was so much I wanted to tell him about the edge I'd just leapt off and into his arms, about sitting in my car and crying from gratitude. Mel was right. I should've practiced talking about my feelings more. This felt as rusty as my childhood bike. But by the way his hands still pressed against my back, he didn't seem fazed by what felt like my inarticulate fumblings.

I tried again. "I mean, it's not weak for me to need people. I've spent my life trying to be the kind of strong I thought I needed to be. But there's strength in a community too."

"Like strength in numbers."

I nodded. "I wanted you to know that…" *That you're welcome to turn my life upside down any time. That you're an integral part of that upside-down life, so I'm vulnerable to you despite the off chance you'll leave, but somehow that doesn't scare me when I know it's you.* "I wanted you to know that I'm keeping you."

Now I sounded like a stalker.

"What I'm trying to say is that you have an important part in my life. And I'm happy to make space for you for as long as you want to be a part of all the craziness."

Well. Those weren't the words I wanted to say, exactly. But these feelings were stuck in my throat, and they were so new, and—

His voice sounded raspy when he spoke. "I'll take any space you give me."

Sweet relief. I wasn't certain what to say next. I wasn't certain I wouldn't ruin whatever was between us. But I knew together, we could do anything.

I tugged at his hair to drag him down for another kiss, pulling at his lower lip when we parted for air.

"Tease," he grumbled. "You're ruining me."

"Can't handle the challenge?"

His expression softened. "I can handle anything for you."

Even my heart? Can you handle that? I think maybe you can.

When I walked into the living room, Phyllis sat a little straighter, and Mom fluffed her throw blanket.

I muted the TV and sat on the coffee table in front of Mom, facing her. "I heard what happened. Are you okay?"

"I'm perfectly fine. It wasn't anything serious."

Phyllis plumped a throw pillow behind herself. "I could've helped her up if I'd had a little more time."

"We were managing just fine," Mom said.

There had to be a way to convince Mom that she couldn't keep her old independence. Life was different now. I was learning to accept it. She'd been happy enough about moving in with me, but this stubbornness would get her hurt.

Toby sat on a chair next to Mom, resting his elbows on his knees and directing his next words at her. "Let's talk about what happened. When did the dizziness start?"

"I was only a little dizzy," she said.

He studied her for a moment. "I think we should look into vestibular issues."

I squinted, thinking of our earlier conversations. I didn't remember him ever mentioning that term before.

He noticed my confusion. "Vestibular issues are like balance problems." He spoke confidently, but his gaze rested on the floor. "Like the dizziness you mentioned experiencing tonight. Have either of you noticed balance problems in the past?"

"I…don't know?" My eyebrows crept up my forehead. Between the doctor appointments and surgery and meds, there was a lot I didn't know. But surely I would've noticed Mom stumbling around like she'd had one too many margaritas. At least I imagined that was what balance issues looked like.

"Your mom is showing good progress with her ankle. Her range of motion is

—" He'd switched to his physical therapist voice, the one he used with Mom.

I lifted a hand. "Just tell me in non-medical terms. I can handle it."

He sighed, staring at his hands. "Her mobility isn't improving like it should. At first I thought it was a mental or emotional block, like she was scared to move around on her own, which is understandable after a serious fall, but now I wonder if she's been having balance issues for a while."

Scared to move around on her own. Images flickered through my mind. The stack of water glasses on Mom's nightstand so she wouldn't have to get up in the middle of the night. The dirty dishes in the sink took on a sinister tint, like she couldn't stand steady long enough to rinse a plate.

"You think that's why she fell the first time?" I asked.

"Possibly. Hard to say."

If Mom had balance issues, vestibular issues, whatever issues, what about her quality of life moving forward? Dollar signs flashed in front of my eyes at the thought of a retirement home or visiting nurse.

I tried to swallow, but my mouth felt too dry. "What does that mean in terms of care?"

His tone turned regretful. "I don't know. I promise I'm not being cagey on purpose. A solid answer will take more time to figure out. But her second fall, which happened purely because of dizziness, is a fairly strong indication that my hunch was right."

I glanced at Mom. Her usually straight posture had wilted into a slump in her recliner. She stared at the throw blanket on her lap.

I wrapped my arms around myself, wishing Toby was hugging me instead.

But Toby stayed where he was, concern wrinkling his forehead. "It could mean more physical therapy. It could mean needing more long-term care. It could also mean needing professional help."

Mom's health was clearly in jeopardy. If I'd noticed sooner, maybe I could've saved her a broken ankle.

Toby's eyes shone with sympathy. "I know that's not news you want to hear." He opened his mouth to say more, looked toward my mom, and stopped.

My nod was automatic. "That's okay. Thanks for telling us. I'd rather know than not."

I thought of Toby's words on the phone. I couldn't do this on my own. But with Toby, Cameron, Mel, and even Phyllis, we could take care of Mom. I shoved away the guilt for not noticing Mom's dizziness, for my daydreams of an art career. No more judging myself, and no more pity for my life as it was.

Instead, I clutched at the gratitude I'd felt earlier. My friends were good people. We would figure out what to do. Everything would be fine. Toby was a big part of that—an important part.

I turned to Toby. "Do you know how to do balance tests?"

"Sure, but you'll need a neurology specialist to have an official diagnosis, or even an ear, nose, and throat doctor since balance issues sometimes start in the inner ear."

"I'm curious. Let's try some." I stood from my perch on the coffee table and gestured him forward.

Mom balked with about half as much spunk as she normally would have. "What tests? I didn't agree to any tests."

I moved to sit next to Phyllis on the couch. "But they might help us figure out ways to prevent future falls. Right?" I glanced at Toby for affirmation, but he didn't meet my gaze.

"I fell because I'm growing older."

"Just humor me, okay?"

I watched as he maneuvered her through various exercises, his hands capable. As she struggled through the motions, he explained what vestibular issues meant, why they happened, what could be done about them.

"Well," Mom said after a few of the tests. "What's the verdict?"

Toby lowered her ankle. "You should call an ENT doctor. I can get some contact information for you at work tomorrow. They'll be able to give you an official diagnosis."

"But what do *you* think?" I asked.

His chest broadened on a deep inhale, his dark eyes fixed on me. "It looks like vestibular issues."

I nodded, already thinking ahead. "So what can we do starting immediately, in practical terms?"

"We'll need to set some rules about what you can and can't do when you're home alone," Toby said to Mom. He began outlining steps, like keeping her phone fully charged and on hand at all times, or having Phyllis come over to help while I was gone during the workday, or maybe considering a medical alarm necklace, which she instantly refused.

I watched and listened, feeling relief ease over me. Even if it weren't for the bright colors in my head, I would find his voice soothing and optimistic. *We have a problem*, it seemed to say, *but together, we've got this.*

CHAPTER 39

IVY

Mel: Happy your mom is okay, and glad Toby was there for you. Have you talked to Toby about your feelings yet?

We spent the rest of the evening exactly like I'd hoped we would. Toby stayed for dinner. The four of us—because of course Phyllis stayed too—dished out leftovers and then watched the latest episode of *The Bachelorette*.

My first hint something was wrong happened when Toby helped me add more toppings to our leftover salad. Usually he entertained me with ridiculous stories from his workday, dramatizing each part with gusto. Normally he used every opportunity to brush his hand against mine when I handed him a plate, or he leaned close to reach for an ingredient.

Not tonight. He didn't tell any stories. Our fingers never touched. He didn't happen to need a utensil from the drawer beside where I stood. He was quiet, withdrawn even. His smiles came a moment too late, a wattage too dim compared to his usual Toby-level brightness. I wasn't sure what worry looked like on Toby, but I was starting to get an idea.

Thinking I was imagining it, I leaned a little closer to him on the couch while we watched TV. His only response was to stare at where our thighs touched.

My stomach bottomed out. I'd been on a high ever since our phone call in the parking lot at work, and I'd been soaring ever since our conversation in the garage. Now I was in a free fall. What had I missed? Had I said something? Had I *not* said something?

Not that we could talk about this with Mom and Phyllis sitting nearby, arguing in favor of their chosen bachelors. They would lose interest in their debate the instant they thought our conversation was worth eavesdropping on.

Old instincts told me to cut my losses and run. I shushed them immediately. He'd told me he wasn't going anywhere. He'd told me he could handle anything I gave him.

Before my imagination could wail like a banshee about the millions of ways our relationship was over before it started, I reminded myself of the ways Toby and I were good for one another. His optimism balanced out my pessimism; his lively energy complemented my mellowness; his positivity bolstered my cynicism; and I hoped my traits anchored him more firmly in reality than he otherwise would be. I could be more when he was less. I could also be there for him when he needed me.

Maybe that was all this moment was. For the first time since I'd known him, Toby needed me. Something was bothering him. And I could, *would* help.

Yes, a big part of me worried about whatever Toby was facing. But stubbornness worked both ways, and I would happily wrestle my way into his life like he'd wrestled his way into mine.

My thoughts were interrupted with a loud protest from Van, who reluctantly left Phyllis's lap as she stood to go home. Mom also stood, making her way toward the stair lift and telling us goodnight.

Toby and I carried plates to the kitchen. Neither of us tried to start a conversation as we listened to Mom's movements upstairs, the floorboards creaking and her bedroom door finally squeaking shut. I'd never known Toby to go so long in silence.

He spoke as soon as the house quieted. "Could we talk for a minute before I head home?"

Is it possible for my stomach to bottom out even lower? I'd hoped he would spend the night.

"What's on your mind?" I asked.

He moved to the other side of the room, his motions slow, like distance between us was necessary but unwanted. He shoved his hands deep into his pockets, stretching the fabric taut. He looked everywhere but at me. "I haven't told you everything."

I grinned. "What, are you secretly married?"

He frowned, unmoved by my humor. "No."

This was more serious than I thought. Toby's default facial expression was a smile.

I mentally reviewed the last few hours. Earlier, in the garage, I'd told him how I felt, or as best I could, and he'd responded with assurances. He'd said he wasn't going anywhere. I still believed that. So what was going on?

He paced a few steps in front of me, pivoted, and then paced the other direction. "I knew your mom would fall again. I mean, I didn't *know* know, but I knew it was likely because of the vestibular issues. I should've told you."

I frowned. "But you weren't sure of her vestibular issues. You only had a hunch."

"I ignored that hunch because I was worried about your stress levels, and I didn't want anything to ruin what we…" He let out an exasperated sigh. "It doesn't matter. I should've told you."

He should've told me; that was true. He'd overstepped, like when he'd tried to protect me from his brothers' noisiness. But his good intentions tempered any annoyance I felt. Only several hours ago we'd spent the night together—we were still sorting out our relationship. Sometimes we would triumph, and sometimes we would fall flat on our backs.

Maybe it was my euphoria from my earlier revelation, or maybe it was his overwrought concern that left me feeling optimistic, but the conflicting emotions in his expression seemed to me like a mere blip in our day, not an obstacle in our relationship.

"Like I said earlier," he continued, "I can refer you to experts who can give you the help you need to take care of her. If…if you prefer, I'll find a different physical therapist to continue our arrangement."

"Don't be ridiculous."

Nobody could replace Toby. It wasn't just about the salted sidewalks and dedicated attention to Mom's ankle. It was about all the little ways Toby was involved in my life, all the ways I'd come to not just need him but enjoy him. I wasn't willing to let that go because of misplaced regret.

As he scrubbed a hand down his face, I caught a glimpse of the emotions in his eyes. This wasn't just about professional responsibility. He felt guilty.

Now was when I needed to step up to his side, wrap my arms around his middle, and tell him everything would be okay because we could handle it. The two of us could handle anything.

I moved toward him. "Is Mom in the hospital?"

Toby stilled, watching me.

"Did she reinjure her ankle?" I closed the distance a little more.

"That's not the point. I betrayed your trust. I kept this—"

"I probably would've done the same thing in your position," I said.

He didn't answer, looking at me with wariness and concern. And…anger? No, remorse.

Toby reached for his coat and duffel bag, tucked under the kitchen table from earlier. "I let my feelings get in the way of taking care of your mom as her physical therapist, of helping you as your…" His throat moved in a swallow. "I'm sorry."

Over the past weeks, he'd kept me laughing when I needed it most, and he'd held me when I fell apart at my lowest moment. I wanted to be there for him now that he was struggling. Because that was what you did when you loved someone.

My mouth opened, but no words came out.

Each one of the walls I'd built to protect myself had disappeared the moment I'd decided to step off the cliff and trust him to catch me. I had a name for that step. Love.

Maybe I'd always felt this way about him, with the way that intrinsic part of me had perked up and paid attention the moment I saw the colors of his voice for the first time, with an instinctive part of myself that my conscious mind had no control over. But now that my conscious mind knew, too, my chest felt like it was about to rupture with a kaleidoscope of emotions. I wanted to tell him I loved him, I wanted him to lean on me like I'd leaned on him so many times before, and I reached out—

Toby took a step back, a pain-filled frown on his face. "I'll be back to check in on you all tomorrow night."

Without another word, he turned and walked away.

For several moments, I stared at the empty place where he'd stood. Van padded into the kitchen, twining around my legs until I picked him up. Absentmindedly, I stroked his fur, analyzing the conversation we'd just had, exploring my thoughts, coming to one conclusion.

Toby was worth fighting for.

CHAPTER 40

TOBY

Ivy: Missed hearing from you today. Can't wait to see you tonight.

All night, I brainstormed ways I could earn back Ivy's trust, jotting down a list in my notes app. The majority of my guilt centered around this truth: I'd broken her trust, which I'd worked so hard to gain, hurting her and her mom, when it was the last thing I ever wanted to do.

I also wrote a speech, complete with an apology and tangible objectives I could use as measurable outcomes to prove I'd learned from my mistake in future months.

Assuming Ivy wanted me to stick around for future months.

I wouldn't give up on us unless Ivy directly said that's what she wanted. So I needed to win her back. With a speech and tangible objectives and maybe some Take It Cheesy takeout, too.

By the time morning came, my eyes felt permanently squinted from so much time on my phone in my dark bedroom.

The workday wasn't much better. Everything was a struggle. Traffic was extra slow, my patients were extra stubborn, and Deke's clipboard was extra clipboard-y. No, I didn't know what that meant, but it was true.

When I got to Ivy's doorstep, I'd rehearsed my speech two dozen times. I'd memorized my list of ideas to earn back her trust. I was as ready as I'd ever be.

Tonight was Mission Win Back Ivy. Failure wasn't an option. *This tape will self-destruct in five seconds.*

With the *Mission Impossible* theme song playing in my mind, I debated opening the door with my spare key and letting myself in, like I'd always done. Somehow that habit felt too personal tonight. Spare keys, and the freedom to let yourself into someone else's home, was reserved for people you trusted. Ivy might not trust me right now. I didn't blame her.

I knocked, deja vu taking me back to the beginning, when I'd stood here with a bouquet not too long ago.

Ivy opened the door. Confusion creased her brow, but a smile curved her red lipstick. "Hey. I'm glad you came tonight."

I blinked. Ivy being glad to see me wasn't part of my practiced script. If only someone could stand behind her and hold up cue cards for my next line.

"Did you forget your key?"

"No, I just…" Didn't want to overstep again? Didn't want to push too hard? How was I already doing this wrong, and how was Ivy acting so normal? Maybe she wasn't upset about this like I was, but I'd hurt her, and we'd parted poorly last night. By all appearances, she'd shrugged it off while I spent all night agonizing about how to recapture what we had before.

I cleared my throat. "How are you? How's your mom?"

"Come in and find out." She moved aside.

Stepping across the threshold, I nodded at Phyllis, who sat in her usual spot on the couch. Irena was in her recliner. They both watched me.

I set down my duffel bag, which I'd stocked with various braces and Icy Hot bottles and patches. I'd wanted to be prepared for anything. "How are you feeling today?"

"I'm fine." Irena's eyes fixed on me in an open stare. "A little sore, but fine."

We paused, the air thick with unspoken words.

Ivy straightened the hem of her black shirt. "Would you like a glass of water?"

I nodded. "Sure. Yes. Great."

She stepped around me and into the kitchen.

Now even Van watched me from his vantage point on the back of the couch, his eyes peering out of his fluffy fur. I shifted on my feet, half expecting Rod Serling to walk into the room and introduce me to *The Twilight Zone*. But instead of Rod Serling's voice, I heard the TV volume increase, blaring a commercial about a cruise vacation being exactly what New Englanders needed this time of year.

The TV must be acting up. I should watch some YouTube tutorials and see if I could fix it, or maybe I could find someone—

But Irena's hand rested on the remote, her finger on the volume button. In a gesture I'd seen Ivy make a million times, Irena rolled her eyes. She lifted her hand in a "go on then" gesture toward the kitchen.

Was Irena…helping me, giving me and Ivy some obviously much-needed privacy? This really was *The Twilight Zone*.

I didn't waste time. I found Ivy in the kitchen, an empty glass in her hand as she faced the sink.

"I'm sorry. I let my feelings blur the lines when it came to your mom's care, and I won't let it happen again."

Before I could finish speaking, Ivy had wrapped her arms around me in a hug. She felt perfect, her blond hair soft beneath my chin, her fingers splayed against my back. But I couldn't let myself get distracted. Resting my palms on her shoulders, I tried to put some space between us so I could continue my apology. Her arms tightened further.

I half-heartedly tried to loosen her grip. "Let me finish my speech."

Her answer was muffled. "You don't need to give a speech. I'm not letting you go."

"But it was a really good speech."

She tilted her head back just enough to look at me. "Then you can finish your speech like this."

My hands, the rebels, moved in a slow slide from her shoulders to her upper back, then lower. At the expression on her face, the worries that had weighed so heavily on me for the last twenty-four hours began to still.

What was I doing again? Oh, yeah. Speech. But who could think about speeches when Ivy fit snugly against me, her arms banded around my waist? What did speeches matter when a wisp of blond hair drew my attention to the sensitive place just beneath her ear?

Speech…

"Honestly," I admitted, "I can't remember it now."

She pretended to think this over. "Wonder what could be distracting you?"

I closed my eyes, struggling to focus. *Mistake*, my brain warned a moment too late, because now I felt her rib cage rising and falling with each breath.

"The gist," I managed, "is that I feel responsible for your mom's fall yesterday, and I feel guilty for hurting you, and—"

"You didn't hurt me."

My eyes opened. "But I betrayed your trust when I wasn't honest with you."

She tilted her head to the side, considering. "Why can't I be the judge of whether I'm hurt or betrayed by something you did?"

Well. I had no counterpoint to that. Ivy's hurt and betrayed trust was a foregone conclusion, or so I'd thought. Of all the ways I'd imagined this conversation playing out, it wasn't anything like this. I mentally ran my script through my brain's shredder.

"Yes," Ivy said, "you should've told me sooner, but I don't feel betrayed. That's too strong of a word. How could I ever be mad at you when you've done so much for me?"

She was letting everything from yesterday go? Just like that?

"So I don't need to start from the beginning to woo you all over again?"

She smiled. "Consider me wooed, okay?"

I wanted to twirl her around the small kitchen, but I settled for resting my forehead against hers. Relief swept away my fears.

She inched onto her tiptoes, pressing her lips against mine in the briefest of touches. "Next time you need to process something, stay with me. We could've talked last night."

I lingered, kissing the corner of her mouth, liking how her red lipstick smudged because of me. "I wanted to stay. You have no idea how much I wanted to. But I have this habit of jumping in headfirst. I didn't want to do that with you before you were comfortable with it. I didn't want to stay last night if all I was doing was running too far ahead."

"You weren't, but even if you were, we still could've talked it over."

"Next time I'll stay." I leaned closer, eager to kiss her again.

She leaned away to stop me. "I want to help you sometimes too. I know my life is chaotic right now, but that doesn't mean I can't support you the same way you support me."

That sounded nice, being able to rely on someone. It also sounded foreign. With nearly everyone else in my life, I was the supportive one. How would it feel to bank on someone else for a change?

I tucked my face into her neck. "I'm not used to asking for help."

"I wasn't either until you came along. How the tables have turned."

Smiling, I leaned lower, determined to smudge her lipstick even more, but she tilted her head away again.

"We need to clear up something else," she said. "You're my boyfriend. Last night, we left your last sentence hanging, and it kept me up all night. I wanted to clarify, and since I don't have Mel's way with words, I'll just be direct. I'm your girlfriend, and you're my boyfriend. We're together."

Warmth radiated through me. This was more than I could've hoped for when I spent all night debating between saying "I'm sorry" and "I apologize." I'd thought I'd pushed too far, too hard. I thought I'd wanted more than she did.

"Yesterday," she continued, "I told you you're an important part of my life, and you agreed to take any space I could give you. I think we should see what our space together looks like." She tugged me closer. "What's the best that can happen?"

CHAPTER 41

IVY

Ivy: Yes, I told him my feelings. All is right with the world.
Mel: ALL of your feelings?
Ivy: Hush.

Later that night, Toby sat on my bed and talked about his day at work while I stood in my en suite bathroom, washing my face free of makeup. Mom was in bed, and Phyllis had gone back to her house, so it was finally just the two of us. Toby was explaining Deke's spontaneous handshake.

Toby's fingers traced a seam in my comforter. "He wants to team up with me to update the employee handbook. I'm not surprised he's redoing the handbook, but I'm surprised he asked me. I think Hudson put him up to it."

Did he really not see how admired and liked he was by his patients and colleagues? Deke may have been the supervisor in name, but Toby had more experience and people skills.

I glanced at him in the mirror's reflection. "Maybe Hudson put him up to it. Maybe not."

"What would be the other option? It has to be Hudson. He told me to include Deke more, which I've been doing. I guess 'inclusion' extends to working on a project together."

"Maybe Deke wants to be friends with you."

"Are robots capable of friendship?"

I rolled my eyes. "I'm serious. Everyone at your job loves you. I saw that even on my first and only visit. Maybe Deke wants to learn from you. Or maybe he just genuinely wants to spend more time with you and can't figure out a natural way to do it."

His expression turned skeptical. "We are talking about the same Deke, right? My supervisor? Remember that time you told off said supervisor right in front of me? And then got mad at me for not telling him off myself?"

I lifted my hands. "I'm just saying, maybe he has some issues that make it harder for him to get along with people. Sometimes synesthesia makes it hard for me to get along with someone. I used to have a coworker whose voice sounded like vomit brown. I could hardly tolerate her for two minutes. Maybe Deke struggles with social skills because of something like that. Some variation of OCD, or social anxiety, I don't know."

Toby's eyes fixed on the seam in my comforter again, his brows pulled together in thought.

Stepping out of the bathroom and toward my closet, I smiled at him. "Not everyone is a natural social butterfly like you are. Give Deke a chance to learn how to be human."

"Maybe you're right," Toby said. "Look at you cracking the Deke code."

Despite his lighthearted quip, I could hear the appreciation in his voice. He would tuck away this conversation for later thought.

I faced away from him as I shimmied out of my pants and sweater and slipped into my nightshirt. Feigning innocence, I moved past him and crawled halfway under the covers before he tackled me.

"Tease." He burrowed his face into my hair, sliding under the covers with me and tugging us close together.

"You knew that the day we met." I tried to turn in his arms so I could kiss him, but he held me still.

"Go to sleep."

I bristled. "You don't get to tell me when to sleep."

It wasn't fair that he could keep me in place with one tree trunk of an arm while he reached to turn off my bedside lamp.

"You're right, I'm not that patronizing. But don't think I missed those yawns you tried to cover up all night."

"I'm still awake enough for some fun." I wriggled against him.

Toby held me tighter until I couldn't move. "Let's give it ten minutes. If you're still awake by then, we'll reevaluate."

"Reevaluate? This isn't a physical therapy session," I scoffed. "Make it five minutes."

His laugh puffed warm air against the back of my neck. "So you agree with me? You don't think you'll be awake in ten minutes?"

I grumbled under my breath. "Fine. Ten. Just to prove you wrong."

"Goodnight, Ivy."

"See you in ten."

I hated that he was right. I woke up a few hours later, still wrapped in his tree trunk arms, his chest rising and falling behind me.

I pictured how the last few days would have gone without him. I would've come home to find Mom and Phyllis way over their heads in a situation they couldn't handle. They could manage online shopping for a BB gun, sure, but for bird-like Phyllis to help Mom back to standing, juggling crutches and a healing ankle? Disaster. I would've rushed to call an ambulance again, costing us more than we could afford to pay. I would've hyperventilated on the phone a second time. Instead I had reheated leftovers for dinner and watched some TV with Toby, Mom, and Phyllis.

I pictured how the day would have gone if Mom had never broken her ankle and still lived at her own house. My home would've been quiet. Van would've meowed for his dinner. After some TV and relaxing, I might have painted, might have gone to bed early.

My silent home had been my safe haven from the world. Now the thought of retreating to silence at the end of the day felt empty. Now, walking through my door to Mom and Phyllis bickering about their reality TV shows, hearing Toby's rumbly laughter, watching Van glare from his perch on top of the refrigerator— those sounds and the colors they brought were my picture of home.

I wasn't sure what that meant. I wasn't sure what to do with the feelings circling in my head and heart. But I knew I needed some paint.

As soundlessly as possible, I crept out of bed and down the hall to my studio. I slipped the key out of hiding and unlocked the door. My blank canvases greeted me in the warm overhead light. I picked up a brush.

Hours later, I set down my paintbrush and stared at my canvas.

I'd been wrong about kissing my creativity goodbye. It was alive and well, and the proof stared back at me.

The sketches I'd doodled at work came in handy. I'd posted them around the room, choosing different canvases that fit each piece. Then I'd tackled each one, bringing my black-and-white scraps to life with bright colors and thick textures.

These paintings were worth something. Snapping a few pictures with my phone, I saved them to edit and share later. Time for Ivy Lunden to re-emerge onto the art scene. The worst I could do was fail so completely that I had to quit all over again. I'd survived that once. I could survive it again.

My favorite piece leaned against the far wall in a place of honor. Brilliant, bold colors, kaleidoscoping into prisms and angles. The colors wove between a line of dark paint distinctly outlining a man's broad frame.

Toby.

I stood from my art stool, arching my back until it cracked. Despite the kinks, I felt equal parts relaxed and energized. Painting always did this to me. Sleep seemed unlikely tonight, even as appealing as it sounded to curl up next to Toby for the last few hours until morning.

After locking my studio behind me, I made my way downstairs, cringing when the old floorboards creaked. The light from the refrigerator outlined exactly what I wanted: my box of sangria chilling on the top shelf. It made a satisfying splash into my wineglass.

Sipping slowly, I wandered through my home. Mom's recliner sat empty in the living room. Her African violets peeked their little purple faces through the fuzzy green leaves, and Van sat in their midst on the windowsill, his tail twitching as he watched me from his faux jungle. I took in the other ways Mom's life mixed with mine: her novels on the coffee and end tables, her knitting needles poking from a bag of yarn, her favorite mug with a coffee ring stain at the bottom.

I left the living room, settling on the bottom step next to the stair lift. I ran a finger along its metallic edge and paused where Chester had drilled screws into the wall. A little bit of the paint and plaster had chipped away.

These changes were permanent now. But what did "permanent" mean in the face of Mom's health?

What was it Toby had said about grief the other night? Maybe grief was what Mom felt after her fall or selling her house, being forced to give up what she'd always known. Maybe we were both grieving in our own ways over the realization that we had limited time to spend together.

A memory drifted back, of me and Toby in the kitchen when Mom interrupted, riding down the stair lift. Its motor had the most grating whirr. The sound smeared rust inside my head, flakes flying everywhere. And then Toby had danced with Mom until she laughed.

This was part of my future now. Obtrusive stair lifts, interrupted romantic moments. But what else was part of my future now? Laughter with Toby, finding humor and joy during one of the most stressful seasons of my life. Love with Toby, even if it was too soon for me to tell him.

In the middle of havoc, Toby was the one who kept me going. He was unstoppable in the best possible ways. The calm to my chaos. The light to my shadow. The Alfred Stieglitz to my Georgia O'Keeffe.

Feeling oddly energized and optimistic, I stood. Time to go to the basement and sort through some of Mom's boxes. I would set them aside for her review and then hopefully donate them. My home wasn't big enough for two individual households. We were a family, after all.

CHAPTER 42

TOBY

Toby: About that make-up date. What if I took you to a different sushi restaurant?
Ivy: Let's just skip ahead to your second-date agenda: pizza and a movie.
Toby: Whoo! Look at us blazing through my dating plan! We'll be in love before you know it.

Sprawled across Ivy's bed, I stared at the dark ceiling above me, watching the reflected headlights of passing cars. I wasn't sure when Ivy left, but she'd been gone long enough that her side of the bed was cold to the touch. I didn't like it one bit.

This had been happening for several nights now. We would fall asleep together, and no matter how much I ordered myself to hold her all night, she would disappear at some point. I'd wake up and sit here. Worrying.

I wasn't a worrier. I was a mover and a shaker. I saw a need (Ivy's icy sidewalk) and I filled it (salting the sidewalk). I didn't sit around gnawing over decisions or emotions. I did things, I did them efficiently and optimistically, and I did them well. But Ivy's late-night escapades had me nervous. Where did she go? What did she do? Would she feel cornered if I asked?

Most importantly, did I have a right to ask? I thought I did. She'd said it herself—we were together. The fact that I had strong feelings for her didn't mean she had strong feelings for me, but given how she jumped into my arms when she came home at night, she felt something. Not to mention the incredible sex. Not that anyone was counting. (It was eight times, and I was totally counting.) But that didn't mean Ivy wouldn't bristle if I asked her where she ran off to each night.

So I worried.

I remembered all the times Cameron had agonized over Mel, telling me his frustrations. At the time, it'd made me twitchy. Why couldn't the man just make a decision? Now here I was, doing the same thing. I much preferred being on the giving end of the advice.

Another car drove past, lighting up the ceiling into fragments of white. I couldn't spend forever sitting here like this. I tapped out a quick text to her phone, but she didn't reply.

I settled on a plan. The best way to play this was to act like I woke up needing a glass of water. People did that all the time. She wouldn't think anything of it. She'd shrug and go back to doing whatever she was doing. I could satisfy my worry that she was okay without being too clingy, and, bonus, I could see what she was up to. Perfectly mature, adult behavior on my part. And if I found her hiding bodies under the floorboards, we would have a mature, adult conversation about her hobby and how it would affect our relationship moving forward.

The hallway was empty. Her mom's bedroom door was closed, and so was the art studio. The kitchen light was on, but Ivy wasn't there. Van followed me on my journey, weaving between my legs in the living room before he sat in front of the basement door and meowed as if to say, "Over here, dummy."

Maybe I was anthropomorphizing a cat. I didn't care, because he was right, the crack beneath the basement door shined a bright streak of light across the floor.

The steps creaked ominously under my weight. Van wisely chose to stay upstairs, distrustfully eyeing the musty cobwebs in the rafters. Boxes towered nearly to the dusty ceiling, creating a fortress within Ivy's house. I heard something from the far-left corner. Was that…hiccupping?

"Ivy?" I made my way through the maze of boxes. "What are you doing down here?"

Rounding a corner, I found her sitting on the floor, her face crumpled in sobs. A shoebox sat in front of her, its contents scattered all around.

I was by her side in a few long strides, my hands on her cheeks. Tears flowed freely from sad, red-rimmed eyes. Ivy wasn't a pretty crier. Somehow knowing that drew me closer to her.

"What's wrong?"

I needed to help her; I needed to fix this, whatever it took. I glared at the boxes surrounding her—were they too dusty? I could bring an air purifier. My eyes darted to the ceiling—spiders and other creepy crawlies were probably lurking in dark corners, and even though her sobs were a little dramatic for arachnophobia, in my opinion, I wasn't about to judge, so I should bring a pesticide and—

Shifting a box out of the way, I sat next to her and pulled her close. "Tell me what's wrong."

My words only made her sob harder. My stomach dropped.

She handed me some papers from the shoebox in front of her. "It's all my a-art stuff." She hiccupped. "She kept it all this t-time."

One arm still wrapped around her, I used my free hand to sift through the clippings and flyers and random drawings. The artwork ranged from a lopsided dragonfly with a childish signature, to a napkin with detailed sketches of hands at a variety of angles and a date and signature from last year. Ivy had found her mom's box of keepsakes, treasures showing her little artist's growth from child-hood to adulthood. It was beautiful.

Relief melted through my chest. "This is why you're crying?"

"She saved all this stuff, all this time. She loves me so much." Ivy sobbed harder.

I didn't quite follow the reasoning, but that didn't mean I couldn't hold her through it.

Her next words were whispered. "I save stuff from you."

My heart stumbled, beating twice as quickly when it recovered. "You do?"

She nodded, her hair slipping around her face so I couldn't see her clearly. "The sticky note you left in the kitchen about eggplant parmigiana that first night. The red necktie you forgot here after our date. Our fortunes from our fortune cookies."

Apparently the Lunden women were like crows, collecting shiny bits that struck their fancy. And it meant she felt more for me than she was willing to say in words.

"Stalking me is nothing to be sad about, Ivy."

Stalking me was wonderful news, actually. Stalk away, baby. What else did she need? My car keys? Social security card?

A fresh wave of tears strangled her voice. "I'm not stalking you, and I'm not sad, because I love you, and it's scary, and I wanted to wait to tell you until I had the right words, or maybe a painting that could show you how I feel—"

My arms instinctively tightened around her.

She loved me. *She* loved *me.* She *loved* me. Could I ever repeat the words enough that they lost the ability to snatch my breath from my lungs?

I'd thought I would have to bide my time. Wait a year, maybe longer, before I could tell her how I really felt. I didn't think she could admit her feelings to herself yet, let alone to me.

Now here we were. *She loves me.*

But she still didn't sound happy. She sounded miserable.

I leaned my head against hers, inhaling the scent of her shampoo. "I love you too," I whispered into her hair. "I'm scared too."

"Nothing scares you."

"You scare me."

"I do?"

"Mm-hm. Your ugly cry is a force to be reckoned with."

She rolled her eyes at me.

"My love for you scares me," I said. "It's bigger and deeper than anything I've ever felt before."

Taking her hand and holding it to my heart felt a little overdramatic, but a moment like this needed some dramatics. "I love you, Ivy Lunden."

I watched her face closely. After several moments of studying me, her lower lip stopped trembling, and some of the tears cleared from her eyes. She blinked up at me. I tucked some loose hair behind her ear, letting my fingers brush along her cheek.

She reached for me, her free arm wrapping around my neck, her lips firm against my cheek, then moving toward my mouth. I complied, of course.

We landed in a heap among the boxes.

Yes. I would've fist-pumped if I hadn't been so busy kissing her, holding her everywhere my greedy hands could reach. Each movement was better than the last.

EPILOGUE

IVY

Several months later

Ivy: Can't wait to see you all at 7!
Mel: Ivy? What alien abducted you and replaced you with someone sociable?
Cameron: We're so proud of our little social butterfly.
Ivy: It's all Toby's fault.
Mel: But we're serious—we ARE so proud of you!

Colors. Every shade spun in my mind. I delighted in it, closing my eyes for a moment to watch the variations twist and unfold.

Voices of every age and octave surrounded me. I didn't listen to the words. What mattered was the thrum that echoed within and without me, Mel's higher pitches from across the room when Cameron leaned close and teased her, Toby's rumbles of laughter as he became best friends with a complete stranger. It was pure joy, and I reveled in it.

My once empty life, where I hid behind blackout drapes and locked doors, now brimmed over with light and laughter. Now, every blind—proverbial and literal—had been thrown open, with sunlight pouring into every crevice I'd covered up in the name of independence. These days, Van curled in the windowsill, basking in the rays and African violets. My home hummed with life.

Before, my quiet house felt peaceful. It was the space I needed to feel restored for the next gray day. Now, it didn't feel like home if I didn't hear Toby's laughter or Mom and Phyllis bickering about their reality shows. The noise didn't drain me; it inspired me—enough that I'd cashed multiple large checks from sales of my original paintings. *Original!*

But that was at home. Here, at the art gallery downtown, my life brimmed over with a new kind of light and laughter, one I hadn't heard in years.

Apparently the reemergence of Ivy Lunden onto the local art scene was a bigger deal than I could've hoped. I'd been apprehensive about relaunching my career, but so far I had no regrets. Several of my old art contacts had already come and gone at tonight's event, and several others were due to arrive any minute, but their opinions weren't what I was giddy about right now.

I found Toby easily enough, the colors guiding me. Taking his hand in mine, I smiled at the man he spoke with and excused us from the conversation.

Toby beamed at me. "I never doubted you, but this turnout is fantastic. Are you happy with it?"

"Of course." I steered him in the direction I wanted, to a specific painting with the best placement in the entire gallery.

"I met that one art critic you mentioned, and I started to brag about you, but Mel dragged me away. She said I needed to let him 'take it in' or something."

I laughed, picturing how this must have played out. "You did great."

"Okay, good."

We were facing the painting now, where everything began. The kaleidoscopic colors, the outline of a man's frame. It was my favorite.

"What do you think?" I asked, nodding at the canvas.

He nodded and smiled. "It's great. Love the colors."

I rolled my eyes. "That's what you say about all my art."

"I have limited vocabulary for this. I'm doing my best. Do you want me to talk about depth or perspective or…panache?"

"Panache?"

"It has confident, um, majesty. There. Do I sound like high society now?"

I laughed. "Toby, no, that's not—"

"I could—"

"It's you." I cupped his chin in my hand and turned his face back to the painting. "I painted you, and how your voice sounds in my head. This is how I hear you, how I see you."

He blinked, eyes wide, lips parted.

"This is a painting of the day we first met. I was fighting with that stupid—"

"Octopus," he murmured.

"—printer. I heard your voice before I saw you, and something in me just knew."

He turned to me with wonder in his eyes. "Is it acceptable in high society to kiss the artist at a gallery showing?"

"Not just yet." I gestured to the other paintings hanging along this particular wall, which curved into a semicircle. "Look at the others. What do you see?"

He glanced over the sushi painting, but he stared at the next one for a moment before he recognized the slate-blue, pale blush colors and sharp angles as the mountain of boxes in my basement, where we first said we loved each other. The next canvas was that April, when we took a freezing cold ride on the Ferris wheel by the river, the background a sheer white, a few minimal hints of spring green. Then came—

His hands cupped my cheeks, and he kissed me before he got to the fourth painting. "All of these are us," he whispered. "Every single one."

"Along this wall, yes." I covered his hands with my own, smiling at his teary eyes. "You've made my life more than I could've hoped for, Toby Azumah."

Kissing Toby here, surrounded by everything and everyone I loved most, felt right. Immensely, incredibly right.

Someone cleared their throat behind me. I turned, finding Mom. Her hair was combed and styled, and her makeup was artfully done like when I was growing up. She'd set aside her fluffy paisley robes in favor of a violet sweater dress tonight. She stood perfectly still, her eyes darting between us and my portrait of Toby.

"Hey, Mom. The show went quickly tonight, huh?"

"Your work is beautiful," she said, her voice wavering. She glanced at Toby. "It's obvious where she gets her inspiration from."

Toby's posture straightened at her words, his gaze turning back to me. "The inspiration is mutual."

Mom watched us, her expression softening into affection. It had taken time, but she'd gradually accepted him more and more, until she began texting him about the weather and traffic too. He'd looked positively boastful when he showed me the first weather text she sent him: *Icy bridges 2day. B careful.*

I noticed her purse slung over her shoulder. "Are you going somewhere? Some of us were heading out for drinks after, and I thought you might want to come."

"I already have plans."

Toby grinned. "Is Phyllis taking you home to watch *Swamp People*?"

"No." She tilted her head, clearly loving the mystery and drama of her secret. "I'm going out."

"Is Phyllis taking you to that new diner we saw down the street?" I asked.

I could see it already, Mom and Phyllis hassling the servers at their chosen restaurant about the exact ingredients and preparation of each food item before they ordered. They would have suggestions for the not-quite-clean restrooms. They would stuff their leftover containers with all of the salt, pepper, sugar, and condiment packets they could reach.

"No," Mom said, "not me and Phyllis."

I tried not to worry. Honestly, I did. But my imagination took a dire turn toward another broken ankle or even worse. I'd thought these conversations would get easier, but so far they hadn't. Her broken ankle had healed, and she had her mobility back, but her life would never look the same. My world was gradually opening up because I'd been willing to set aside my stubborn pride; Mom didn't get any such reward for setting aside her independence.

I took on a coaxing tone, hoping I sounded compassionate like Toby. "Mom, it's not safe for you to go alone. I can take you wherever you need to go tomorrow." I reconsidered at the thought of how long it took her to get ready to come to the gallery. "Or even later tonight since you're dressed up—"

A familiar figure, topped with a head of thinning hair, ambled into our conversation. "Evening," Chester said.

I blinked, unsure why he stood in the art gallery in a button-down plaid and khakis. Toby looked as confused as I felt.

"Hi, Chester," I said.

He nodded in my direction. "Good to see you. Your paintings look great."

Not even my confusion could hold back my beaming smile at that. "Thank you. I've already sold several pieces."

He nodded again. "Instant sensation, isn't that what they're saying?"

"Social media has been kind to me."

I glanced at Mom. I hated to bring it up again with Chester around. I didn't want to embarrass her. But I couldn't let her go out alone. It simply wasn't safe. What if she fell on a sidewalk or in a public restroom? Who would help her?

Chester fixed his eyes on Mom. "Ready?"

Faint bubblegum pink colored her cheeks. Mom adjusted her purse strap over her shoulder. "Enjoy your evening, Ivy. I'll see you in a few hours."

Mom paused before she stepped away. Patting Toby's arm with one gentle hand, she nodded. Then, shoes squeaking against the flooring, she turned to Chester. She smiled at him as he tucked her hand in his elbow and grinned down at her.

I'd never seen her smile like that before. My gaze stayed fixed on Mom as the pieces came together. Mom's violet sweater dress and pretty makeup. Chester's business casual clothes. Were they…? It wasn't possible, was it…?

With Toby by my side, I followed a few dazed steps behind Mom and Chester. They walked out the door, which closed softly behind them. I went to the glass front of the gallery and watched them guide one another down the side-walk. At the street, he helped her into his truck before walking around to the driver's side.

Toby's awestruck voice echoed my own thoughts. "Did they just…?"

Cameron came to stand next to us, his arm draped over Mel's shoulders. "Ivy, I don't know if you realize this, but your mom's a cougar."

Mel stood on her tiptoes to catch a final glimpse of Chester's truck as it drove away. "That was so sweet."

Toby tucked me under his arm. "I can't wait to see how you paint this moment."

I couldn't wait either. This collection, the next cliff's edge, our life we were building together were the smartest moves I ever could have made.

AUTHOR'S NOTE

It's a complicated process to explain how characters gradually grow in a writer's mind. I'll summarize by saying that when I realized Ivy is neurodivergent, I knew her story needed to be treated with care, sensitivity, and accuracy. I did extensive research on synesthesia, and I based Ivy's perspective on first-hand accounts of life with synesthesia. I hope I have given these real-life experiences the care and thoughtfulness they deserve.

ACKNOWLEDGMENTS

I still can't believe I get to write stories and characters that I love and then share those stories and characters with you. Thank you for picking up *Smart Move* and reading about Toby and Ivy. I hope they made you smile!

Smartypants Romance, thank you for making my dream come true—twice! Penny Reid, Brooke Nowiski, Fiona Fischer, and my fellow Smartypants Romance authors have made the such a fun-loving, supportive community.

Thank you to Krista at Mountains Wanted Indie Author Services and Publishing. You jumped in when I needed you most. I was desperate, having a finished manuscript but no editor at the last minute, and you calmly talked me through my panic.

Kymberly Krogh, my alpha (and beta) reader, thank you for reminding me that Ivy might be stubborn, but that's one of her greatest strengths. I wanted to give up on Ivy multiple times, but you encouraged me to try again. And again. And again.

Thank you to my team of beta readers: Dawn Koontz, Kelsey Pennington, Claire Stoner, Emily Stoner, Karen Sutherland, Vince and Melissa Winner, my husband, and my parents. Your feedback is invaluable. You are beyond supportive with listening to my endless rambles, helping me brainstorming, and keeping me smiling.

Thank you to my Rupp family, for never doubting my ideas, as crazy as they might sound when I first try to put them into words. You've encouraged me to make my own niche for my stories and chase my dreams.

Thank you to my Pennington family for keeping me laughing and smiling when I'm running on too little sleep. Your kindness and encouragement mean so much to me. I couldn't ask for a better in-law family.

My family, friends, and mentors who have supported me from the first, thank you. I would never be writing without you—your encouragement makes the writing process so much better!

Thank you, in particular, to my husband, Gregg Pennington. I never would've started this writing journey in earnest if it weren't for you encouraging me every step of the way. When I'm stuck on characters or plot, when I'm overwhelmed, when I'm inspired, when I'm ready to give up or push forward, you're always the solid ground I come back to.

ABOUT THE AUTHOR

Amanda Pennington lives outside Louisville, Kentucky with her husband in their fixer-upper house. When she's not writing, Amanda loves traveling, running, and reading anything within reach. More information is available at www.amandacpennington.com.

Facebook: https://www.facebook.com/amandacpennington
Instagram: https://www.instagram.com/amandacpennington_author/
Newsletter: https://bit.ly/3qielLI
Twitter: https://twitter.com/seeamandawrite
Goodreads: https://bit.ly/3fdsvHH
Pinterest: https://bit.ly/3tm3uT0

Find Smartypants Romance online:
Website: www.smartypantsromance.com
Facebook: www.facebook.com/smartypantsromance/
Goodreads: www.goodreads.com/smartypantsromance
Twitter: @smartypantsrom
Instagram: @smartypantsromance
Newsletter: https://smartypantsromance.com/newsletter/

ALSO BY AMANDA PENNINGTON

Book Smart

Smart Move

ALSO BY SMARTYPANTS ROMANCE

<u>Green Valley Chronicles</u>

<u>The Love at First Sight Series</u>

<u>Baking Me Crazy by Karla Sorensen (#1)</u>

<u>Batter of Wits by Karla Sorensen (#2)</u>

<u>Steal My Magnolia by Karla Sorensen (#3)</u>

<u>Worth the Wait by Karla Sorensen (#4)</u>

<u>Fighting For Love Series</u>

<u>Stud Muffin by Jiffy Kate (#1)</u>

<u>Beef Cake by Jiffy Kate (#2)</u>

<u>Eye Candy by Jiffy Kate (#3)</u>

<u>Knock Out by Jiffy Kate (#4)</u>

<u>The Donner Bakery Series</u>

<u>No Whisk, No Reward by Ellie Kay (#1)</u>

<u>Dough You Love Me? By Stacy Travis (#2)</u>

<u>Tough Cookie by Talia Hunter (#3)</u>

<u>The Green Valley Library Series</u>

<u>Love in Due Time by L.B. Dunbar (#1)</u>

<u>Crime and Periodicals by Nora Everly (#2)</u>

<u>Prose Before Bros by Cathy Yardley (#3)</u>

<u>Shelf Awareness by Katie Ashley (#4)</u>

<u>Carpentry and Cocktails by Nora Everly (#5)</u>

<u>Love in Deed by L.B. Dunbar (#6)</u>

Dewey Belong Together by Ann Whynot (#7)

Hotshot and Hospitality by Nora Everly (#8)

Love in a Pickle by L.B. Dunbar (#9)

Code of Matrimony by April White (#2.5)

Code of Ethics by April White (#3)

Cipher Office Series

Weight Expectations by M.E. Carter (#1)

Sticking to the Script by Stella Weaver (#2)

Cutie and the Beast by M.E. Carter (#3)

Weights of Wrath by M.E. Carter (#4)

Common Threads Series

Mad About Ewe by Susannah Nix (#1)

Give Love a Chai by Nanxi Wen (#2)

Key Change by Heidi Hutchinson (#3)

Not Since Ewe by Susannah Nix (#4)

Lost Track by Heidi Hutchinson (#5)

Educated Romance

Work For It Series

Street Smart by Aly Stiles (#1)

Heart Smart by Emma Lee Jayne (#2)

Book Smart by Amanda Pennington (#3)

Smart Mouth by Emma Lee Jayne (#4)

Play Smart by Aly Stiles (#5)

Look Smart by Aly Stiles (#6)

Smart Move by Amanda Pennington (#7)

Lessons Learned Series

Under Pressure by Allie Winters (#1)

Not Fooling Anyone by Allie Winters (#2)

Can't Fight It by Allie Winters (#3)

The Vinyl Frontier by Lola West (#4)

Out of this World